THE SHADOWS OF LONDON

THE SHADOWS OF LONDON

NICK JONES

**BLACK
STONE**
PUBLISHING

Copyright © 2021 by Nick Jones
Published in 2021 by Blackstone Publishing
Cover design by Bookfly Design
Book design by Blackstone Publishing

Printed in the United States of America

ISBN 978-1-6650-4200-0
Fiction / Science Fiction / Time Travel

1 3 5 7 9 10 8 6 4 2

CIP data for this book is available
from the Library of Congress

Blackstone Publishing
31 Mistletoe Rd.
Ashland, OR 97520

www.BlackstonePublishing.com

PROLOGUE

Shock surges through me as vast amounts of information assault my senses, one world swapped for another in a blink. I shield my eyes against the midday sun, heart pounding in my chest, and take in my new surroundings. It appears I've traveled from the biting chill of a midnight thunderstorm in Cheltenham to the blazing warmth of a summer's day in a bustling city. And not just any city. I crane my neck as I look up at Big Ben towering above me. I'm in London.

My throat tightens. My legs want to fold. I've jumped back in time before, but my trips were within Cheltenham, which puts this London jaunt in a different league altogether. How did I get here? I'm a hundred miles from home. Have I been shoved through some kind of wormhole? More worrying, though, is the amount of years I've traveled back through time. This looks like the 1960s. A constant stream of people glides past me. Women with huge hair and dark makeup, adorned in colorful mini-dresses; men in somber suits and smart hats.

I'm surrounded by sights I've only glimpsed in history books or grainy YouTube clips. Black cabs and iconic double-decker buses, the circular signage of the Underground, half familiar, but all in a vintage style.

I spot a well-stocked newsstand with a selection of broadsheets mounted on boards and float toward it in a daze. I'm transfixed by the headlines. the

Daily Mirror's front page reads: "PROFUMO QUITS! He lied over Christine to save his family!"

I pick up a copy and peer closer to check the date. This cannot be. I rub my eyes in panic.

"Just woken up, 'ave ya?"

I stare down at a round pudgy-faced man seated between bundles of newspapers.

"Pardon?"

"You're still wearing your pajamas!" he says gleefully, the gap between his front teeth whistling.

I glance down. He's right. Pale-blue silk pajamas and navy velvet slippers. Hardly the best getup for a trip to the capital. I grab the newspaper, the ink as fresh as the breaking story on its cover. Right beneath the *Daily Mirror* logo, it reads: Thursday, 6 June 1963.

1963?

"You all right, mate?" the man asks, adjusting his cap. "You seem a bit lost."

"A bit lost . . ." I echo his words. "That's the understatement of the year."

"You need to pay for that." He points at the paper in my hand. I give it back to him and wander around Parliament Square in a daze. I slap my face a couple of times, just to make sure I'm not dreaming. Nope. Still here.

The last thing I remember is reaching out to touch the radio in my shop, and then—*bam!*—I landed here. My thoughts turn immediately to W. P. Brown, the jovial chap who turned up in my shop this morning, offering to be my time-traveling mentor. I told him I'd only just got home from saving my sister, Amy, and I wasn't interested in doing any more traveling. I was polite, but I think the sneaky so-and-so must have done something to the radio, charged it up with you're-going-to-travel-whether-you-like-it-or-not energy, and sent me here. Whatever he has planned for me, he's going to be disappointed. I'm not doing it. I'm staying right here until I travel home again.

Speaking of which, why am I still here? When I was trying to save Amy, the farther back in time I jumped, the less time I spent in the past. I used to think of it a bit like an elastic band—the more I stretched it, the less time

I spent in the past and the faster it pinged me home. This is 1963, which is, well, *decades* farther back than I've ever traveled before. In the middle of the street there's a policeman, busy directing what appears to be stationary traffic. Cars, taxis, and buses beep their horns. People yell pointlessly out their windows. What if I'm stuck? What if I never get home? Acid bubbles in the pit of my stomach.

I pull my mobile phone out of my pocket to check the time: *9:47 p.m. No signal.* Of course. I scan the clear blue sky above me. Suddenly, there's a rush of air, a strong smell of sweat, and my phone is snatched from my grasp. "Hey!" I call out in shock. I see the back of a man with baggy trousers, a dirty blue shirt, and dark greasy hair running away from me at full speed, my phone in his hand.

For a second, I'm frozen in indecision. It's 1963, I'm wearing my pajamas, and it's just a phone. And the man might be violent, if I can even catch him.

Then, an irritatingly righteous sense of responsibility kicks in. That tiny slab of glass contains a computer that's probably a million times more powerful than the ones they will use to put men on the moon in a few years' time. I can't be responsible for letting that kind of technology loose this far ahead of its proper launch date. Anything could happen if it got into the wrong hands. I might get home to a world run by vindictive robots who shoot antiques dealers on sight.

Head down, I give chase. Not easy in slippers. I push through the crowds, laser-focused on Greaseball, forcing my legs into another gear, knees popping. My vision blurs, and I lose him.

I lurch across an intersection. On the other side, the road forks. I mentally toss a coin and choose the street that leads to the left, and as I round the corner, I catch sight of the thief ahead, darting into an alley. I follow at a sprint. The alleyway is long, with featureless brick walls stretching up on either side. The robber has tired, and I finally catch up to him.

He's young, maybe late teens, but he looks like he's about to have a heart attack. His cheeks are red and blotchy, and his lank hair is wet and slicked against his forehead. He stares at the phone. Luckily, it's asleep and the screen is black.

"What is it?" he pants. "Looks expensive."

"Give it back," I tell him, doing my best to appear tough. Not easy, considering I look like I'm ready for a spa treatment.

"How much money have you got on you?"

"None," I say, shaking my head. "I don't have anything."

He looks me up and down. "Are you a perv?"

I'm in pajamas in the middle of a city street. It's a fair question.

"I just really need that back," I say.

The kid thinks about it for a second, looks behind me, then grins and chucks the phone over my shoulder. "Fetch!" he cries and runs off down the alley.

The phone lands in a pile of black bags in a small gated courtyard at the rear entrance of what I suspect is a restaurant. Relieved, I walk over to the gate. It's locked, but the fence surrounding it isn't that high, so I climb over it carefully. Touching down on the other side, my nose is immediately invaded by the rotten stench of a week's worth of old food and kitchen scraps. I pinch my nostrils and crouch down, gingerly moving bags around. After a few minutes, I spot a glint of something shiny and pull at a heavy bag with both hands, but just as I raise it up off the ground, it splits, spewing a foul mixture of tomato sauce, fish bones, and meaty entrails all over my pajama bottoms. "Oh, for the love of—" I stop midsentence as I nearly heave. "Mind over matter," I mutter, picking out the phone and wiping down the screen as best I can.

I'm about to climb back over the gate when a woman appears, a dark silhouette against the bright, sunlit street behind her. I freeze. She looks briefly over her shoulder and then runs along the alley toward me. As she gets to the courtyard—no more than six feet away—she pauses, turns, and looks directly at me. She's in her early thirties, a neat figure dressed in a black skirt with an apron, brown eyes bright with fear.

Another figure enters the alleyway; a man, his outline solid and stocky. The woman sees me looking, glances behind her, then runs on. The man walks purposefully up the alley in my direction. Instinctively, I crouch down and flatten myself against the wall. I hold my breath as he stalks past, his forehead glistening with sweat.

Forcing myself to move, I slide silently along the wall and peer out just enough to see the man's back. He's about thirty feet away. In front of him is the woman. She's stopped running. Her escape route at the other end of the alleyway has been blocked by a car, a cream Rolls-Royce parked sideways across the path.

A man steps out of the rear door.

He's tall and lean, wearing a fitted cream suit that matches the color of the car exactly. His hair is ginger and neatly brushed to one side. Sunlight glints off him. He tips his head forward, revealing deep angular features, and walks deliberately toward the woman. I can't see her face, but she stands taller as he approaches. He has a gold cross around his neck. He closes his eyes and touches it to his lips. I hear his voice, low and menacing, and hers, higher and more insistent, but I'm too far away to hear what they're saying. I can tell that they're arguing though. The stocky man, clearly a thug for hire, watches them. I glance back down the alleyway to the gap where I came in and wonder if I can get out of here without them noticing me.

Then the voices get louder, the woman's voice shriller now, her words more rapid. I decide it'll be safer to wait it out.

I watch as the red-haired man nods to his stocky accomplice, then turns and saunters back toward the car. Suddenly, I understand what's about to happen. The thug pulls something from his jacket.

Icy dread runs the length of my spine.

It's a gun.

I open my mouth, about to shout, but then the alleyway fills with the bark of gunfire. Two shots.

The woman collapses forward. The thug walks over to her, grabs her handbag, then follows the red-haired man toward the car. I watch in mute terror as they climb into the back, the door slams shut, and the car pulls away.

I let out a long shuddering breath. My vision blurs, the edges darkening, and for a moment I'm frozen by fear, huddled in a ball. Once I'm sure the coast is clear, I climb back over the fence. I make myself turn and look back at the motionless figure on the ground. I should have intervened, tried to stop this, but I was too afraid. I have to do something to help. All I can do now is call an ambulance.

I stagger out of the alleyway into a sea of faces. People are pointing and staring at me. The deafening ring of a siren explodes in my ears. A police car screeches to a halt in front of me, blue lights rotating and blinking like all-seeing eyes. Three policemen scramble out of the vehicle and immediately begin interviewing people on the street. The tallest one, a man with a large bulbous nose, walks straight to me and places a firm hand on my shoulder. I'm not sure whether he's propping me up or holding me in place.

"Are you all right, sir?" he asks. "What's going on?"

"Ambulance," I say thickly, my mouth dry. "Somebody call an ambulance."

A man in a flat cap points at me. "He just came runnin' out of that alleyway. Very dodgy if you ask me."

The policeman shakes me gently. "What's just happened?" he says.

I clear my throat. "There's a woman down that alleyway. She's been shot. I think she might be dead."

A woman standing nearby gasps in horror and covers her mouth with one hand. She points at my legs with the other. Looking down, I notice the red stains all over my pajamas. I look as though I'm covered in blood.

Talk about being in the wrong place at the wrong time.

PART 1

1

Sunday, January 5, 2020
14 hours earlier

After weeks of failed attempts, storms, barbed wire, science, intuition, and dead ends, I finally managed to travel back in time and save my little sister, Amy. While I was trying to work out how to save her, only three people knew about it: my best friend, Vinny; my science-genius buddy, Mark; and my ex-almost-girlfriend, Alexia.

Now I've changed history, stopped Amy from drowning, and no one remembers any of it, except for Amy and me.

Or so I thought.

William P. Brown stands in the center of my antiques shop, smiling confidently and rocking gently backward and forward on the balls of his feet. I say *my* shop, but it really belongs to a previous version of me, one I replaced. Let's call him "Other Joe," because it sounds so much better than "the man I unintentionally deleted yesterday." He's just offered me the chance of more time-travel adventures, and he's acting like I'm going to take it.

"Hold on," I tell him. "Where did you say you were from?"

Mr. Brown dips his head politely. "I'm sorry, Joseph," he says. "I realize this must be quite a shock. I believe you only returned from saving your sister"—he checks his watch—"yesterday, correct?"

He waits for confirmation, but I don't move a muscle. How does he know so much about me, about what I did? He knows that I'm a time traveler—does he know that Amy is too? Part of me wants to ask, but I decide to keep my mouth shut for now. I don't know anything about this man, or why he's really here. I'm not going to give anything away.

"I work for an organization," he continues, "a group of dedicated time travelers."

"Organized time travelers?"

"Indeed," he smiles. "New recruits are often taken aback by the fact that we work together, but it's rather comforting, don't you think?"

No, I don't. The thought freaks me out. Discovering I had the power to travel through time and change my own life was one thing—let alone finding out that Amy was a traveler too—but the idea of a load of other people with different goals and values wielding the same power is frankly alarming. I think about my previous jumps back in time. Was Brown—or someone else—watching me? Was I followed? The hairs stand up on the nape of my neck.

"How did you find me?" I ask.

"It's quite simple," he says. "In the same way that you're attracted to objects, I'm drawn to new time travelers. When people like you change a key moment in their own lives, I am able to discern that history has been retold. I feel it in my bones that a new traveler has harnessed the gift. It's incredibly exciting."

His eyes glint again, but I couldn't say if it's with excitement or madness.

"I realize it must sound bizarre to you," he continues, "but so much of life is, don't you think? 'Truth is stranger than fiction,' as dear Byron said."

He gazes out the window, as though reliving a memory. I wonder if I should make a run for it. He turns back and takes a step toward me.

"Once a new traveler is 'born,' if you will, then in due course, I am given the opportunity to visit," Mr. Brown says, almost conspiratorially, "and to invite the new traveler to become a member of our merry throng. And thus, here I am, inviting you."

He grins broadly and makes a *ta-da* gesture with his hands, as if he's expecting me to applaud.

I smile back, half-heartedly, buying myself a few seconds to think. If this guy is a nutjob, I need to try and keep him calm. If he's for real, I need to tell him I'm not interested in joining his gang. Either way, I want him out of my shop. I must be careful though. He knows a lot about me, but he hasn't explained how, at least not in a way that makes sense to me. I'm certain there are things he's not telling me. He's charming enough, but I've seen all the movies: the nastiest villains are often likable, charismatic, and engaging, tricking you into dropping your defenses and then going for your throat when you least expect it.

"I'm grateful for your offer," I say hesitantly, "but I only time traveled to save my sister. Now I have her back, I don't need to travel again—in fact, I don't *want* to."

"Everything is just the way you want it, right?" Brown asks.

It's a rhetorical question, and his tone isn't entirely neutral. I take it as a warning.

"Precious few have the ability to travel, and only a tiny proportion of those who do ever change anything," he continues. "That already makes you special."

Special? My gut growls a warning. I am many things, but special isn't one of them.

"I just want to live an ordinary life and stay out of trouble," I tell him guardedly.

"It's a little late for that, don't you think?" he muses.

"What do you mean?"

"Ordinary people don't travel back in time and change the entire course of history."

I almost laugh. "I didn't change 'the entire course of history,'" I correct him. "I just put my family back together. It was my fault we got torn apart, so I fixed it. That's all."

"You're too modest, my boy," he says. "You overcame almost impossible odds to save your sister, all the more impressive when you consider how long it took you to discover your ability. Most travelers hit their stride in their teens or early twenties. You, Joseph, were a late starter. Your window of opportunity almost closed, but then you completed a double jump in order to get back to Amy. That's very rare indeed. Ingenious, in fact."

Shivers travel down my spine. Once I knew I could travel, I felt many times that I'd wasted years of my life, that Amy's disappearance was just too far back. I was frustrated by how little time I had in the past and desperate when I realized I couldn't reach 1997, the night of the fair. Alexia and I spent many hours together working on that double jump. She even came back with me halfway, to help me focus. How does Brown know about all of this?

"You have an incredible gift," he insists. "But you need training and guidance if you are to learn how to use it fully. And that is why I'm here. Your skills need to be developed. I can help you tune in to your intuition and enhance your psychometry." His body is taut with excitement, and his face is lit with expectation. "This is just the beginning, Joseph. There are other people who need your help, other stories to be rewritten. You won't *believe* what you're capable of!"

The more excited he gets, the more I feel my heels digging in. I'm not only unnerved by how much he knows, but I don't trust his motives. I have a new life now. I have my sister back, a business to run, a relationship to rebuild with Alexia. My focus is firmly on the present. I only ever traveled back in time to fix my life. I had a specific goal, and I achieved it. Job done.

"That all sounds great and everything," I say politely, folding my arms over my chest, "but I'm not interested. I think I've made myself clear."

Brown heaves a long sigh. "I understand," he says. "I often get accused of being a little overzealous. Forgive me. I must admit, I've never been drawn to a recruit so soon after a first mission. I must try to remember you've only just returned from the past." He wanders to the far side of the room, where a row of a dozen glass cabinets holds a diverse collection of objects. He walks slowly past each one, perusing the contents and nodding approvingly now and again. He stops in front of an oak table laid with a marquetry chessboard, its ebony and ivory pieces set out in tidy rows. "I suspect though, as is often the way, that events will unfold just as they should. There will be a reason. There always is." He says this with absolute certainty, regarding me thoughtfully.

I move to the door and flip the sign to Closed. "As you already seem to know, Mr. Brown, I risked everything to get Amy back. Now I'm home, and I plan to stay here. Thank you for your offer, but I mean it. I'm done with time traveling."

I hold my breath, hoping he isn't going to make this difficult. The only sound in the room comes from the clocks on the wall, ticking out of rhythm with one another.

"It's your decision," he acquiesces, pulling his watch out of his jacket pocket and checking the time. "Ah, such a shame, I don't have long. I should inform you that I will be drawn to you again, two or three times." He sees my expression. "I appreciate that you have made your feelings on this matter exceedingly clear. However, being drawn to you is not a process I control. Perhaps—at the very least—we could share a glass of something convivial, and you can tell me how things are going in your new life."

What can I say? Hopefully, next time I'll see him before he sees me so I can run a hundred miles an hour in the opposite direction and avoid him altogether.

His body shimmers, like oil and silk dancing across water. "Good to see you, Joe," he says with surprising warmth, as though he's taking leave of an old friend. For perhaps a second, he is translucent, then he fades neatly into nothingness.

There's a temporary short circuit in my brain as I attempt to comprehend the empty space. I watched my little sister disappear like this only yesterday. I can still see the sparkling outline of her body cut like crystal through the rain, the drops of water falling silently to earth. No matter how many times I see this flickering out of existence, I'm never going to get used to it.

I sit down heavily in my desk chair and rub my eyes. I'm relieved to be alone again, but feel profoundly disturbed. I had no idea there were other travelers, other people who somehow knew what I was doing, and his offer is beyond weird.

I nearly jump out of my skin when the drawer in front of me starts to hum. Yanking it open, I see a mobile phone spinning itself around in half circles as it vibrates. Without thinking, I pick up.

"Hello?" I answer, nerves jangling.

"Hi, Joe."

It's Amy. I'm so happy to hear her voice. When she left me here in the shop last night, it was difficult to let her go after just a few short hours. I can't wait to get to know my grown-up sister.

"Are you there?" she asks.

"Sorry, yes. I'm here." *And so are you.*

"You sound out of breath. Is everything OK?"

"Fine. I just . . . ran across the shop to get to the phone. How are you?"

"I'm all right," she says. "I didn't sleep that well, but I'm OK. How are you settling in?"

"Good. Great!" I reply, keen to reassure her. "I just had a . . . tricky customer who didn't realize we were closed, but I managed to get rid of him. It wasn't a problem." At least I hope it won't be.

"Well done," she says. "Every customer you meet, it'll get easier. I was wondering, would you like to come over for a bite to eat? I thought we could talk about tomorrow, make a plan, decide what we're going to tell everyone."

My heartbeat steadies. Everything is OK. Amy's OK. I'm going to have lunch with my sister. It sounds so banal, but for me, it's a dream come true.

2

Amy lives in a pleasant, up-and-coming part of town, mostly inhabited by young families and single professionals. I arrive outside her building and gaze appreciatively along the tree-lined street. Nearby is a gated park with tennis courts and a playground, and there's a bus stop across the road. It feels safe, a good place for my sister to be.

I make my way up the path and press the button for Amy's flat. She buzzes me in, and I climb the stairs to the second floor. I ring the bell, and Amy opens the door. She smiles and hugs me. I hug her back, trying to soak in the fact that I have a sister again. My old life is gone. I have a new story now.

Amy pulls away. "Come in," she says. I'm struck again by her grown-up face and the startling echoes of Mum at certain angles. She's dressed in a red hoodie that's way too big for her, cropped, flowery trousers, and bright purple and silver Converse All-Stars. Her hair is down and kind of messy. She exudes the kind of effortless, bohemian style that many women attempt but few achieve. I follow Amy into the living room. It's spacious and airy, with high ceilings, fancy cornices, and tall windows.

"How did you sleep?" she asks me, picking at her nails. "Did you find everything OK?"

"I slept fine," I tell her. "The apartment's great." Actually, I feel as though I've moved into a dead man's home before his body is even cold, but I suppose

I'll get used to it eventually. "Amy, I was so relieved when you invited me over. There's a lot to talk about. I'm not sure where to start."

"It's huge," she agrees. "I've known this was going to happen for a long time, and I've thought about it loads, but nothing really prepares you." She shrugs. "Would you like a drink? Cup of tea? Or something stronger maybe? Beer?"

"Beer sounds good, thanks." It's only just past midday, and I hardly ever drink before 6 p.m., but this is not your average day.

"I think I'll join you." She sits me down on the huge sofa and heads to the kitchen. "I'll be back in a minute."

I lean into a heap of colorful cushions and survey my surroundings. In the center of the room are two huge sofas and a carved wooden coffee table, sheesham maybe. Berber rugs hang on two of the walls, and on a third, tall shelves crammed with books flank a huge mirror in a gilded frame. Everywhere I look there are ornaments, carvings, and knickknacks. Some people might describe it as untidy, but to me it's charmingly chaotic. Even though it smells like a health-food shop in here, with a strong scent of weird hippie oils and a faint whiff of licorice, I already feel more at home here than I do in Other Joe's flat.

I spot some photos on the wall and walk over to take a closer look. There's a picture of Amy, a little older than I remember her, at a gymnastics competition. Photos of a teenage Amy messing about with college friends on a beach somewhere. Amy smiling, Amy hugging people, Amy dancing, Amy living. Evidence of a full life, more than twenty years, thousands of days.

Unexpectedly, a complex set of emotions wells up. I missed all these years with my baby sister, and I feel stabs of envy toward Other Joe, who got to experience it all firsthand. But if I hadn't gone back to save her, none of this would have happened. I should feel proud, not jealous.

Amy appears with two beers and a bottle opener.

"Nice photos," I say, returning to the sofa. I try to keep my voice level, but it catches.

"Thanks," she says, with a hint of concern. She doesn't push me further though, and I'm grateful. She deftly removes the caps, hands me a bottle of beer, and sits opposite me on the other sofa. "So," she says. "What would you like to talk about first?"

There's so much whizzing around in my head, it's overwhelming. I decide to start with what's right in front of my nose. Yesterday Amy and I decided we'd tell everyone that I have amnesia. It seemed like an easy way to explain all the history I've apparently "forgotten." I've thought about it more though, and I've realized we're going to need a whole story.

"I'm feeling pretty nervous about opening the shop tomorrow," I say. "I'm up for this amnesia thing. I think it's going to work, but we will need to explain to people how it happened."

Amy takes a sip of beer. "I was thinking we would say you had a mountain-bike accident."

"Mountain bike?" I say. "I've never been mountain biking."

"Actually, Joe—I mean Other Joe—used to go most weekends," she says. "He loved it. He was quite an adrenaline junkie."

There is no part of me that's interested in throwing myself down a hill on anything. I wonder how, and when, Other Joe discovered that he liked that kind of action. "OK, mountain-bike accident it is."

"Cool," Amy says. "I'll give Molly a call later today and tell her." Yesterday Amy explained to me that Molly is the shop manager. Amy had given her the weekend off so that she wouldn't be around when I got back from 1997. "Then I'll give Martin Watts a call and let him know too. Martin's your accountant."

Hearing a familiar name is like an oasis in the middle of a desert. Martin used to cause me all kinds of administrative nightmares—to be fair, he was just doing his job, and I was generally the cause of the nightmares—but he was also my cupid. He set up my first hypnotherapy appointment with Alexia. I will be forever grateful to him for that. "I know him," I say. "In my old life, he used to look after my shop finances."

"He still does your shop accounts, but he also runs the property development business for you."

"Property development business?" I say. "God, Amy, I don't know anything about property development!"

"Don't worry," she says. "Other Joe used to oversee his businesses, but he let people like Martin and Molly run things. You can do the same. You have great people all around you, Joe. I'm sure they will do everything they can to support you."

Cripes. I take a long swig of beer. There's so much to learn, basically everything. I'm determined to make this work for the sake of my family, and Other Joe's legacy, but it's going to take effort and patience, and not just from me. I wonder how actual amnesia patients cope. It must be dreadful.

"I think I probably ought to tell Mum and Dad about your 'accident' today too," Amy continues. "If I don't, Martin will probably let it slip, and I'll never hear the end of it."

It's strange hearing Amy talk about our parents. "It's going to be a big deal for me, seeing Mum and Dad again," I tell her.

"I can imagine," she says softly.

I decide it's time to ask her what she knows. "Amy, the day I came back from the fairground, you told me you'd traveled forward a few times as a child, that you'd seen the future."

"That's right," she replies.

"What did you see?"

She pauses for a second, remembering. "Mostly I didn't know where I was, or how far I'd traveled. I was only little, and I guess I was just starting to understand what *the past* and *the future* meant. And I was scared. A couple of times though, I landed at home, in my bedroom."

"Really?" I think about all the times I passed Amy's room, too scared to open the door and enter the shrine we'd left untouched. What if I'd walked in and found her?

"I know," she says, and I can see in her face that she's thinking it too. "At first, I wondered if I'd traveled at all. My room was the same as when I left it. Nothing had changed. Of course, now I understand why. One time I remember looking out of the window and seeing Mum in the garden. She was a lot older. She was crying. She looked up, as if she knew I was there." Amy glances at me. "I often wonder if she saw me that day. If she did, she must have thought she'd seen a ghost."

"She never mentioned anything to me."

"She probably wouldn't have wanted to worry you."

"I suppose so," I say. "Did you ever see me? Or Dad?"

"No, neither of you. And then, after you saved me, I didn't ever visit that version of our life again."

"Well, that makes sense. Because it didn't happen."

"Right. You changed it." She brushes a lock of hair away from her face. "Joe, can I ask you something? About your life before you saved me?"

"Of course," I say.

"The day you came back, when I told you that Mum and Dad were OK, it was obvious how relieved you were. You specifically asked me to confirm that Dad was all right. What happened to him?"

I shiver. My past is nothing more than a memory, just like everyone else's, but mine belongs only to me, and it moves through me periodically, like aftershocks. "Are you sure you want to know?"

"Yes," she says. "I want to know what you went through."

I just need to say it. "He committed suicide."

"Oh no!" she murmurs and puts her hand over her mouth. "How awful." She takes my hand and gives it a squeeze. "What about Mum?"

"She developed dementia. It seemed to come on quite quickly after he died. It was the stress of it all, I think."

"Poor Mum," Amy says. "I know I didn't have any control over what happened, but I can't help but feel partly responsible."

"Amy! There was nothing you could have done," I say fiercely. "It was just a terrible, terrible tragedy. For all of us." I straighten up. "But it didn't happen, and we don't need to think about it anymore."

Amy hugs and holds me as she talks. "That night in the summer of 1997, when you saved me, you saved us all. You fixed everything." She pulls away and holds my gaze. "Now it's our turn to help fix you."

"I'll be all right. It's just a matter of time."

"I know," she says. "I hope that when you meet Mum and Dad again, the sad memories will fade away like a bad dream, lose some of their power."

"I hope so too," I tell her, and I'm surprised when my fear is side-lined by a flash of excitement. "When are they back from their trip?"

"They'll be away for another ten days yet," she reassures me. "By then you'll be well into the swing of it." She puts her beer down. "Would you like to see a photo of them?"

I want to, but I'm afraid I won't be able cope with the magnitude of my feelings. "OK," I say hesitantly. "That would be good."

Amy walks to the other side of the room and lifts a framed picture off the wall. She brings it back and hands it to me. "This was a session we did in a photographer's studio about three years ago," she says.

There they are, the Bridgeman family. Mum is radiant, with the polished, centered poise of an older woman. Dad stands proud and upright, one arm around Mum and the other on Amy's shoulder. Amy beams brightly at the camera, her nose wrinkled in a moment of mirth. Other Joe grins at me. He wouldn't be smiling if he knew what was coming. I study these people, my own family, the people I grew up with, and yet I hardly recognize them. I pore over the details: their healthy faces, their smart outfits, their confidence. We all rode the same train until I was fourteen, and then the track split violently in two. Another sadder version of my parents and I were confined in a cramped carriage and sent down a hellish, tortuous route which pushed my mother to the brink of insanity, drove my father to suicide, and pretty much destroyed me. Meanwhile, these guys got to take the scenic route. I know there's no such thing as a perfect life, but they seem happy and healthy. And there are four of them. They're the proof that circumstances change everything.

I hand the photo back to Amy. "Do you think Other Joe knew what was going to happen to him?"

"I'm pretty certain he didn't," she says. "I was with him yesterday morning when it happened."

"Oh God," I say. "I didn't realize you were there. That must have been so hard."

She shakes her head. "I don't think it's really sunk in yet, to be honest. He didn't suffer, he wasn't scared. He just went. It was instantaneous."

I shiver. "Amy, I hadn't really thought this through, not till now, but you lost your brother yesterday."

"No, I didn't," she assures me. "He's sitting in front of me. *You're* right here."

It's kind of her to say, but she has memories of a brother who no longer exists. "Am I anything like him? Was he like me?"

"Try to think of him as someone on the same team," she says. "He always made sure I was safe. Just like you."

I think of the man I replaced, looking out for his sister, happily living his life until I came along and canceled him out. Guilt hits me in a wave. "I feel terrible, Amy," I say. "He disappeared . . . to make space for me. I feel so guilty."

"You mustn't," Amy tells me firmly. "It had to happen. If it hadn't, I wouldn't be here. Listen, Joe. Once upon a time, I died at the age of seven. You came back to save me, and you gave me my life back. I will never know how to thank you for that. I owe you everything. But if I hadn't died, none of this would have happened. If anyone should feel guilty, it's me."

"No, Amy, that's crazy talk," I tell her.

"No crazier than what you were saying," she retorts. "But it's all in the past now. We are where we are. Can we agree to focus on the future?"

"I guess," I say, still trying to work out how I feel.

"Good," she says determinedly. "Listen to me. Your only job now is to get to know your new life here. Get to know your family and friends, decide what you want to take forward, and enjoy yourself. Keep talking to me, and I'll keep talking to you, and we will be fine."

We hug, and the world feels almost good again.

3

The sky is ominously gray, and I'm rushing to get home before the heavens open. I turn off the street and take a shortcut through Imperial Gardens. In the summer, the flower beds would be in full bloom and the green would be teeming with office workers, mums with dogs, kids playing, and strollers. Today it's quiet, just me and a couple of others, shoulders hunched against the cold. The trees are barren, the flower beds bare patches of soil, waiting for the weather to warm and the days to lengthen. I push my hands deeper into my pockets. Amy and I are sowing the seeds of our new relationship, picking up where we left off all those years ago. I hope she won't be disappointed.

The thick mist finally gains enough density to break into a fine drizzle. "Wetting rain," as Grandma Bridgeman used to call it. Is there any other kind? I walk for a while along soaked streets, avoiding the puddles. My brain's frazzled. Conflicting images whip through my mind. Seven-year-old Amy drifting away from me in the lake. Grown-up Amy welcoming me to her home this morning. My mum in the nursing home, and then in that photo of the four of them, happy together. My old house, full of bitter memories, and the cool luxury of Other Joe's apartment. It's enough to drive a man mad.

I stop walking and discover that I'm standing across the street from Alexia Finch's office. Clearly, my subconscious had a plan. Alexia is a talented hypno-therapist and, quite possibly, the world's best listener. She's kind, funny, and gorgeous. She helped to unlock my time-traveling abilities, and she promised she would be waiting for me when I got back. She wasn't.

I lean against a tree and gaze up at her office. It's dark, clearly empty. I wonder where she is, who she's with. The pain of memory hits me again; our short, intense history together wiped clean. When I returned from 1997, Alexia didn't remember anything about what had happened. I called her to let her know our plan had worked and that Amy was OK, but Alexia didn't know what I was talking about. I think she thought I was losing my marbles. It was horrible.

No part of me wants my old life back, but I miss Alexia—the warmth of her smile, the softness of her kiss. I drift into a flight of fancy, imagining myself running across the street, bounding up those steps, and bursting into her office, hand on my heart, declaring my undying love. That would be romantic, wouldn't it? She'd take me in her arms, and we would waltz off into the sunset together. But real life doesn't work that way. The reality is that I'm a rain-soaked stalker, gazing longingly at the office of a woman who doesn't remember that she had feelings for me once.

Distant thunder rumbles. The rain becomes a downpour, sheeting down and pelting my head. It's like a message from the universe: give up and go home. I lift my collar and jog the last few streets back to the shop.

By the time I get to Montpellier Road, the bruised clouds are a dirty shade of yellow. As I hunt for my keys, a fork of lightning cracks and lights up the shop like a camera flash, whitewashing everything in the window. The zoetrope is still sitting there, where I left it this morning after W. P. Brown left the shop. I unlock the front door and go inside, grateful to be in the warmth again. I feel the slight give of the old wooden floorboards beneath my feet and appreciate the musty, leathery, polish-laced scent that hangs comfortingly in the air.

"This is my shop," I say quietly, testing the words. They sound alien, but it feels as though the shop is listening and recognizes its new owner.

I'm soaked. Water pools at my feet, which feel like blocks of ice. I dump my phone on the desk and lock the front door, then I go upstairs to my flat and take a hot shower. I know it's not bedtime yet, but I'm not going anywhere, so I put on a new pair of smart blue pajamas I find. I make myself a hot toddy—purely for medicinal purposes—and decide it's finally time to check out the top floor of my apartment. Amy said she thought I'd like it.

I walk through the snazzy kitchen with its spotless tiles and sparkly worktops, past the den, and up the wide glass staircase at the end of the corridor. The steps are lit with bright white LEDs. I feel as though I'm ascending a stairway to heaven.

When I get to the top, the lights flicker on. I find myself in a large ultra-stylish space with a vaulted ceiling and exposed wooden beams. The walls are bare brickwork, dotted at regular and precisely measured intervals with industrial light fixtures, smart loudspeakers, and pieces of abstract art. It's not to my taste, but everything looks very expensive. The pale wooden floor-boards are polished to a glossy sheen and spanned by a wide cream-colored carpet from the top of the stairs to the glass doors at the other end of the room. To my right is a bar with stools and a classic American car depicted in LEDs on the wall. To my left two battered leather sofas huddle on either side of a wood-burning stove, laid with paper and kindling and ready for action. Directly in front of the fireplace sits an enormous sheepskin bean-bag on a fake leopard-skin rug.

The whole room is chic and cool, reminiscent of a bar in a boutique hotel. It's basically a bachelor pad, a rich boy's playground. Wasn't Other Joe a bit old for all this? For a moment, I feel the gulf between his life and mine. Then, I pull myself together. Imagine if he'd already been living here with a partner. Or had children, even. My skin crawls, and I shake my shoulders, grateful beyond words that Other Joe hadn't settled down with anyone before I came back. Of course, I would have done the right thing and tried to make it work, but I want to take each step at my own pace with some-one I've chosen, not start smack-bang in the middle of someone else's life, playing happy families with strangers.

I walk across the room. It's dark outside now, but as I reach the bifold doors, lights flicker on, and the terrace is illuminated in the glow of a thou-sand lightbulbs.

Wow.

I pull open the doors and step out onto the terrace. It's small and shaped like the bow of a ship. Rain hammers the smoked-glass awning. And ladies and gentlemen, I have a Jacuzzi. The water is lit with twinkling blue and green lights, and it's steaming lightly in the chilly night air. I've not long dried off, but it looks so inviting that I consider taking a dip.

A wood-paneled building the size of a large shed turns out to be a sauna and shower. Inside, stacks of soft, fluffy towels sit on wooden shelves next to a cupboard full of loofahs, facecloths, oils, and shower gels. I'd have a go if I could work out how to turn the sauna on, but there are no obvious controls. I presume Other Joe has a central tech hub hidden away somewhere, perhaps behind the bar or downstairs. I'll check with Molly tomorrow.

A sudden, violent gust of wind blows rain horizontally into my face, and I hasten back inside. It's building up to be a mother of a storm. Padding back across the room in my posh slippers, I notice some photos on the wall behind the bar. As I approach, I realize they are all photos of Other Joe. Many of them have friends in too, or Amy and my parents. But they all include him. In my old home, I had almost no pictures up, just one of the Christmas before we lost Amy. I had tons of photos, but they were all in boxes in the loft. They were too hard to look at, dredged up too many painful memories. I guess Other Joe had nothing he needed to forget.

I study him more closely. He's leaner, dresses sharper, and there's something subtly unfamiliar about his features. They're mine, and yet not. I guess his face wore different expressions and displayed different emotions over the years, and that affected the muscles, wrinkles, and lines.

Looking at these pictures gives me an odd, disconnected sensation, as though one of my mates has photoshopped my head onto the body of a bloke who likes fantastic adventures in far-flung places. I don't remember any of them.

In one picture, I'm playing rugby, probably in my late twenties. In another, I seem to be backpacking with friends in Thailand, maybe. I get a weird and unexpected pang of jealousy.

A smaller photo catches my eye, a group shot in Cheltenham Town Hall, everyone dressed to the nines. Other Joe stands near the center of the group, his arm around an extremely attractive red-haired woman in a very short black dress and vertiginous heels. Everyone else is beaming, but Other Joe and the woman are remarkably serious. Beneath the picture, written on the mounting card, is a handwritten note: "Love you babe. Two years! Karen xx." Amy told me that Other Joe hasn't had a serious relationship recently, and I wonder what happened to Karen. If she was an ex, how come he still has the photo on the wall?

I spend a couple of hours walking down new memory lane, listening to music, trying to settle in. As midnight approaches, I decide it's time for bed. I'm just about to turn the lights off when they flicker. A brilliant flash of lightning is followed by a fizzing pop, and I'm plunged into darkness. I stand still, hoping the lights will come back on, but nothing happens. Either the power's been cut or the fuse has tripped, but I don't know where the fuse box is. I hear an insistent beeping from somewhere downstairs. It's probably the alarm warning me that it's been disconnected from the mains. I don't want it to go off at full volume, so I head to the end of the corridor and down the narrow staircase to the shop.

As I feel my way down the stairwell, another huge rumble of thunder vibrates the walls, and a cold bead of sweat trickles down my spine. I feel a massive urge to run back upstairs and lock myself in.

"Don't be so ridiculous," I mutter. "Get a grip, Bridgeman."

My foot finds the floor at the bottom of the staircase. As quietly as I can, I slide the bolt and gingerly push the door open.

By day, Bridgeman Antiques is a wonderland filled with intriguing treasures, but by night, it's Stephen King's favorite shop of horrors. The wind howls, shaking the front door like an angry ghost. Rain hammers the huge bay windows. A streetlight bathes the shop in a sickly aqua light, transforming channels of rain into swaying seaweed that dance playfully over the ominous shapes of the antiques. Shadows reach out like broken fingers, waiting to drag me into the darkness.

I fumble for the light switch and click it up and down a few times. Nothing. The beeping is louder now, and I think it's coming from somewhere near my desk, toward the front of the shop. I notice a strange light flickering randomly near the front door, like static on an old television. I can hear buzzing too, like electric cables crackling in fog.

"Is someone there?" I call out. The power of my voice belies my fear.

The wind howls an ominous warning, and thunder crashes directly overhead. I take a few steps toward the ghostly light. As I approach the door, I notice that one of the cabinets is open. It was closed when I got home, I'm sure of it.

Then my heart all but stops. Someone is crouching on the floor beside the cabinet! Dressed in dark clothing and a hoodie, the person faces away from me, fiddling with something on the floor.

I freeze, rooted to the spot. What do I do?

The hooded figure suddenly turns to me. Lightning flashes, and the burglar's dark, catlike eyes stare at me. Then the infiltrator jumps up, grabs a bag off the floor, and flees through the front door.

I walk quickly to the door, close it, and dead bolt it. There are no signs of forced entry, no broken glass or splintered wood. Leaning back against the door, I breathe slowly and try to think clearly. Did I leave the shop unlocked? At least the intruder had only a small bag and couldn't have taken much. I'll chat with Molly tomorrow, ask her to check whether any stock is missing, and report the break-in to the police. No point in getting anyone out of bed now.

That's when I notice it: a Roberts radio. Cherry red and brand new, its round dials white and gleaming, its grille polished, the waveband display clear and well-lit.

Static electricity ripples over my skin. The buzzing sound is back. It changes quality, becoming sharper, the whistle and whine of a radio scanning the airwaves. I glide toward it, like a man in a dream, drawn to it as though the radio is luring me. Then, the dial begins to turn, all by itself. It locks onto a signal, filling the shop with deafening rock and roll, a fast tremolo guitar riff—A minor into G major, a progression I recognize instantly. It's Del Shannon's "Runaway." He croons in his famous falsetto, wondering where she'll stay. The keyboard solo howls, and the song gets louder, building to an almighty crescendo.

I reach for the volume dial, raw power crackling between my fingers and the radio. As my finger connects with the dial, I hear a loud, shattering pop, like a roomful of lightbulbs blowing in unison. The world becomes a blinding ball of light, and Bridgeman Antiques is no more.

4

I'm in the back of a police van, bound by handcuffs. It's June 1963. I'm a murder suspect, and for all I know, I could be stuck here indefinitely. The sound of gunfire still rings in my ears. My retirement from time travel isn't exactly going according to plan.

Seated opposite me is a fresh-faced police constable. He looks about twelve, all freckles and no discernible stubble. His brown hair is neatly chopped and oiled. He's wearing a standard uniform, black with a pressed blue shirt and tie; his belt is high on his waist. He tucks his helmet under his arm and offers me a thin smile.

The van is hot as a sauna. I'm still wearing my pajamas, which are covered in drying ketchup and exude a nauseating combo of sweat, rotten food, and disinfectant. The van comes to a stop. I hear voices, and the doors open. The sudden bright light forces me to recoil. We emerge onto a street that's eerily quiet for London's East End. The police station is a slab of red brickwork with dark metal windows. In the present, buildings like this are grubby and run down, the embarrassment of every architect and planning officer that signed off on them.

I'm guided up stone steps that lead to a large oak door with blue police lamps on either side. A maroon sign on the wall reads "Limehouse Police Station" in cream letters. Inside the heady odor of bleach and fresh paint hits my nostrils. I am very close to puking now. Two officers march me along a corridor, shoes squeaking on the linoleum floor, and we end up in a small room in the basement. It's stacked with radio equipment that wouldn't be out of place in an episode of *Star Trek*.

I'm introduced to a cherubic-looking man who I'm told will be my custody officer. His fingers are covered in ink. He explains that they can only hold me for twenty-four hours.

"It won't matter," I tell him. "I'm not staying."

He glances at the officers on either side of me and explains that I'm allowed a phone call and a lawyer. I just nod, feeling as though I'm watching events unfold from a distance.

"You've been arrested on suspicion of murder," the officer says. "You don't have to say anything, but anything you do say could be used against you in a court of law."

I nod again. I've heard this a thousand times on TV.

My fingers are inked and rolled. It crosses my mind that my prints shouldn't exist yet. I haven't even been born.

The custody officer asks me to empty my pockets.

"What's this?" he asks, discovering my iPhone. He presses the circle— because that's just what you do—and the future comes to life with a glow. The officer's mouth hangs open. "Well I never . . ."

"Er, can I keep that with me?" I ask.

"Afraid not," he says. Helplessly, I watch him place it in a cardboard box with "EVIDENCE" written on the side. There's nothing I can do. Hopefully, it'll get shoved in a locker and forgotten about until, at some point, it pings back to the present. "We will lock it up, and you'll get it back . . . later."

He doesn't say, "when you're released," because guilty men don't get released, and he looks like he's made his mind up about me already. They all do, apart from the very young-looking constable who rode with me in the van, and who now escorts me to a cramped cell block.

"My name is Police Constable Robert Green," he tells me. "I'll try to get you some clean clothes. If you need anything, let me know."

"Thank you," I reply. "What happens now?"

"You'll be interviewed shortly." He gestures for me to enter the cell.

Although he's young, his cool gray eyes are those of a much older man, one with confidence and obvious kindness. "For now, make yourself at home."

I walk in, and he locks the cell door.

The sound sends a fresh wave of panic through me. I glance around the cell. It's been tiled like a swimming pool in mustard yellow with white trim. There is one small window, barred, but at least it lets in some light from outside. A thin mattress lies on top of a bench, which is bolted to the wall. The steel sink and toilet are stained with the debris of previous occupants.

There is no way I'm getting out of this. That poor woman was murdered, and as far as the police are concerned, they have their man.

How did this happen?

All avenues lead to W. P. Brown. This is obviously his doing. It's no coincidence that he turned up in my shop this morning, extolling the wonders of time travel, offering mentorship. And then this happens. He seemed harmless, but I was wrong. I told him no, but he clearly decided I was going to travel whether I liked it or not. What's he trying to achieve? Why would he try to persuade me, only to send me anyway?

I never thought I would crave brain freeze, that reassuring icy chill that signals my impending return to the present. It hurts, but its complete absence now is worse. I think back again to the storm, the radio, feeling powerless to stop myself from reaching out and touching it . . . it has to be the reason I'm here. But why?

Thirty minutes later, when I hear keys rattling in the cell door, I'm no nearer to an answer. The door swings open. It's PC Green. He's holding a pile of folded clothes. "Hopefully, these will fit you," he says. "Get changed and put your old clothes in here." He hands me a bag. "Detective Inspector Price is ready to see you now."

The interview room is clearly designed to suck the life out of people. It's windowless, small, and cold. Nothing but a square table with two chairs. PC Green stands in the corner and tells me to sit down. I do as I'm told. It's good to be out of my stinking pajamas, but the shirt and trousers are a tight fit and smell musty and sour.

A man enters the room. He's in his early fifties, I would guess, medium height with a heavy build, broad shoulders, and an air of superiority. He acknowledges PC Green, sits down in the chair opposite me, and runs a hand through his receding gray hair.

"I am Detective Inspector Price," he announces. I detect a hint of a Yorkshire accent, but London appears to be winning the battle. "Do you wish to speak to a lawyer now? Or have one present during this interview?"

"I don't have a lawyer."

"We can appoint one for you."

"I don't need one. I'm not guilty."

Price glowers at me, sizing me up. "Please state your full name," he says, only his lips moving.

"John Smith."

"Address?"

"I don't live here."

"It's a police station," he shoots back sarcastically. "No one lives here."

"I mean I don't have an address."

"You're homeless?"

"Yes."

Price leans back in his chair, his brown tie stretching over his belly. He pulls a cigarette from his pocket, lights up, and slides the pack across the desk. "Help yourself."

I shake my head, noticing that his hands are strong and calloused. The clock on the wall reads 2:45 p.m. The second hand ticks, my heart beating three times per tick.

"You seem nervous, Mr. Smith."

Of course I'm nervous. A wave of nausea flutters up through my gut. "Would you mind not smoking?" I ask him.

He exhales smoke from his nostrils, looking genuinely confused. "Why don't you start by telling me what happened?"

"I heard a gunshot," I explain, working through the story I've been practicing in my mind. "I stumbled upon the woman in the alleyway, ran to the street, and raised the alarm."

PC Green looks like he believes me. DI Price, not so much.

"So who killed her then?" Price asks.

"I have no idea. I found her like that."

"Shall I tell you what I think?" He doesn't wait for an answer. "I think you were together last night, and she ran out on you this morning, hence the pajamas. You caught up to her, had a fight, shot her in cold blood, and then hid the murder weapon."

I shake my head.

Seconds pass. His slate-gray eyes remain fixed on me the whole time.

Eventually, he says, "Then, for some strange reason, you covered yourself in her blood and walked in the direction of the sirens. Unbearable guilt, maybe?"

"It's not blood," I tell him. "I was scared, I fell over. Then I ran. All I was trying to—"

"You think we're playing games?" Price smacks his hand on the desk. "A woman is dead, Mr. Smith, and you don't even seem bothered."

"It's terrible. But it has nothing to do with me."

Price stubs out his cigarette, stands up, and paces the room. "I can't figure you out," he says. "I know a criminal when I see one, and I don't think you're a bad man, John."

"I'm not," I agree enthusiastically.

"Then it's time to start telling the truth," he says. "Tell me what you saw."

It's tempting to spill the beans, but until I understand why I'm in 1963, I think the less I say, the better. I've changed history just by being here. If I tell them what I saw, I could set events in motion that might have a catastrophic impact on the future. "I told you, I didn't see anything."

He leans back and sighs. "Call it a copper's intuition, Mr. Smith, but . . . has someone threatened you?"

"No."

"We can protect you," he assures me. "You just need to tell the truth."

I feel a weakening in my resolve. When a traumatic event happens, you want to tell someone about it, anyone who will listen, but I can't. Not here, not this time. I feel sorry for these men, decent people just doing their jobs. All they want is the truth. The problem is, they couldn't handle it if I told them where I was really from. All I have to do is keep my mouth shut and wait.

"I'm sorry, but I can't tell you anything if I don't know anything."

"This is important," Price says. "If you go to trial, a jury is going to wonder why you withheld information. It could harm your defense. Do you understand?"

I assure him I do. Undeterred, DI Price chips away at me for another ten minutes or so, turning the screws. I stick to my script. It isn't hard, there are only two words: "No comment."

Price glares at me, tapping a pen on the desk. His fierce expression suggests he would like to stab me in the neck with it. "You think you're smart, don't you?"

"Actually, I don't."

He grins, which is worrying. His eyes remain cold. "Stick him in with Trevor."

PC Green frowns but shakes it off quickly. "Yes, Guv."

"Who's Trevor?" I ask.

Price shows me his teeth. "No comment."

PC Green escorts me to my cell, which reeks with the sour stench of whiskey, like a steel-caged distillery, and the pungent, underlying odor of old sweat and urine.

Trevor—I presume that's who he is—paces the cell, shouting and gesticulating. His hair is oily, unkempt, and scraped back over his head. His gray beard doesn't hide a couple of unpleasant brown stains around his mouth. He looks like he's been wearing the same clothes most of his life.

He is busy telling London that he's dying, that he needs a doctor. I watch him nervously, desperately trying to avoid eye contact until the main lights go off, leaving us in a gloomy half-light.

Trevor staggers over, his smell forcing me to cover my mouth. He begins to speak, then pauses, as though suddenly confused. An almost infant-like expression falls over him, and then he belches. "That's better," he says, his weepy, bloodshot eyes focusing on me. "Is it bedtime?"

"Yes, mate," I say slowly. "Time to go to sleep."

From inside his beard, a smile appears, revealing surprisingly perfect white teeth. He claps his hands and starts hopping on one leg, telling me that he was important once, that he had a life.

Yeah, didn't we all.

Trevor's ranting continues on a loop and includes some quite loud screaming. No one comes to help. I slide my fingers into my ears. Eventually the cell falls quiet, and I am alone with my thoughts, which soon settle on Alexia. They say absence makes the heart grow fonder; well, fifty-plus years adds fuel to that fire.

Alone here, it's easy to imagine being forgotten, slipping between the cracks of time. When I was younger, I often thought how cool it would be living in the sixties. Not so much in prison though, without my family, or friends, or hope.

What if I am stuck? I could go on trial for murder, sentenced to life before I'm even born. I have to figure out a way to get home.

I think back over my previous jumps, when I was trying to save Amy. I was always fighting to go deeper into the past, to stay as long as I could. In the end, though, time would always send me home, and the farther back I went, the faster that would happen. There were rules. I had to learn them, and then break them, in order to achieve the impossible. Do I have to try and do the same again? I consider how the radio seems to have enabled a new, very different way of traveling through time. There must be some similarities, some common ground.

Has all this been reversed?

W. P. Brown probably knows.

I think about Alexia. She taught me to rethink what I consider to be *now*. She taught me reset the past, to make it feel like the present. I wonder if that could be the key to getting home.

I close my eyes and steady my breathing. I listen to Trevor's rhythmic snoring, like a metronome crossed with an elephant. Noisy but reliably consistent.

All I have is the present. All I am is now.

When my surroundings begin to slide away, I feel a sense of relief, but soon I feel a familiar sensation, like slipping beneath the veil of sleep, and yet I'm fully awake and aware.

I'm about to have a viewing, I realize.

And I have no choice but to follow it down the rabbit hole.

5

The scene builds in front of me like an establishing shot in a movie. I'm high up, as though on a crane, thirty feet above a busy London street. Below and ahead of me sits an impressive stone building, the distinctive black horse of Lloyds Bank above the entrance.

A woman comes out the front door, holding her handbag tightly against her body, and runs down the steps to the street. I recognize her immediately. It's the woman I saw gunned down in the alleyway. Her eyes dart around, apparently searching for someone. It's like those near-death, out-of-body experiences. I'm drifting down to street level, toward the woman, except I'm not returning to my own body. Instead, I feel myself moving into hers. I begin to see the world through her eyes, and I become immediately aware of how tense she is.

She walks quickly toward a young man in his late teens leaning against a nearby wall. As she approaches, he throws his cigarette to the ground and stands on it, blowing the smoke hastily over his shoulder. She decides not to berate him. Not today.

"What's going on?" he asks. "Why are you in such a rush?"

He's taller than she is now, muscular and strong, but he is still her boy, and it's her job to keep him safe. She cups his cheek lightly in her hand. "Something terrible has happened. We are in danger, Gus. We need to leave London. I'm sorry." Her heart aches. This is all her fault. She wishes she had never taken that job at the Unicorn.

"What kind of danger?" He looks at her searchingly. "If you've been threatened by one of your customers, I can sort them out. I know some good moves. They won't know what's hit 'em." He balls his hands into fists and stands a little taller.

"This is not the sort of thing you can fix with punches. We need to go somewhere else for a while—a few months, at least." She says this, knowing they will never come back.

"A few months!" Gus exclaims. "But my life is here, Mum. All my friends!"

"You'll make new ones."

His gaze hardens. "I'm fed up of starting again. I've had it with running. If we don't face up to people, they'll just keep hounding us. We need to show them we're not afraid."

"Some people are too powerful to face up to," she says.

Gus shakes his head. "Listen, Mum. I used to respect Tommy Shaw, but then people started saying he was going soft, and the next thing you know, he's been smacked over the head and he's a vegetable. That's what happens if you don't stay strong. We need to stand our ground." He frowns. "Hey, I bet Frankie would help. The Shaws know everyone. Frankie's always sorting stuff out for other people."

"No!" she says forcefully. Gus is obviously shocked at the power of her response. "The Shaws are connected with this," she says. "They are part of the problem."

"Really? How?"

"I can't tell you," she says. "I don't want to put you in more danger."

"What's going on? What have you done?"

She takes hold of her son by the arms. "Listen to me," she says, her voice low and urgent. "I have always put you first. I'm not saying it's forever, but we have to get out of London for a while. I need you to trust me."

Gus's face is impassive. "You go then, if you have to. I'm staying here."

He inherited his father's dark hair and his stubbornness. She tries another tack. "Remember when you were little, and we used to have *yes* days? You could ask for anything, and I would say, 'Yes,' if I could?"

"Mum, no! It's not the same."

"Yes, it is. I don't ask much of you, Gus, but I am asking you to do this. Please."

He thinks about it for a minute. She sees herself in his eyes, her own indecision. She tries not to rush him, although she is afraid that they are running out of time.

"OK," he says finally. "I'll come with you."

"You must not tell anyone what we are doing or where we are going. Not even Father William. Promise me."

"All right."

"Say it."

"I promise, Mum, Jesus!" he says, raising his hands in surrender. "What's the plan?"

"We need to go home and pack, then I've booked us train tickets to the coast."

They're walking toward the bus stop when a flush of adrenaline floods her stomach. Across the street, she sees a cream-colored Rolls-Royce crawling slowly along the curb. "Gus, I just remembered I need to pick up a couple of things for our trip," she says. She moves a little, so that Gus turns his back to the car. She pulls an envelope of cash from her handbag and hands it hurriedly to her son, her heart thudding in her chest. "Take this and go straight home. I'll meet you there in a bit. Call a cab for an hour's time, to Victoria Station."

"Mum, I'm not leaving you."

"You must, *tesoro*, please! I won't be long." She gives him a gentle shove. "Go now. Remember, don't talk to anyone. I'll see you soon. *Ti voglio bene.*"

She watches as he jogs along the street and jumps onto the back of a double-decker bus. Her shoulders drop with relief as it pulls away, but it's short-lived. Turning back, she sees that the Rolls-Royce has parked. A tall, stocky man in a leather jacket gets out of the back. He clocks her and prepares to cross the road. Casting her eyes around, she spots a small alleyway beside the bank that cuts through to the next street. Holding her bag tightly, she runs back past the bank and into the alley.

Up ahead there's a break in the wall, maybe a good place to hide. As she reaches the little courtyard, she barely registers a man, dressed in pajamas, rummaging through the bins. She's focused on escaping danger.

She runs on, up the alleyway.

Hearing footsteps, she glances behind and sees the man in the leather jacket gaining on her. Her heart is pounding in her chest. She turns back, ready to run, but then stops in her tracks, her body rigid. The Rolls-Royce is blocking the other end of the alley.

A red-haired man climbs languidly out of the back door and positions himself imposingly in the middle of the alleyway. A heavy gold crucifix glints below his neck.

She tries to catch her breath, determined not to show her fear. "Frankie Shaw! What are you doing, following me?" she says indignantly.

"You going somewhere, Lucy?" the redhead asks.

"It's a free country," she replies.

"Not when I'm paying you to be somewhere else, it isn't," he says. "Tony called and said you'd only just started your shift when you suddenly ran away. I was worried about you." His tone shifts, becoming unnervingly empathetic. "Where's Gus? I saw him with you outside the bank. Is everything OK?"

Lucy folds her arms. "I'm not feeling well, Frankie. I need to go home. Can you let me past, please?"

"Tell you what," he says casually. "Tell me what happened to my brother, and I'll let you go."

The skin prickles across the back of her neck. "Seriously? This again? I've told you already, I don't know anything."

He puts his hands in his pockets and sighs. "The thing is, Lucy, I've got a God-given gift. I know when people are lying to me. I'm a reasonable man, as you're well aware, but I can't stand a liar." He clenches his jaw, and his face grows paler, accentuating his freckles. "What happened to Tommy?"

"I don't know! Frankie, I swear!" She swallows and tightens her grip on the handbag. "And anyway, I heard the good news, that he's getting better."

Frankie smiles, but it's a cruel sneer. "You heard he's coming out of the coma then?" he says softly.

"Yes," she says, "and when he wakes up, you can ask him yourself what happened." Lucy searches his face, trying desperately to convince him. "You'll see I had nothing to do with it."

Frankie shakes his head and harrumphs. "You're the worst thing that ever happened to him. You gave him ideas, delusions of a quiet life in suburbia. You sent him soft." He scans the summer sky above, composes himself, and then looks Lucy dead in the eye. "Tommy died this morning," he says.

She feels as though all the blood has drained from her legs. "No!" she says. "But I heard he was getting better! Tony said he was communicating, starting to open his eyes?"

"I spread that rumor," says Frankie, spine-chillingly calm. "I wanted to flush out the dirty rat who did this to him. And it's you who's running."

Lucy struggles to hide her shaking.

"Before he died," Frankie says, "Tommy told me it was you."

"I don't believe it."

"I didn't believe it either. But if there's one thing I've learned, it's that innocent people don't run."

He reaches for his crucifix and lifts it to his lips. He closes his eyes and kisses it, his mouth moving in silent prayer.

Lucy senses what's about to happen. "Murder is a sin, Frankie," she says slowly. "If you kill me, you will go to hell." Gus's face flashes into her mind's eye. *I can't leave him.*

Frankie chuckles. "God and I have . . . an understanding. This is one of those eye-for-an-eye situations. You see, after what you did to my brother, killing you sort of gets . . . *canceled out.*"

Lucy turns and runs, knowing, waiting for the sound of gunfire. When it comes, there is no pain. There is only darkness.

PART 2

6

Self-awareness surges through me like the shock of a defibrillator. I heave oxygen into my lungs. I'm back in the prison cell. Moonlight streams in through the barred window. Trevor is asleep on his front, somehow snoring. It's 1963, and I'm alive.

I reassure myself that it wasn't me who was brutally gunned down in that alleyway. And yet, the sound of gunfire rings in my ears, and the cold specter of death clings to me like a disease. My heart hammers away. I sit and lean forward, waiting for the speckled dots in my vision to subside.

That poor woman.

Lucy.

I could feel her emotions. Fear. The building panic, the shock and realization that Frankie Shaw meant to kill me.

"To kill *her*," I murmur, forcing myself to acknowledge that the experience was a viewing. It didn't happen to me. Still, I felt it all. I felt her take her last breath.

This isn't the first time I've seen life through another lens. Far from it. Objects have shown me their secrets since I was a teenager. Officially, it's called psychometry, but I call them *viewings*. I get a sense of a person connected to the object, and the feelings and emotions associated with it.

But that viewing was nothing like I've experienced before.

For a start, there was no object to trigger the viewing. And usually, the object feels delicate, its associated stories like soap bubbles. I have to coax the viewing out. This wasn't like that. It came to me during a moment of meditation. It arrived and it owned me, no permission required. That's never happened before. And that's just the technical aspect. The viewing itself was much longer and more detailed than I've ever seen before. I got an entire narrative, a coherent piece of a story.

My hands tremble as the adrenaline finally runs out. I can taste its coppery tang. The radio may have sent me here, but I don't think that's why I saw the murder in such detail from Lucy's perspective.

They say the eyes are the windows to the soul. I wonder if Lucy and I formed some kind of emotional connection when we first met in the alley. It was brief, but we did make eye contact, both of us shocked and afraid. Was that all it took?

Why now though? Why hasn't this happened to me before? Is it because she died? Is this some sort of message from the grave?

W. P. Brown's words come back to me, like the lyrics to a song you hate but can't get out of your head. He talked of developing my gift, said that I would tune in, told me not to be afraid. Is this part of it?

I hold my head in my hands, despair sinking in. So many questions, and I am still no closer to getting home. I wince, my head pounding like it's being squeezed in a cold vice.

Hang on.

Wait one time-traveling minute!

"Brain freeze!" I cry, standing up in a euphoric surge of joy. I have never been so happy to be in pain. "I'm going home!"

"Can I come with you?" Trevor asks, standing up.

I take a nervous step away from him. "I'm sorry, mate, but this is a one-way trip."

Trevor steps into the moonlight, suddenly lucid. "You don't look right," he says. "What's happening to you?"

I peer down at my hands. My skin shimmers like the scales of a fish in a beam of light. "Listen, Trevor, it's going to be OK."

His lips tremble. His eyes fill with water. "I'm never drinking again."

"That would be good," I say. "*Really* good."

"Are you a ghost?" he asks, but before I can say another word, he screams—and I mean he wails, like a banshee on fire.

I plead with him to be quiet. "This is all a dream!" I try to reassure him, but his eyes widen and become a little redder, and he turns the volume up a notch. I cover my ears as the cell turns a wonderful shade of blue.

Normally, the return process takes around fifteen minutes, but this time, the brain freeze rushes at me.

The present is almost here.

The cell floods with light. PC Green runs in. "What is all this noise?" he demands.

Trevor rushes to the bars of the cell, gripping them hard, eyes so wide they look like they're trying to escape from his head. "He's a demon, come to kill me!"

"Are you OK, Mr. Smith?" PC Green asks. "You've gone awfully pale."

My hands are semitransparent now. Thankfully, this is 1963, so there are no CCTV cameras to record my disappearance. "You're about to see something you are not going to believe," I tell him.

He leans back against the wall and folds his arms. "I've seen it all and heard it all before," he says, with the slow, worldly tone that only the young can manage. "Don't tell me, you're planning to escape."

I suddenly feel very sorry for this poor young man. At the moment, life makes total sense to him. That's about to change.

"I'm about to disappear," I explain, breathless with relief that I'm homeward bound. "I mean, I'm going to do a proper Houdini. When you think back on this, just know that you aren't going mad. This is real. It's just hard to explain."

The young policeman laughs, but then his expression slackens. His mouth hangs open, eyes agog. "What's happening to your . . . your face?" he says, his voice catching.

The room floods with the cool blue of time travel, like the ocean of the present crashing over us. As the cell dissolves before me, I catch sight of PC Green, his expression uncomprehending, and hear the echoing sound of Trevor's scream fading into darkness.

But I don't go home.

I slip into a place that exists between times, a dark void where floating windows serve as portals through time. I remember this place. When I was trying to navigate my way back to Amy, I used to find myself here. I likened it to being inside a zoetrope. Back then, I wanted to be here. I was trying to go back deeper in time. Now though, I'm confused. My mouth dries up. Does this mean I'm going even farther back?

I study the windows revolving around me. Colorful, animated scenes framed with soft edges that bleed into empty space. Through one, I see Cheltenham, my shop, small details like the furniture, brickwork, and wooden floors. I see my terrace with the Jacuzzi, but it passes quickly. Eight or nine different scenes go spinning past at nauseating speed.

I try not to panic. Timing is everything. I bob my head along to the rhythm of the passing windows, trying to psych myself up to jump. The terrace goes by again, and I decide that will be my target.

I feel the zoetrope tipping, like a tent being pulled from the ground by a hurricane. If I don't jump now, I might spin off into nothing, forever . . . I glance up and see only darkness, an impossible void. Instinctively, I know that time doesn't exist out there.

I watch the terrace window make another revolution, and then, with a guttural screaming sound that I am *not* proud of, I run. The zoetrope continues to tip against me. I launch toward the image of my terrace. Wind rushes; my stomach drops. I pinch my eyes shut and jump.

It's a shock when my feet hit earlier than expected. My body slams down at a horrible angle onto what I realize are roof tiles, slimy and wet. My fingers gain no purchase, and I slide straight down the tiles. My slippers fly off, and now it's just my bare feet skidding over rough terra-cotta. It hurts like hell, but I get a slightly better grip.

I crack straight through some plastic guttering and fall, expecting a sickeningly long descent, but I hit the wooden deck of the terrace and stagger backward, tumbling into a chair and tables. My hands are still ghostly, pulsing and shimmering. I stumble backward, arms flailing, and fall into the Jacuzzi. It's warm and welcoming, and after everything I've just been through, it feels pretty good.

I sit up, bathed in neon-blue froth. "I'm alive!" I cry, wiping water and tears from my eyes. Eventually, I spin my legs over the edge of the circular tub and place my feet back onto the deck, reassuring myself that I really am home, that this is the present.

It's light outside. I feel queasy, like I've been on a roller coaster.

But the ride is over now. I'm home.

I slide open the bifold doors, step into the warm loft, and close the doors again behind me. I'm struck by how modern everything is, a stark contrast to the sixties. The clock on the wall tells me it's 8 a.m. When I travel, time passes at the same speed in the present. It was midnight when I touched the radio, which means I was in the past for eight hours. Desperate for a shower, I make my way across the loft toward the stairs, but my nostrils are assaulted by the smell of burning metal, like soldering. At first, I assume it's my senses adjusting to the aftermath of time travel, but then I notice a set of metal ladders leaning against the wall, beside a speaker with cables protruding from its rear. I look around but I can't see anyone.

"Hello?" I call out. "Is someone here?"

There's a scraping sound, followed by a whimper. Gingerly, I creep toward one of the leather sofas.

Leaning over I discover a large man on his backside, pressed up against the wall. His bald head shines beneath a blanket of LEDs, slick with perspiration. He's wearing Doc Martens, faded gray jeans, and a black T-shirt that reads, "No Fear." Ironically, he looks scared out of his mind.

I sigh with relief.

"Vinny!" I say. "Are you OK?"

My best friend chews his lip feverishly. "Yeah, I'm fine, absolutely fine."

In my previous life, Vinny helped me in my quest to save Amy— although only I remember our adventures together—and I haven't seen him since then. It's good to see him, but my happiness dissipates quickly. Vinny isn't just surprised by my sudden appearance. He seems utterly petrified. Perspiration beads from his forehead, and he is horribly pale, almost yellow.

"What are you doing here?" I ask him.

He gets up off the floor, dusts himself off, and stares at me. "What am I doing here?" Vinny repeats my initial question. "I'm installing your new Sonos system, *like you asked me to*." He fishes a brown glass bottle from his pocket, shakes some pills into his trembling hand, and munches them down, grimacing like he's chewing soap.

"Ah," I say, thinking that Vinny can be my first test case for the amnesia story. "The thing is, mate, I had an accident on my mountain bike. I banged my head, and now I don't—"

"I won't tell anyone," he gasps, eyes wild with fear. "I'll just forget all about it. This could be like a secret or something. I promise I won't tell anyone!"

"Whoa, Vin, what are you talking about?"

"I didn't see anything, I swear!" He's begging now, his voice getting higher and higher. "Please don't kill me!"

"Kill you?" A nervous laugh escapes me. "Don't be ridiculous! Why would you say that?"

"I saw you . . . I was up on the ladders, and I was looking through the window, and you just . . . fell out of the sky!"

Oh dear.

"Listen, Vinny, whatever you think you saw, I can explain," I say as reassuringly as I can. "I'm not going to kill you. We're friends."

That line does not have the desired effect. "Now I *know* you're not him!" Vinny holds up a screwdriver, his hand shaking. "Oh God, I don't want to die, not like this . . . not *hungry!*"

"Vinny, I am not going to hurt you."

"I know what's going on here." He takes a deep breath, his eyes darting in all directions. "You're dead, but your spirit isn't rested. You've come back to exact your revenge on me."

"I'm not here to kill anyone, Vin, and I'm not a ghost either."

He points the screwdriver at me. "I know why you don't know anything and why you sound so different. You've been abducted by aliens, and they wiped your memory." He waves at my sixties prison gear. "And look at what they made you wear!"

The memory wipe idea is his closest theory yet.

I attempt a smile. "I was up on the roof and—"

"You appeared out of thin air," Vinny spurts with a manic laugh. "When you landed, you looked like you were made of jelly or something! Do you have to adapt to our oxygenated environment?"

He pulls the bottle of pills from his pocket again, tips back his head, and pours more of them down his throat.

"Vinny," I say, "take it easy on those, yeah?"

He nods as he crunches. "They're for my anxiety," he says. "They help me sleep too, although I'm not sure I'll ever sleep again. Not now I've seen proof."

He works his way along the wall toward the stairs, his gaze fixed on me. "Listen," he says. "People who know me, know that I've done quite a bit of the old *wacky baccy*. Do you understand what wacky baccy is?" I nod. "I'm a total airhead, so they wouldn't believe me if I told them. Not that I *will* tell them!" He draws a line across his lips with his thumb and forefinger. "I'm just going to walk out of here, nice and slow, and you're going to let me go, OK?"

"Yes," I assure him, feeling terrible for scaring him so badly. "And, Vinny, try not to worry, yeah?"

He smiles stiffly and then darts down the staircase without looking back. He thunders down the stairs two-at-a-time and is gone. Poor guy. I'll give him some space, then go and see him later. Who knows, I might even tell him the truth. I did that once before, and he took it well.

Meanwhile, the Amnesia Protocol is a go.

7

I kick my filthy convict gear into the corner of the bathroom and step into the shower. A multitude of jets hose me clean from every angle like a human car wash. It feels good. Grounding.

Finally, I begin to process the last few hours of my life, starting with my unexpected arrival in 1963. The murder, my subsequent arrest, and then the powerful viewing from Lucy's perspective. I keep thinking about how this all began with the radio, but that's not quite right. Life got weird the minute Mr. W. P. Brown walked through the door. It wasn't him who burgled the shop, but I can't believe he's not connected.

Waves of exhaustion wash over me, like maximum jet lag. Add to that the shock and intensity of my recent trip, plus the feelings of insecurity and disconnection from my life here in the present, and what does that equal? A recipe for a total meltdown.

That makes me think of Vinny. I was so wired and so relieved to be back, I wasn't thinking straight. I can't leave him overdosing on anxiety pills and thinking I'm from another planet. I must go and see him today. I turn off the shower and grab one of the towels from the rack. My hands are still shaking. How the hell did my life get so complicated again?

I notice my convict clothes have disappeared, and I'm not really surprised. That's how it works. When objects are dragged through time, it takes a little while, but eventually time seems to realize they're out of sync and pings them back to where they're supposed to be. I guess my pajamas will have arrived back in Limehouse police station in the present, and my iPhone too, hopefully before anyone back in the 1960s had the chance to examine it too closely. Back then, sixty years ahead of its time, it had the potential to change the entire course of technological history, but now it's just another lost mobile phone, one of millions.

I survey the racks of clothes hanging in Other Joe's bedroom. Rail after rail of classy threads, all designer brands, organized by color. Everything feels a bit snug, apart from the shoes. On that front, at least, we're exactly the same.

It's just after 9 a.m. Time to face my life here. This really is day one of my new job, and it's suddenly feeling alarmingly real.

I head down into the shop.

Golden shafts of dust-filled light drift across my antiques wonderland. In my previous life, I had a shop, but I lost it due to a lack of focus. Deep down, I didn't believe I deserved success or happiness. It's going to take a long time to accept this place as my own, but I absolutely love it: the smell of dust, age, and varnish; a chorus of clocks ticking; the enchanting aura of very old things, each with their own unique story, treasures and fascinating artifacts waiting to be claimed.

Bridgeman Antiques appears to be open for business, but there are no customers yet. I'm thankful. It means I have time to ease myself in.

A woman emerges from the storeroom. She's in her early sixties, I would guess. She carries herself well, shoulders square, chin lifted, hands clasped at her waist. She's dressed in a cream blouse, dark-brown trousers, and sensible lace-up shoes. Her thick gray hair is short and wavy.

"Ah, there you are," she says, removing her glasses.

A name appears in flashing lights in my mind's eye. "Molly!"

"So you still know who I am, then?" she says. "Amy told me you fell off your mountain bike and gave yourself amnesia." She looks at me expectantly.

"I bounced down the hill on my head, and now I can't remember much about anything."

"You weren't wearing a helmet?" she says, failing to hide her disapproval.

"No. I forgot. But the doctor says my memory will come back eventually."

"Oh dear, oh dear. What a terrible to-do. Are you sure it's amnesia?"

Her pale green eyes are now laced with concern. "How much can you remember?"

"I remember the basics. I know about antiques, and I know my family. The rest is a bit of a blur at the moment."

She purses her lips, deep lines etched on her forehead. "I don't know, Mr. Bridgeman. You don't seem right at all. Your voice sounds different, and I have to say, the idea of banging your head so hard that you don't know what's what, and then carrying on as normal—well, it doesn't seem right." She works her gaze over me slowly, as though checking for wood-worm in an old piece of furniture. "Have you been properly assessed?"

"Yes," I lie. "Lots of tests and stuff. Apparently, things should settle down and my memories will come back. Hopefully."

"I see," she says. "Amnesia is rather rare though, isn't it? You were terribly unlucky. No helmet though, Mr. Bridgeman . . ." She trails off, shaking her head.

I feel as though I'm being scolded by a schoolteacher. "Sorry, Molly," I mumble.

"I'm not sure about any of this at all," she says, folding her arms. "Are you sure you should be at work?"

"The doctor said I'll get better much faster if I'm surrounded by people who know me, who can talk about my life and help to jog my memory. I would really appreciate it if you could do that for me. Just take me through the process of how we do things. I'll do my best to keep up."

She heaves a big reluctant sigh. "Well, if you're absolutely sure."

"I am, Molly. Go for it."

"Right," she says briskly, suddenly infused with businesslike efficiency. She walks over to the desk and opens up the diary. "We've got a busy day today. Where would you like to start?"

I feel a momentary nibble of panic at my lack of a plan. Then I remember that I've forgotten everything. "Why don't you start by telling me what we normally do? Just give me a rough idea of what a normal day looks like."

She appears agitated. "There's no such thing as a normal day."

I decide not to bite. I just wait.

Eventually, she says, "I usually make you a nice cup of tea, then we run through the diary. Then I stay here and handle all the deliveries, customers, shipping, and stocktaking."

"And what do I do?" I ask.

"You handle the purchasing. You find all the stock for the shop. You choose everything yourself."

I smile in relief. "I'm sure I can handle that."

"You don't spend much time here," she continues, "but when you do pop in, you chat with customers, tell them the provenance of the items they're interested in. They like that. Very much."

"OK," I say, looking around the shop, wondering, not for the first time, whether Other Joe may also have had some psychometric ability.

Molly's watching me the whole time. "Do you really not remember any of this?" she asks.

"It's going to be fine, Molly," I tell her, as confidently as I can. "I'm already feeling better."

She looks at me dubiously and then waves a hand in the air, as though swiping away my madness. "If you say so, Mr. Bridgeman. Shall I pop the kettle on now?"

"That sounds good." She glides away to the kitchenette at the back of the shop, and I'm alone again with the antiques. This feels like my first day at school. It will probably take a few months to settle in, but this might just work.

Molly returns and hands me a cup of tea. "Just how you like it," she says.

I am desperately in need of a caffeine hit, but I decide not to claim that my bump on the head has turned me into a rabid coffee drinker. I'll leave that for another time.

"Thank you," I say politely.

Molly waits for me to take a sip. Hesitantly, I do just that. It's weak, lukewarm, and tastes horribly sweet and milky. I almost spray it across the room. I put the cup down on the desk. Molly sucks air through pursed lips. "We might have forgotten who we are, Mr. Bridgeman, but let's not forget our manners." She picks up the cup, hands it to me, watches me take another sip, and shakes her head. "Last night I received an alert on that app you installed for me."

"App? Sorry, I'm not sure what you mean."

"The security app." She smiles, but it's almost a grimace. "The alarm was tripped last night, although I can't see any sign of a break-in."

"I think it was the storm," I tell her. "The power went out."

"Oh, that reminds me." She goes into the stockroom and returns holding the red Roberts radio. "I found this radio this morning, but I don't recognize it. It's not on the stock list either," she says, as though that's a cardinal sin and it's my fault.

The sight of it sends my guts into a spin. I flinch and step back. "Can you please put that down?" I say, trying not to sound snippy.

She frowns. "It's just a radio, Mr. Bridgeman. Did you take it in?" Her tone suggests that would have been a bad decision. I couldn't agree more. Being near it is making me feel ill, although I'm getting no sense of the energy that I felt from it last night.

"No, I didn't," I say. "Can you get rid of it?"

"Certainly. I'll pop it in the charity pile."

"Actually, I'd rather you just took it somewhere, away from here. Today." I try to sound calm, but she looks at me askance.

"Whatever is the matter with it?" she says, examining the radio.

"Nothing. I just don't want it . . . in the shop."

Around ten o'clock, a man comes in searching for a hat stand. We have an enjoyable conversation, and I make my first sale. It feels good. I do my bit, and Molly takes care of the money. Miraculously, she seems satisfied and tells me appreciatively that I still have "the magic."

That may be, but if I don't get some coffee soon, I won't be responsible for my actions. I yawn, a little too loudly.

"Would you like another cup of tea?" Molly asks.

Just the thought of another tepid, tea-flavored milkshake makes me heave. "Actually, I'm going to head out and grab some lunch," I tell her.

Molly checks her watch. "It's only eleven o'clock. Isn't that a little early?"

"I suppose so, but I feel a bit jet-lagged today."

"Jet-lagged? Why? Where have you been?"

"I slept really badly, that's all," I tell her. "So, is it OK if I go out then?"

She frowns at me in confusion.

"What?" I ask defensively.

"Why are you asking for my permission?" She seems genuinely bemused.

"That's not normal, is it?"

"No." She shakes her head. "You usually do exactly as you please."

"Well, Molly," I say, "some things are going to change around here, starting with better communication."

"Oh, excellent," she says with a heavy dollop of passive aggression. "Perhaps you could start by returning your calls."

"Have I missed one?"

"Martin called me last night, said he's been trying to get hold of you." She folds her arms. "He was not at all happy," she adds, sounding almost gleeful.

"I'll call him," I say. "Although that reminds me. I've lost my phone."

Molly's brow narrows. "Lost, as in you can't recall where you left it?"

"No." I think on my feet. "It got smashed, you know, during my biking accident."

"Would you like me to arrange a new one for you?"

"Yes, please. If that's OK?"

"Of course."

"Do you need anything while I'm out?" I ask.

She seems surprised. "We're nearly out of tea bags," she says. "Although I can get some at lunchtime, if you like."

"It's OK," I say. "I'll pick some up on the way back."

I pull open the door and the bell jangles.

"Mr. Bridgeman?" Molly calls out. I turn back toward her. Her expression is pained, but then it softens. "I just wanted to say . . . I'm glad you weren't badly injured. This place wouldn't be the same without you."

8

Out on the street, I take a moment to admire the shop. I glance up at the sign above the door, written in a dark-gray serif font with gold edges. The frontage looks smart, a dark-blue door flanked by stone pillars. It's inviting, with large windows displaying an enticing range of genuine antiques. I've lost count of the number of times I was told, within the close-knit community of dealers in Cheltenham, that a shop like this would never work. Too hard to turn a profit, too many tourists and bargain hunters. Yet somehow, Other Joe made a success of it.

No doubt with a ton of help from Molly.

It's going to take time to properly assess and learn the cast of characters in this play that has become my life, but first impressions count. Molly seems like an efficient, capable, and loyal employee. And like Amy said, it seems like Other Joe let her run the place. I plan to continue with that approach, so that I don't destroy his legacy and his business. I do need to be careful.

The fresh air is good, but it's not enough. I scan my mental GPS for caffeine hot spots between here and Vinny's shop. As I walk, I think about how incredibly lucky I am to have landed so squarely on my feet. I feel humbled, almost embarrassed. That thought inevitably makes me think of Lucy, gunned down in the alleyway. She wasn't so fortunate. I feel terrible about what happened to her, but it was a long time ago, and it really has nothing to do with me. Whatever happened with that radio, I need to put it behind me.

Ten minutes later my coffee radar perks up. I smell the beans before I even see the Daily Grind, an independent establishment, with lots of wood paneling and industrial lighting. KT Tunstall warbles sweetly through the speakers, welcoming me into the café. The small queue quickly dies down, and the server—a hipster with a groomed beard and a checked shirt—seems to recognize me.

"The usual?" he asks.

"If my usual is a three-shot flat white, then yes please."

"Sure," the hipster says, clearly surprised. "No problemo."

My gaze is drawn to two customers. Both have beards, like most of the men in here. They are kids really, and acting *way* too positive, loud and enthusiastic with lots of nodding and back slapping. I smile. Maybe nothing bad has happened to them yet. Good for them.

A heavily tattooed girl calls my name. I grab my coffee and take a desperate sip. It's heaven.

"Did you find everything you were looking for today?" the girl asks with well-practiced enthusiasm.

This generic question is one of my pet peeves. I consider asking the girl how likely it would *really* be for a person to find *everything* they were looking for in a coffee shop—when a woman enters. Sound fades away, as though someone has spun the world's volume dial. My peripheral vision fades around the edges as she glides across the room.

Alexia Finch.

Seeing her again is like seeing her for the first time. She looks radiant, classy in tight black jeans, chunky brown boots, and a long swaying coat. Her hair is shorter than the last time I saw her, almost bobbed. Her skin glows. My stomach tightens. A wave of panic and adrenaline rushes up from the ground and climbs all over me, and I'm rooted to the spot.

Alexia reaches the counter, and slowly, reality leaches back into my senses. She hasn't seen me yet. I blink, wondering what to do next. Last time we spoke, it was awkward. She opens her bag, and fate offers me a solution when she drops a stack of papers.

"Dammit!" she says, crouching down to the floor.

I kneel next to her, gathering up folders and envelopes like a love-struck schoolkid. I smell the soapy sheen of her hair and the subtle spice of perfume beneath. She glances up at me, and I notice the freckles dotted around her mouth. When our eyes meet, I'm transported to the night of our first kiss on Leckhampton Hill. She frowns.

She doesn't know this version of me, but that doesn't stop me from wanting to tell her how much I've missed her. I know this moment is going on way too long, but I can't help it; I just stare, eyes swimming in hers.

"What are you playing at?" she asks as we stand up. Her voice has the husky quality I remember, but it's laced with something new. She seems annoyed.

"I'm just trying to help you," I say, handing her a pile of folders.

"I don't mean *now*." She grabs the papers from me, her voice sharp and accusing. "I mean what on earth was that phone call about?"

She's referring to the call I made to her when I got back from saving Amy, which was when I realized that she didn't remember any of it. That was a horrible moment. I mumbled some pretty lame excuses about a bad dream. It's a blur, really, but I was surprised to discover that although she had no memory of helping me save Amy, she recognized my voice and said we knew each other. It's been playing on my mind.

I keep my voice low and calm. "Listen, I'm sorry about that call. It must have been confusing and scary."

"It was." She stuffs the papers into her bag, orders a three-shot flat white—see, we are *meant* for each other—and then scowls at me. "But that was just a warm-up for the main event, wasn't it!"

"What do you mean?"

"How long had you been planning it? You must've already sent it when you called me!"

"Sent what?"

"Look. It's business, I get it. All I'm saying is, I would have appreciated a little more notice." She glances at the door. "As you can imagine, I now have a lot of sorting out to do."

Right. Decision made. Time to execute the Amnesia Protocol and find out what she's talking about. "Can I walk you to your office?"

She shakes her head.

"Please. I need to explain something to you, and it's important."

She shrugs. "It's a free country, I suppose." She stalks out of the coffee shop. I follow behind. Alexia walks so fast I have to jog every third or fourth step to keep up. "I'm not sure what you think I've done," I say, already out of breath, "but whatever it is . . . I mean *was* . . . something's happened, something's changed."

"What are you talking about?"

"Alexia, this is going to sound weird, but I have amnesia, which means I don't remember what I've done to make you so angry."

She stops abruptly and glowers at me, incredulous. I've seen this expression before. "Amnesia! You're serious?"

"Yes." I nod earnestly.

She folds her arms. "Go on then, what happened?"

"I fell off my mountain bike. It was bad," I say, trying to choose my words carefully. "And now, I don't remember much about my life, but I know you."

And that's the most honest thing I've said all day. I *do* know her. We've eaten lunch together, walked her dog, Jack. We've kissed. I try to stay on course. "I can tell you're upset with me. The problem is, my amnesia means I don't remember why."

She folds her arms. "You fell off your bike, and now you don't know why I'm upset with you?"

"That's right."

"You're unbelievable," she says. "Listen, I don't know what little game you've cooked up this time, but I'm not playing."

She strides off again, and I follow, keeping a safe distance until we arrive outside her office. She pauses at the bottom of the stone steps that lead to the front door.

"Alexia, please."

She turns and stares at me, brow furrowed. "And I suppose now you're going to say you don't remember sending me the letter."

"What letter?"

Her office door opens, and a man appears. He looks physically fit, well-dressed, and exudes an air of superiority. "Are you OK?" he asks Alexia, sounding genuinely concerned.

"Yes, I'm fine." He holds open the door for her and she walks up the steps.

"Who are you?" I ask him.

"I'm Gordon," he replies, peering down his long nose. "And you are?"

"Joseph Bridgeman."

"Ah." He narrows his gaze, then glances at Alexia. "Are you sure you're OK, Alex?"

"Never been better," she smiles at him. She turns back to me. "I think we're done, aren't we?"

Alex. He just called her *Alex.* My eyes dart between them, then settle on Alexia. "Please tell me—what was in the letter?"

Gordon looks at me, bewildered. "Are you having a laugh?"

Alexia finds a thin smile. "Look, it doesn't really matter anymore. I'm leaving Cheltenham, and maybe that's for the best."

"What?" I say. "You can't leave."

Gordon shakes his head. "But it's your fault, for heaven's sake!"

"I told you, I don't remember. I don't understand."

Alexia walks back down the steps to me. "OK, if this is the game you want to play, let me tell you what happened. Out of the blue, my landlord just gave me one month's notice. I say, 'out of the blue,' but I think you and I both know what's going on here." I wish I did. She carries on. "It's pretty obvious that you can't stick to anything. Your word being your bond is just another lie, isn't it?" She doesn't wait for an answer. "Let me ask you something: Do you ever stick to what you say you're going to do?"

My mouth is hanging open. Words aren't happening though.

Alexia's expression shifts and she suddenly looks almost relieved, as though these feelings have been bottled up, and I just popped the cork. "Maybe I should thank you," she says. "Maybe this will be just the push I need to start a new chapter in my life."

"What are you saying?"

"I'm saying thank you for evicting me."

She goes inside. Gordon moves to follow her but turns back to me. He takes the time to cast his gaze over me, then smirks. "She's moving on to bigger and better things," he says. "I think it's best if you leave her alone now."

9

The sky is overcast, the clouds heavy with rain. The air feels damp and clammy on my skin as I walk through the gates into Sandford Park. The wide expanse of grass is empty this morning, and the bare-branched trees at the edge of the park do nothing to break the icy gusts of wind that nip at my collar.

My conversation with Alexia has left me feeling dejected. I already knew she didn't remember helping me to save Amy, but the next best thing would have been if she didn't know me at all. That way, we could have started over from square one. Unfortunately, this is the worst-case scenario, because she knew Other Joe; he was her landlord and she's upset with him for evicting her. Why did he do that? Maybe it was "just business," like Alexia said, but I need to find out more and, if I can, make things right. I make a mental note to ask Dad or Martin about the eviction at the next opportunity.

I'm emotionally exhausted after my trip to London, and the lack of sleep is making me miserable too. My imaginary bump on the head means that people will give me some slack, but building a new life is hard work.

I pass through a gate into an enclosed woodland. Snowdrops are pushing up through the sodden earth, the first promise of spring. I breathe deeply and roll my shoulders a couple of times, trying to shake off the blues. I stride out across the putting green. With perfect timing, it begins to rain, so I jog toward the bandstand on the other side of the park to take cover until the shower passes. The rain gets heavier, streaming down my forehead and blurring my vision. I lower my head and sprint the last hundred yards or so, and I'm out of breath by the time I get to the bandstand. Wiping my eyes, I look up and straight into the face of W. P. Brown.

I nearly leap out of my skin. "Where did you come from?" I splutter.

"I didn't mean to startle you," he says.

Shock turns to anger. Indignant fury erupts in my chest. "Actually, I'm glad you're here. You've got some explaining to do!"

His face is impassive. "I can understand why you're angry."

"Too right I'm angry!" I say, bounding up the steps two at a time until I'm level with him. "I told you I didn't want to travel again! Why did you send me to London?"

He sits heavily on one of the wooden benches around the edge of the bandstand and rests his cane across his knees. He's wearing a thick brown coat with shiny black buttons and an ivy-green scarf. His shoes are black patent leather, perfectly shiny. It strikes me how out of place they seem in this muddy park.

"I didn't send you to London, Joseph," he says. "What happened to you had nothing to do with me."

He must think I was born yesterday. "So it's just a coincidence, is it, that a few hours after you appear in my shop, and I turn down your offer of a glittering career in time travel, I touch a bewitched radio and get thrown back to 1963?" I pace back and forth in front of him. "I had no idea what was going on. It was terrifying! I didn't know if I was ever going to get home again!"

He takes a handkerchief out of his pocket and wipes his nose. He looks tired. "I can only imagine how alarming it must have been. The whole situation is most unfortunate."

"*Unfortunate?* That's got to be the understatement of the year."

"It wasn't supposed to happen. You weren't supposed to go." He puts the handkerchief back in his pocket and rests both hands on his cane.

"What do you mean, I wasn't *supposed* to go?"

"I think I mentioned I was part of an organized group of time travelers."

"You did. What is it, some kind of shady government operation?"

He frowns as though the idea is repugnant. "We are a fully independent and privately funded organization. We monitor the past for 'change events,' opportunities to put things right when they've gone wrong. The radio was what we call a 'focus object,' a powerful link in time to one of these events. It was stolen from us. We think someone planted it in your shop."

I think back to the night of the storm and the person I saw running out of my shop. Their bag looked empty, and when Molly confirmed nothing was missing from our stock, I presumed I'd stopped them before they had a chance to steal anything. I don't have any reason to trust the man sitting before me, but I don't have any evidence that suggests I should *distrust* him either. What if he's telling the truth and the burglar's bag was empty because they'd *already* placed the radio in the shop?

"OK," I say slowly. "Let's just park, for a second, the whole concept of how touching a radio could throw me back to 1963. Why would someone want to do that to me?"

W. P. Brown folds his hands. "It's a good question. We believe it was a deliberate attempt to bond an inexperienced traveler to a critical mission."

"Mission?" I almost laugh. "You mean like covert ops? Do you realize how mad that sounds?"

"I do," he says, "but this one is of paramount importance. The woman you saw murdered, Lucy Romano, must be saved."

I feel like this is all getting out of hand. "Look, I don't know what to make of this, whether or not to believe you, but it doesn't really matter. I'm back now and—as I already told you—I'm not traveling again. Read my lips. Ever."

I'm already halfway down the steps when Brown speaks again, his voice now unexpectedly powerful.

"I'm sorry, Joseph. It's not that easy."

I turn back to him. He's standing now, his cane tucked under one arm, his eyes glistening sharply like ice crystals.

"Are you threatening me, Mr. Brown?"

"No, I'm advising you. I came here today to make sure you're as prepared as possible. Because you *will* travel again. It's no longer a choice."

"Says who?"

"As I explained, the radio was a link back in time to an event that needs to be put right. The mission to save Lucy Romano's life had already been assigned to one of our most experienced time travelers, but when you touched the radio, you became bonded to it instead."

"Bonded?"

"Bonding is a form of quantum entanglement. It's permanent."

"Well, you can just untangle me. 'Debond' me or something."

"Once the bond is made, it cannot be undone. You can't fight it."

"But the radio's gone," I insist. "I won't touch it again."

"That makes no difference," he says.

"There must be a way. You have to get me out of this!"

"Joseph, the connection isn't a physical one anymore. You were sent back to witness the final act in Lucy's story, and in due course, you will travel back again and be given the opportunity to change it. You and the story have become one. This is the mystery of the universe at work. The radio was a pathway, opened and joined to you. You are bonded to Lucy and her story until its conclusion."

"Whose idea was that? Who would design a system that works like this?"

"It wasn't designed by anyone. This is a natural process."

I decide to try a new approach. I walk back up the steps of the bandstand. "Look, Mr. Brown," I say, more calmly, "I'm sorry about what happened to Lucy, but it's not my responsibility. It has nothing to do with me."

"When I asked if you would allow me to become your mentor," he says, "I was excited, because you're an exceptionally gifted time traveler." I grit my teeth. I resist flattery at the best of times, but when it's designed to persuade, I hate it. "I know this mission is a great responsibility on such inexperienced shoulders," he adds, "but I also believe that you already have the skills to complete it successfully."

He's not giving up. Neither am I. "Helping other people is a good thing to do," I admit, "but we're not talking about giving a vulnerable member of the community a hand with the groceries here, we're talking murder. I went through hell to get Amy back, and I'm not going to risk losing everything just because someone got reckless with a radio. I have my sister back, a family here that needs me, a business, a whole life to catch up on. I'm sorry about London, really I am, but someone else is going to have to do it."

Brown sighs and rubs his chin. He looks suddenly deflated. I think he might have got the message.

"So be it," he says. "I've done my best to persuade you. I've done everything I can think of to convince you to take on this mission." He shakes his head. "I wish it didn't have to be this way."

He opens his coat and pulls his watch out of his waistcoat pocket. Slowly, he twists the dial, winding it up. The rain suddenly stops hammering on the roof above our heads, but the air remains filled with droplets of water. The rays of sunlight streaming through a crack in the clouds transform the air around us into a sparkling, hyperreal network of myriad rainbows. The trees are motionless. The birds pause midflight, and all sound ceases.

Who *is* this man?

He takes a step toward me. "I'm sorry, Joseph, but you've left me no choice."

10

We appear in a field. In the distance I see a familiar sight: a large canvas tent, its red and yellow stripes floodlit against a fading summer sky. A flag dances from its peak. King's Funfair, 1997. The night Amy disappeared. My gut flips.

"Why have you brought me here?" I ask.

W. P. Brown studies me, calm and assured. "Because you said no." He turns on his heel and walks determinedly toward the fair. I follow him, my mind spinning like the carnival rides around us, trying to guess his next move. He walks between the stalls, through the throngs of people, nodding elegantly. By the way he's dressed, they probably expect to see him later as the ringmaster.

Lights strobe. The scent of toffee apples and spun sugar mingles with diesel fumes on the dust-filled summer air. We arrive at the Ferris wheel. There is no queue.

"What's this about?" I ask. "What are you doing?"

Brown's expression is cold. "Sometimes, to see the way forward, we must go back. I have brought you here for a sense of perspective."

Without asking, he pays for us both, and before I can explain that I'm afraid of heights, he gestures for me to climb into the metal death trap. A metal bar descends over our heads, the wheel starts to turn, and we rise up into the air.

I hear the popping of the shooting gallery, and below us I see the man

I labeled the Artful Dodger when I traveled here the first time. I see Sian Burrows too, the Julia Roberts look-alike who distracted my original teenage self on this fateful night. By my calculations, there are now four versions of me here. It's beginning to feel a little crowded.

I see myself, aged fourteen, and seven-year-old Amy. Then I watch two versions of my adult self, one arguing with a security guard.

My stomach clenches. I see Amy in her bright-blue dress, running away from the fair, and I see myself giving chase. I would soon learn that Amy was a time traveler, just like me. On this night, once, she traveled into the future and was lost forever. It was her fate to die, and then I changed it.

Slowly, a dark realization pinches my heart. My body tenses, and my fingers grip the cold metal bar. "You can't mess with this," I say to Brown, without looking at him.

"I don't *want* to," he says, "but I will do whatever it takes to make you listen."

My fear digs deeper. "You're blackmailing me," I growl, my lips curled in impotent fury.

"You've left me no choice," he says, his voice so calm it's driving me insane. "I have to ensure that—"

"How dare you!" I spit with rage. "I went through hell to save my sister." I turn to him, eyes burning. "She was just a little girl. She didn't deserve to die."

He studies me with unsettling composure. "Did you really think you could do whatever you wanted?"

I glare at him. "What do you mean?"

"You changed time, altered history to suit yourself. Did you honestly believe this would come without a cost?" He takes my arm. "You have a debt to pay, Joseph. Lucy Romano must be saved. You must commit to the mission and mean it. If you do that, then I will leave this night alone."

I feel the fight draining out of my body. "Why?" I ask wearily. "Why is Lucy so important?"

"She must raise her son, Gus. He needs his mother to help shape who he will become."

I frown at him. "But none of this has anything to do with me."

"You of all people know we're shaped by what happens to us," he says. "With the support of his mother, Gus goes on to do great things."

"What things?"

"I can't tell you any more, for fear of altering the Future Change Index."

"The Future what?" I ask.

"If I give you too much information, it could alter your approach and change time in ways we cannot foresee."

"Right," I mutter, confused.

"Joseph, the past is not set. Your mission could return it to its optimal state. You can put right a terrible wrong. Believe me, saving Lucy is for the greater good."

He sounds like he actually believes it. "Who are you to decide what's right and wrong?" I ask. "Who are you to make the call on what needs to be changed?"

"You made the same call," he says, "when you traveled back here to save your sister."

"That's different!"

"Is it?"

I stare at my hands, cursing the moment I reached out and touched that damned radio.

The Ferris wheel descends. I'm in turmoil. Do I believe what this time traveler is telling me? I don't know what he's capable of, but based on what I've seen, he has some advanced skills and will do what it takes to get what he wants. I survey the dark woodland, knowing that a version of me is saving Amy right about now.

Now I need to do the same, again.

"Let's say I do this." My voice is jagged. "I will have paid my debt?"

He nods.

"And I won't have to do anything else? No more traveling?"

"If that is truly your wish, then yes. No more traveling."

The Ferris wheel comes to a stop, the safety bar lifts, and we are back on the ground.

My blackmailer walks, his stride purposeful. I trail behind him until we are back in the field where we arrived just a short while ago.

It's amazing the difference a few minutes can make. The world feels undone.

"How do you sleep at night?" I ask him.

"I understand why you feel that way," he says. "In time, though, I hope you will understand why all of this was necessary."

"I doubt that very much."

He pulls out his bronze pocket watch and clicks open the front. "It's time to decide," he says, snapping it shut again. "And you must mean it."

What choice do I have? He has total control.

"I will do it," I tell him, bitterly.

His shoulders drop and he sighs, clearly relieved.

"But you should modify your pitch a bit, next time you try to recruit someone," I add. "Make sure you tell people how you blackmail travelers into doing your bidding."

He regards me impassively and holds out his right hand. "We have one more piece of business to attend to."

I stare at his hand. "Are you serious?"

He looks back at the fair, then fixes his steely gaze on me. "Unless you want to stay here?"

I take his hand. As we connect, I feel raw, malevolent power surge between us. We return to the bandstand instantaneously. Cheltenham. The present. But time is still frozen here.

"How are you doing this?" I ask, unnerved by the sight of people transformed into statues. A woman, her mouth stretched in a silent laugh. The man holding her hand, surrounded by a million droplets hanging in the air. They look like performance artists, fixed in positions that would be impossible to maintain in real time.

"They can't feel it," W. P. Brown says, his voice eerily calm. "When we are finished here, time will resume, and they won't know a thing about it."

"Oh, that's very good of you," I reply with deliberate venom. "Anyway, you said there was something else you wanted to do. Can we just get this over with?"

He pulls a silver pocket watch from his waistcoat and holds it, dangling from its chain, at eye level. The metal casing has an iridescence not normally associated with silver. It catches the light, highlighting some attractive, ornate engraving that looks like tendrils. Even in the hands of a blackmailer, it's an undeniably beautiful timepiece.

He says, "It's a double half—"

"Hunter, I know." I think he's forgotten I'm in antiques. The front casing has three circular glass windows, so the dials can be read even when it's closed.

"The casing is original," Brown says matter-of-factly, "but the mechanism has been heavily modified, fitted with an array of time crystals." He turns the watch over. It's primarily glass, revealing a beautiful mechanism of bronze and silver cogs, studded with tiny gleaming jewels: sapphire, ruby, and garnet. "Time crystals are extremely sensitive to changes in the fabric of time. Each watch contains twenty-two of them."

"Time crystals?"

"They measure time displacement and fluctuations. It's how our watches are able to accurately predict both departure time and how long we will remain in the past."

It must be obvious that I'm struggling to understand, because he takes a new approach.

"Consider the barometer," he says. "It measures atmospheric pressure, nature's indication of impending change. The information was there all along, just waiting for someone to trap mercury inside a vacuum and take notice. Think of your watch as a barometer of *time*, measuring the pressure created by impending travel. When it is time to travel into the past, the watch will give you a countdown. When you land in the past, it will calibrate and tell you how long you will remain there. On your first jump, your watch will guide you to the change event itself, so that you are clear about the goal of your mission. As you've already completed your first jump, however, you have already seen the goal of your mission."

"The murder of Lucy Romano?" I suggest.

"Indeed. Subsequently, the watch will guide you toward waypoints. Waypoints are the turning points of each story. They are chances for you to move toward solving your mission, either by observing something time wishes you to see, or by making a physical change. In your case, the watch will guide you to key events in Lucy's story." He offers it to me. "Take it."

I hold back. After my experience with the radio, I'm afraid of what touching another unknown object might do to me.

"It won't send you anywhere," W. P. Brown says, correctly interpreting my hesitation. "You have my word."

"Like your word means anything. What possible reason do I have to trust you?"

"You were lost on your first jump to London without this watch. You didn't know how long you would be there, or where you were supposed to be." His gaze never wavers. "To complete the mission and secure Amy's safety, you will need it."

Gingerly, I take the pocket watch. It's weighty but perfectly balanced on its chain. The case feels smooth and cool and fits perfectly in my hand. I turn it over. The craftsmanship is exceptional. A charge of prickling energy travels up my left arm and over my shoulder. It isn't painful. It's almost pleasant, like a caress.

W. P. Brown appears contented. "This watch is yours now, Joseph," he announces. "You are bonded. You cannot lose it, do you understand?"

I just nod, staring, transfixed.

"Why don't you open it?" he suggests.

I press the release button at the top of the casing. The fascia beneath is a creamy oyster color with gold Roman numerals, ornate black hands, and inset radial dials indicating hours, minutes, and seconds. I've seen plenty of pocket watches in my time, but never one quite like this. It looks old, but something is decidedly off about it. It's like watching a sunset on a TV screen, beautiful but not quite real.

"Coming home will be safer now you have this," Brown says. "You won't need to navigate the void."

"The void?"

He blinks in thought. "If I remember correctly, you likened it to a zoetrope. The void is a place that exists outside of time. With the watch, you will bypass the void and travel directly home."

I peer at the timepiece, intrigued despite myself. "OK, so this gives me information . . . I sort of get that, but how does it change the *way* I travel?"

"It's a finely tuned instrument," Brown says. "We discovered that if time crystals could be held in equilibrium, we gained extra stability. That's where the ytterbium comes in."

"What's that?"

"It's a rare earth element. There's a small amount in all of our watches. It keeps the time crystals balanced, so they can measure where you are in time, in relation to where you belong. Your watch not only grounds you and gives you information, it also acts as a homing beacon. It's calibrated to bring you back to Bridgeman Antiques after each trip into the past."

"So when will I travel again?"

"Impossible to say at this juncture, but keep an eye on your watch. You will be given some warning before you travel. Upon your arrival in the past, the crystals will calibrate and display a countdown."

"What determines how long I stay in the past?"

"At this point, it's impossible to say."

"You mean you won't tell me."

"No, I mean no one knows. The length of time you stay in the past is not set by people or machines or an algorithm. Time itself will offer the optimal parameters for success."

I screw up my nose. "You say it as though time is aware."

"Not aware. But time has a deep, irrepressible drive to restore balance. When we are aligned with our purpose, it can feel for the traveler as though time is on our side. There are rules of course, constraints that we must work within, but when done right, you can feel that time *wants* the change, wants us to succeed."

I shake my head, which feels swollen with his ramblings. "So are you saying I could be stuck in the past for months . . . or even years?"

He considers this. "It's true that the length of your stay can be hugely variable. It depends somewhat on you."

I fold my arms in frustration. "Can't you just give me *some* idea? Any clue would be helpful."

He shrugs. "It's hard to generalize, but a few hours is common."

Well, that was a lot harder than it needed to be. "How many trips will I make?"

"That depends—"

"On me," I say before he can.

"Correct. However, if only one jump remains, your watch will display a final warning before you travel." He reaches down into his coat, and instinctively I take a hurried step back. "I'm not going to hurt you, Joseph," he says softly. He hands me an envelope. "There's some cash in here, for your next trip."

I peer inside the envelope and see a sheaf of bills.

"Those banknotes were legal tender from 1960 to 1979," he explains, "so you should be safe."

Dazed, I shove the envelope into my jacket pocket.

"There are a few more things you must understand," Brown says. "You are not to attempt to drag Lucy or Gus through time. Their destinies belong in their own timelines."

"OK," I mumble.

"And you must not tell anyone about this, especially not Amy."

"Why not? What does she have to do with it?"

"Everything is connected," he says cryptically. "Your mission is more important than I can tell you. Saving Lucy will, in turn, save many, many lives." He blinks, seemingly lost in thought, as though remembering something fondly.

"Let's say I do my best, but I still fail. What happens then?" I ask.

"You won't fail."

He seems troubled, which, in turn, troubles me. Usually, when the bad guy has you just where he wants you, he can't help but look pleased with himself. W. P. Brown, on the other hand, appears to take no pleasure in what he's doing.

I remind myself that I can't trust anything he says. I don't know this man any better now than I did when he first walked into my shop and rolled a grenade into my life.

"One final thing," he says. "When you were saving Amy, you may have felt a sense of freedom, of being able to jump back in time in any way that suited you. But it doesn't work that way. All of your jumps were related to saving her. Time decides what must be done."

I reflect on his words, and I think he's wrong. I achieved some very focused and specific jumps, very *intentional* jumps, while I was figuring out how to save Amy. But I decide to keep my cards close to my chest.

W. P. Brown begins to fade, his skin shimmering like wet, oily sand. "Safe travels, Joseph, and good luck."

"That would mean so much more if you weren't blackmailing me."

He lowers his head. The light around his face appears to flicker, his outline loses clarity, and he is gone.

PART 3

11

Walking home, cold and wet, everything feels different. This morning, despite the gray skies, felt like the first day of the rest of my life, and I couldn't wait to live it. Now, I've been backed into a corner and there's no way out.

My mind spins in an endless loop as I tread the sodden streets. If what W. P. Brown says is true, then I owe a debt, and if I don't do his bidding, Amy's as good as dead. Again. But who made him God?

I wish I'd asked him more about who he's working for, this "organized group." I consider the possibility that I'm somehow being played, that for some inexplicable reason he's chosen *me* to do this bloody mission and he's got no control over Amy's life at all. In that case, I don't have to do what he says. I could just ignore him. But the stakes are too high. I've only just got Amy back, and I'm not going to risk putting her in danger again. Feeling trapped and claustrophobic, I undo the top button of my coat and breathe a big lungful of damp winter air, but it just makes me feel like I'm drowning in fog.

As I near the Gustav Holst museum, I become aware of a tall, lean man walking straight toward me with intent. I try to avoid eye contact, but it's too late.

He waves. "Bridgeman!" He's dressed like a catalog model in a long camel coat and smart leather brogues. His skin is lightly tanned, and his teeth have been whitened by a few too many shades. He would look more at home in Los Angeles than Cheltenham. "Joe, fella! Is that you?"

I plaster on a smile.

"Is everything OK? You look absolutely terrible!" He chuckles. He seems like the kind of guy who would laugh even if you told him your best friend had just died.

"I'm fine," I announce confidently. "Great. Good to see you." I keep moving, in the hope that he'll walk on by. I'm not in the mood, and I don't want to start explaining to this guy about my amnesia.

"You're soaked, Bridgeman," he says. "What've you been doing, showering in your clothes? Ha ha!"

"Ha ha!" I fake laugh back. "Sorry I can't stick around. See you soon, yeah?"

"Sure," he says. "Oh hey, will I see you at the club?"

That could mean anything. Cricket? Crochet? Either way, I won't be there. "I'm not sure I'm going to make it," I say. "I'm not feeling great."

"Tough luck, but I'm not surprised," he says, then leans toward me. "You know what I think? You've been burning the candle at both ends again. How's it going with Chloe?"

Before I can stop myself, I say, "Who?"

He bursts out laughing. "Nice one! You're a devil." He pats me on the back. "See you next week."

He strides away. I walk the rest of the way home with my head down, determined to avoid any further interactions. When I get back to Montpellier Terrace, it's only 3 p.m. I'm still soaking wet, and I don't want to start answering twenty questions from Molly, so I cut through the alleyway a couple of doors down and head up the fire escape at the back of the shop. It's an iron staircase that spirals its way up the back of the building and gives me direct access to the roof terrace.

After a short fight with the large bunch of keys I now have to carry around with me, I let myself into the loft room and fling myself gratefully onto the sofa. I kick off my shoes, peel off my socks, and lie on my back, staring at the ceiling. I reach for the chain around my neck and take off the pocket watch. Its pearlescent face stares impassively at me, its three dials calmly marking the passage of time.

I think back on my trip to the fair with W. P. Brown. "Bastard!" I say out loud. I chuck the watch onto an armchair and head for the shower.

Half an hour later, I'm upstairs in the bar. I've lit the fire, and I'm in dry clothes. Although I'd love to add it to Molly's charity pile, I'm keeping the watch close. If Brown was telling the truth, I'm going to be sent back to the 1960s at some point, so I check it every few minutes, like a teenager on social media, to see if there's any indication that I might be about to leave.

I'm watching the flames in the fireplace, drifting in and out of consciousness, when the landline rings. I check the caller display and pick up.

"Hi, Martin," I say brightly, hoping I can pick his brain on Alexia's eviction.

"So you still know who I am then? I'm honored," he says dryly.

"Of course I do," I say. Last time I spoke to him, I was living a different life, but he sounds just the same. "I presume Amy told you what happened?"

"She did," he says. "I keep telling you, that mountain bike will be the death of you."

"I'm not dead yet, Martin," I say. Not this version of me, anyway.

"Good," he says. "Sounds like it was a nasty accident. Listen, do you have a few minutes to talk? I'm willing to hold the fort until you're feeling better, but I need to run a couple things past you."

"Excellent, I need to run a couple of things past you too, actually." I wait for him to laugh at my assertive tone, but he doesn't miss a beat.

"Fire away."

"It's about the George Street office building," I begin.

"On it. We've had the final paperwork through."

"Final paperwork?"

"For the Cotswold Hotel Group deal."

"What deal is that again?"

Martin pauses. "Is this what Amy was trying to tell me? Have you forgotten?"

"I think I might have. Can you remind me?"

Martin whistles. "That really must have been some bump on the head. We're leasing George Street to the Cotswold Hotel Group. Renovations start next month. Twenty-year contract. Ring any bells?"

"But that's Alexia's building," I say, things rapidly coming together in my mind.

"That's right. She's the hypnotherapist. So you do remember?"

"Yes I do," I say firmly. I'm so eager to find out whether there's anything I can do to keep Alexia in Cheltenham, I almost trip over my words. "Is it definitely happening? The deal?"

"Full steam ahead. I've emailed you the contract. I just need the nod from you. We can get physical signatures sorted out later this week."

"OK," I say, "brilliant. But Martin, I was wondering—just for my information really—is there anything that could cause the deal to fall through?"

He pauses. "The only problem I could imagine would be if you signed a new tenant's lease, which you'd be mad to do, of course!" He laughs.

Watch out, world. Here comes Mad Joe Bridgeman.

"I'm actually having second thoughts about the whole deal," I say.

Martin waits for the punch line, but it doesn't come. "Second thoughts? Are you *serious?* You honestly want to back out?"

"Maybe . . . yes."

Silence for a few seconds. I can imagine his face.

"Look, obviously it's your call, but you need to know that before . . . before your accident, you were one hundred percent committed to it." He's trying to sound calm, but I can hear the strain in his voice.

I know I should let Other Joe's business run its course. I made a commitment to do my best to keep his life going. But Alexia and I had something in my previous life, and I want to give that a chance to run its course too. If we're going to have any chance of finding our way back to each other, she needs to stay in Cheltenham. And to make sure that happens, I need to stop this deal.

"Sorry, Martin. I'm just not sure any more."

"Joe, listen to me. The Cotswold Hotel Group have committed to a twenty-year lease. You courted them for months. It took time and effort and a lot of cash. They have contractors coming in next month to begin renovations. If you stop this now, it will have serious repercussions for our business and—sorry, but I have to say this—your personal credibility."

Martin's words stop me in my tracks. "Look, I don't want to cause any trouble."

"I think you need to take some time off," Martin says tightly. "Sleep on it. Are you getting proper medical care?"

"Yes," I say confidently. "I saw a specialist. He said it'll just take time."

"Who did you see?"

"I can't *quite* remember his name," I say, trying to sound as though I'm racking my brain.

"Does Thomas know about this?" I feel an emotional microshock, hearing Dad's name in the present tense. "Joe? Have you talked to him?"

"No, not yet. Amy was going to talk to Mum and Dad, let them know what happened." Before Martin has a chance to move on to the next item I can sense on his agenda, I decide to wrap up the call. "Listen, I need to go."

"We've got more to talk about though," he complains.

I knew it. I imagine him with his massive notepad. "I have a splitting headache. I think I'm going to throw up. I'll call you tomorrow." Before Martin can argue, I disconnect the call.

Damn. For a minute there, I thought I had this whole situation nailed. I thought I could just cancel this deal and Alexia would be able to stay in her office. Sounds like it's a huge thing though, and if I cancel it, I'm going to create a massive ruckus.

A blanket of exhaustion washes over me, thick and cold like a lead shroud. I'm desperate for sleep, but I have to be prepared for the fact that, at any moment, I could go back to 1963. I decide to do some internet research and find out more about Frankie Shaw, the guy who killed Lucy.

I find a few websites about notorious British criminals and spend a couple of hours reading about the rise and fall of Frankie and Tommy Shaw. During my viewing, it sounded like Lucy's son, Gus, had a good relationship with Tommy, but he and his brother Frankie were nasty human beings, charged with some horrific crimes during the late 1950s and early '60s. Tommy ran things for a while, but in August of 1962, he was attacked and left for dead. He was found in the street and slipped into a coma.

There are numerous contradictory accounts of what happened. Tommy wasn't able to tell anyone, because he never woke up. He died on June 6, 1963. The very day I witnessed Lucy Romano's murder. The one thing everyone seems to agree on is that the attack on Tommy was most likely carried out by a rival gang, the Dickersons.

Once Tommy was dead, Frankie Shaw took over the family business and gained the nickname "Mr. Untouchable," although the police caught up with him eventually. Like many tough guys who end up in prison, he cried a lot, confessed to a long list of horrendous acts of violence—which I choose not to read through this late at night—and then hanged himself.

There's no mention of Lucy Romano or her son. I guess she was just another unseen casualty of gangland London. She seems to me like an innocent victim in this story. Frankie obviously believed Lucy was connected to Tommy's death, but I can't imagine she had anything to do with it. Gangsters, though. They scare the bejesus out of me. I'm hardly the world's toughest guy. I wonder again why W. P. Brown picked me.

Yawning, I close the laptop. After witnessing the end of Lucy's life in that alleyway, and then walking in her shoes during the viewing, I feel connected to her. It makes me wonder, if W. P. weren't blackmailing me, would I still try and save Lucy Romano? I brush my teeth, change into pajamas, and collapse into bed. Then, I remember my first trip to London and change back into jeans and a T-shirt, so that if I suddenly travel in the night, I'll blend in well enough. I click the switch next to my bed, and the room is plunged into darkness. Exhaustion blankets me from the top of my skull to the soles of my feet. My joints ache, my teeth hurt, and my head feels like it's caving in. I don't think I've ever been so tired, but I'm convinced I won't sleep. Eventually, though, the slumber I've been so desperately craving consumes me, and I sink into blissful oblivion.

The following day I wake up refreshed at 6 a.m. I feel like a new man. No bad dreams, no storms, just peace. For a few happy seconds, I lie in bed, stretching my arms and legs, reveling in my new life. Then the memory of yesterday's conversation with W. P. Brown invades my head, and I'm crushed by the weight of the impossible task ahead of me.

Brown told me he suspected that someone had deliberately planted the radio in my shop, to make sure it was me who ended up in London. He insisted that it has nothing to do with him, but when I tried to back out of the mission, he blackmailed me. It doesn't make any sense. I think through how the best scams work. The scammers secretly create a problem, then turn up like knights in shining armor and offer to fix it. That's how they reel people in. I guess Brown could be pulling all the strings.

I reach out and check my watch of doom, lying peaceably beside me on the bedside table. Nothing. I press the cold metal to my forehead. If only I hadn't touched that bloody radio.

Wait a minute.

I jerk upright, my mind fizzing. That's it! If I jump back to before I touched the radio and tell myself not to touch it, I can avoid this whole nightmare! I won't get bonded to this stupid mission, and I'll be off the hook!

Saving Amy was my job. Saving Lucy is someone else's. I could reset all of this. But I know I have to be careful about layering up too many changes. What if I make things worse? I consider what would happen if I miscalculate and jump back too far. What if I land before my original return from the fairground? I won't exist here, Other Joe will. But even if that did happen, as long as I keep out of his way, I can't see how that would do any harm. Going back and avoiding this whole mess is just too tempting.

Decision made. No time like the present.

I get up, have a bite to eat, then head up to the loft with a chamomile tea to try what Alexia taught me during my efforts to save Amy: candles, meditation, chanting, the works. Nothing happens. I find not the slightest chink in time's armor. Maybe W. P. Brown was telling the truth. Or maybe he's somehow stopped me from traveling. Either way, it seems I can't travel at will anymore. I'm well and truly stuck in the present . . . for now anyway.

12

I spend the rest of the day in the shop, but I can tell Molly is frustrated with my clumsy attempts to make myself useful. By 4:15 p.m., we've had a trickle of customers, we've made a few sales, and Molly seems to think we've done OK. I decide it's time to check on Vinny.

"Do you mind if I head out for a bit?" I ask Molly.

"Not at all!" she says, much too quickly. "I can lock up at closing time. Will you be in tomorrow?"

"I expect so," I say stalwartly. Disappointment flickers across her face. "Thanks for being patient with me. I'll start to remember things soon."

"I'm sure you will, Mr. Bridgeman," she says amiably. "I'll look forward to that."

I get to Vinny's in record time, and I'm panting as I arrive at the shop door, peppered as always with flyers and gig posters. I push it, but it's locked. That's strange. I step back to scan the shop front and see a single sheet of paper at waist height. Hastily handwritten in marker, it reads, Closed Until Further Notice.

I feel terrible. Last time I saw Vinny, I materialized in front of him and scared him half to death. He was popping anxiety pills like M&M's. I was hoping he'd have calmed down by now, but it seems he's gone AWOL.

I call his cell a few times, but there's no answer. I call his landline, and I've been waiting for him to pick up for nearly two minutes when a man sidles up to me. He's slight, with pale thinning hair that looks like a shredded wheat comb-over. He's wearing a navy velveteen jacket and skinny black trousers.

"Have you seen Vinny?" he asks.

"Not today," I say.

"How well do you know him?" he asks mildly.

"Pretty well," I say. I used to, anyway. I hope I still do.

The man's demeanor changes immediately. "Right, well he was supposed to DJ a party for me yesterday, but he didn't show up. He owes me five hundred pounds. It's unacceptable."

I feel worse than ever. If Vinny's defaulting on DJ gigs then he must be in a really bad way. "I'm not sure why you're telling me," I say.

"He can't keep ignoring me!" The man's head wobbles back and forth as he talks, like a pigeon. "You tell your fat friend to call Carl. Bloody time waster."

When I look at him this time, I don't see his face; I see W. P. Brown's. This Carl guy has chosen the wrong day to push me around. "Vinny is my friend," I tell him, "and you have no idea what might be going on with him. So I'm warning you, unless you want something else to complain about, walk away now."

"All right, mate." He raises his hands, backing off. "Simmer down."

"I'm not your mate." My vision pulses, and there's a buzzing in my head. "*Vinny* is my mate. He's had a bad shock, and you need to leave him alone." I pull my wallet out of my pocket and find a couple of fifty-pound notes. "Here," I say, handing him the money. "Take this for now. You'll get the rest back soon enough. Now just go, before I change my mind."

The man shoves the cash into his pocket and scuttles off. I watch him leave, then notice a figure hiding behind a large beech tree about twenty yards away. For a second my heart misses a beat as I wonder if it's W. P. Brown. I take a few steps toward the tree, and the man pops his head out. He's wearing a flat cap, a long raincoat, and dark glasses, but I can tell who it is straight away.

"Vinny!" I cry, happy to see him, but concerned. "What are you doing?"

"Are you following me?" he asks shakily.

"No, I came to see if you were OK," I say. "Why are you dressed like that?"

"Research," he says. Before I can ask what he means, he pulls a small brown bottle out of his pocket and pops another pill.

"Take it easy on those, mate," I say.

He ignores me. "I heard you talking to Carl." He sounds as frightened as ever.

"Don't worry, I set him straight," I say. "He won't be any trouble."

"It's not that," he says. "You stood up for me. You've never done that before."

"Haven't I?"

"Who are you, and what do you want?" he says fretfully.

"Vinny, it's me! I wanted to make sure you were OK after I scared you the other day."

"There you go again," he says, laughing uncontrollably. "You're nothing like him! You've been swapped! You've been probed and dissected! You've had your mind erased and now . . ." He pauses. "What do you want with us?" I think he means mankind. "I'm really not the best specimen, if you're wanting to abduct a human being with good genes."

I'd have to disagree. Vinny is just about the best specimen of a decent human I know. "Look," I say, "how about we go and get a beer? We could find somewhere that does pickled eggs."

He regards me suspiciously. "How do you know about pickled eggs?"

"I know they're your favorite."

"But how? How do you know these things?"

"That's what I want to explain."

We end up in one of Vinny's preferred watering holes, an ancient pub called Inn for a Penny, which is tucked away down one of Cheltenham's many quiet side streets. It smells of hops, old carpets, and stale cigarettes, though I doubt anyone has smoked in here for years.

"My round," I tell Vinny.

"I'll go and find a table."

I notice a door to the garden at the back of the pub. "All right, but don't run away. I just want to talk to you, that's all. OK?"

He nods. "If this is going to be my last meal, let's make it a classic.

Three pickled eggs and a pint of Guinness, please." He thinks for a second. "Better get a tube of barbecue Pringles too. Just in case."

At the bar a row of old men nurse their pints. I notice a sign that reads, Soup of the Day: Whiskey with Ice Croutons. It's tempting.

I place the order and watch the server pull our drinks. This is the most grounded I've felt for some time, and I'm suddenly aware of how much I need this: to tell someone that I trust what's going on. Cue my nervous tick. I fish out my pocket watch and check it over. It's still blank.

Vinny gives me an appreciative nod when I return to our table with the goodies. He's taken off his raincoat, and his T-shirt advertises the "National Sarcasm Society," with a tagline beneath that reads, "Like we need your help."

He downs one of the pints in about nine seconds, takes a long slurp from the second one, then leans back, folding his arms over his considerable tummy. "Some people think that because I run a vinyl shop, drink like a fish, and smoke a bit of wacky baccy, I'm stupid."

I think about the fun we used to have at our curry club, the hours we spent in his shop on rainy afternoons listening to music no one wanted to buy, the way he would always bring a new perspective to everything and cheer me up when I was feeling miserable. I just want to fling my arms around him.

"I know you're not stupid," I say.

"I'm not," he replies, "and I know what I saw. I watched you teleport into existence in front of me. Plus, you're definitely not the same as before." He crams a tower of Pringles into his mouth. "You might *look* the same, but you're an impostor, and I think it's time you told me what's actually going on."

Whenever you tell someone you're a time traveler, they either think you're joking or they worry for your sanity. Vinny was there for me when I was trying to save Amy, so I'm hopeful he'll take it all in stride, but he's pretty wobbly at the moment, and I don't want to tip him over the edge.

"Vinny," I say, deadly serious, "you need to be sure you really want to know."

He nods determinedly and pops a whole egg into his mouth. "Yep," he says. "Tell me everything."

I glance around the pub to make sure there's no one near enough to hear. "I'm telling everyone else that I fell off my bike and got amnesia."

"Like Jason Bourne," Vinny says. "But you didn't, did you?"

"No."

"I have to say, you don't look like a man who's just had a serious accident. You're too . . . upright. You're not even limping." He downs the rest of his second pint. "So?"

"I'm a time traveler," I say, bracing myself for his reaction.

Vinny searches my face to see if I'm telling the truth. I hold his gaze, unflinching.

"Ha! I knew it," he says, obviously pleased with himself.

"What? How?"

"I told you, I'm not stupid. It makes total sense when you think about it. You've obviously gone back, changed a load of stuff, come home, and *boom*"—he gazes around the pub—"now everything's different, but only for you. You're pretending you've got amnesia, so that nobody suspects. Am I right?"

"Bang on!" I laugh. I'm flabbergasted at how relaxed he is. "I was expecting you to freak out though. How come you're so cool about it?"

"I've got so many downers in my system," he says, "you could tell me you're from Mars and I'd buy it."

I hope he'll still be this understanding once the pills wear off.

Vinny taps the table. "Anyway, if I'm going to be your companion, you'd better spill the beans."

"Companion?"

"Yep," Vinny says earnestly. "Every time traveler needs a sidekick. Think *Doctor Who*. Come on, talk to me. How did it all start? Have aliens been involved?"

"No aliens," I confirm. I tell Vinny about my sad old life, about Amy and how she went missing, and about his part in it all. I explain the rules of time travel, the elastic-band theory, and how all of that has now changed. When I tell him about Alexia, he looks upset. When I tell him about W. P. Brown, he looks angry. And as I talk through Lucy's murder at the hands of vicious gangster Frankie Shaw, Vinny listens quietly, taking it all in. When I finally feel like I've said it all, Vinny is as serious as I've ever seen him.

He whistles through his teeth. "Fair play, mate, you've certainly been through it. I can't believe what happened to Amy. It's weird that I was involved but don't remember."

"It's because I changed it all. When I saved Amy, it changed my entire history and the lives of the people closest to me. Seems that's the way it works. Only the time traveler remembers how things were before the change."

"Right, let me get this straight. This W. P. Brown bloke has you over a barrel," he says, "and if you don't do what he says, Amy is gone?"

"But not only Amy," I say. "Everything else will go back to how it was too. Before I saved her, my dad was dead and my mum was ill. I won't go back to that life. I can't. It's not fair," I clench my fists. "I already saved her once, Vinny. I thought I was done."

"So when are you going back to 1963?" Vinny asks.

"I don't know." I pull out the silver hunter. "This watch will give me a countdown, apparently." I pass it to Vinny. He turns it reverently in his hands. "Brown said it'll help me when I get there too, though I don't know how. And it'll bring me home again. So he says."

Vinny hands it back to me. "Why can't you just travel when you like? Change what you want?"

"No idea. I've tried to travel on my own, like I did before, but I can't." I down the last of my pint and feel a pleasant fuzziness around my edges. Vinny offers to buy another round, and I accept enthusiastically. He disappears to the bar and comes back with four pints. "Two each," he says. "Reckon we need it."

I wonder if I should be drinking like this. What if I suddenly travel again? Should I be sensible and sober up?

"Cheers," says Vinny, pushing one of the pints toward me. "Drink up." I hesitate for a second. I can't live my life on edge, waiting for the watch to flush me down time's toilet. I decide to let my hair down, and if I end up drunk, so be it. We clink glasses, and I take a long draft of beer.

"Now it's my turn to tell you something," Vinny says, rubbing his hands together. "Time might be on your side after all, you know."

"What do you mean?"

"Just so happens there's someone not so far from here who's an expert on classic British gangsters. In particular, London gangsters from the sixties." He winks.

"You!" I say, incredulous.

"Gangs, extortion, fraud . . . the works."

I look at him, astonished. "Are you kidding me?"

"Nope."

"This is amazing!" I gush. "Maybe you can help me figure this whole thing out and save Lucy Romano!"

"What are sidekicks for?" he says. "But listen, Joe. You need to be very careful of Frankie Shaw."

"I wasn't planning to go anywhere near him, if I can help it."

Vinny belches loudly. "The police called him Mr. Untouchable."

"Yeah, I read that. Why?"

"Frankie Shaw was as slippery as they come. He always got other people to do his dirty work, particularly the killing."

That sends a ripple of gooseflesh over my shoulders. "That much is true," I tell Vinny. "I've seen him in action."

"It all caught up with him in the end though," Vinny continues. "Mr. Untouchable ended up behind bars."

I shrug. "Looking back, it's good to know he got caught, but it doesn't change the fact that I traveled to a time when Frankie was on the rise."

A few hours later, Vinny and I are weaving our way home, singing to the empty streets of Cheltenham. The temperature has plummeted, but I'm so drunk I don't really care. I feel as though I might need my stomach pumped, but Vinny continues to fill his. We stop at a food stand, and he orders two large kebabs. He offers one to me. I turn my head and wave it away. "I don't trust street food."

"Why not?" he says. "I have a policy only to eat food from establishments with a two-star or lower hygiene rating." He announces it like a fancy food critic. "It keeps your antibodies keen. I'm telling you, alcohol hand gel will kill us all."

A few minutes later, we're outside his house.

"Thanks, Vinny," I say. "I've had the best night. And thanks for being so cool about everything."

He stretches his arms as though limbering up for a race. "So are we off soon, then?"

THE SHADOWS OF LONDON

"What? Where?"

An eager grin spreads over his face. "Don't you mean *when*?"

"No, Vinny. Absolutely not . . . no way."

He looks like I just smashed his favorite toy. "But I'm involved now," he says. "And it's the sixties . . . I'm your man!"

"I can't drag you into this."

"You dragged Alexia, although I know I'm bigger than she is." He pats his tummy. "Is mass an issue?"

"I don't know," I say, "but it doesn't matter, because you're not coming. This isn't your problem. It's dangerous."

"This isn't all about you, you know," he says with a sharp tone I've never heard him use before. "I've been waiting for this my whole life."

"What do you mean?"

"I'm so bored. I love my shop, but it's been nearly twenty years . . . I need an adventure before it's too late, before I get too old. I need this." His hands are in tight fists. "At least think about it, please?"

I have no intention of taking Vinny with me and putting him in danger, but for now, placating seems like the best option. "OK. I'll think about it."

"Lovely jubbly. Got time for a nightcap and a spot of supper?"

Food is the last thing I need right now. I shake my head. "I'm going home to watch every London gangster film ever made."

Vinny grins. "Not bad homework. Call me if you're going to"—he narrows his gaze—"you know . . . *go*."

"I will."

"I mean it. Call me, OK? The only way out of this is through. You're going to need support."

"Do you think I can do it?"

"You're totally screwed," he says, "but you've got me now, so you'll be all right. A problem shared is a problem doubled."

"Thanks, Vin," I say, my emotions a confusing tumble of relief and apprehension.

"No worries," he replies. "It's what friends are for."

13

I arrive home just after 10 p.m. Molly's taped a note to the door at the back of the shop: "I've left your new phone in the kitchenette." She insists on calling the tiny broom cupboard "the kitchenette" because it's where we make tea, but it barely deserves the title. There's an ugly, badly painted chest of drawers with a kettle and a microwave oven on top, and a small shelf stacked with a diverse collection of tea bags and a couple of mugs. There's no sink. There isn't even a fridge.

I poke my head inside and spot the new phone on top of the microwave, plugged in and fully charged. I press my thumbprint to the screen. It unlocks. All of Other Joe's stuff has been restored onto it, and a notification tells me I have two messages. I press the button, but before it will let me hear them, it asks me to review my prerecorded response.

"Hi!" Other Joe says when I play it. "Thanks for calling. Sorry I can't pick up right now. Leave a message, and I'll call you back. Cheers."

It's so weird to hear him. He sounds like me, but with an injection of pride and ebullience. He's well-spoken, as though he's had an expensive education—the one that was robbed from me after my family fell apart. I press the hash key to keep the current greeting. It's the least I can do.

The first message is a mechanic from the garage. My car is due for a service, apparently. I don't know what car or where it's parked, but I make a mental note to check with Amy.

The second message is from Mum.

"Hello, Joe," she says. "Oh, what a shame, I was really hoping to speak to you."

During the short silence that follows, I try to calm my heartbeat, which thuds in my ears like drummers at a festival. *Hello again, Mum.*

"Your father and I are very worried about you, you know." Another pause. "I suppose you're out. Joseph, please call us as soon as you get this message. Amy told us about your accident. We just want to know you're all right, darling. Bye for now."

My eyes sting. The last time I saw Mum, she was suffering from late-stage dementia, and she barely knew who I was. It's wonderful to hear her now, sharp and present. She can be as demanding as she likes. Part of me is desperate to talk to her, but I can't call back now. I send a quick text instead.

> Sorry I missed you. I'm fine, don't worry.
> See you when you get back.

I unplug the phone, shove it in my pocket, and go upstairs to the flat. My hangover is kicking in already, so I hunt through the cupboards and drawers in the kitchen for some headache tablets. Gratefully, I chase down two of the little white pills with a pint of water and decide to hang out upstairs for half an hour to sober up a bit before I turn in. I refill my glass and climb up the sparkling staircase to my loft. When I get to the top, the lights automatically come on at their brightest setting. It hurts my eyes and my head, so I grab the wall-mounted iPad and press the home button. The screen glows, revealing three icons. I press the first one, and a complicated-looking dashboard appears: "Loft LEDs." I choose PRESET ONE. The room transforms into a mermaid's paradise, bathed in green-and-blue light. Everywhere I look the lighting has changed: behind the sofas, at floor level, on the ceiling, beneath the audio unit, out on the terrace. I choose another preset and, just like that, the entire space is a moody purple. I cycle through the different settings until the room shifts to a soft vanilla, relaxing but bright enough to see what I'm doing. I try to put some music on, but I can't work out how, so I chuck the iPad to one side and let my thoughts take over.

I think about Vinny's supportive response to my time-travel revelations. Just knowing that he knows helps somehow. It reminds me of something Paul McCartney said about the early years of the Beatles, how they coped during the madness of Beatlemania. He said they always had each other's backs, and they helped each other keep it real. For a while I was the only member of Joseph Bridgeman's Lonely Hearts Club Band, but now Vinny has joined, and it makes a hell of a difference.

Suddenly, Donna Summer's "I Feel Love" blares out of the speakers, and I jump out of my skin. I check to see if I've accidentally sat on the iPad, but then, out of the corner of my eye, I notice a figure and turn to see a stunning woman standing at the top of the staircase. I have no idea how she got up here without me hearing her. She's wearing a short cream rain-coat, red miniskirt, and towering black heels. She smiles, revealing perfect teeth framed by glossy red lips.

"Pleased to see me?" she asks, studying me with humorous interest.

"How did you get in here?" I blurt.

"Don't you remember?" she laughs.

"No, I don't—"

"You gave me the code, silly." Her voice is soft and playful. She holds my gaze as she walks slowly toward me, heels clicking rhythmically on the wood floor. She moves with the balanced, confident grace of a supermodel, her suicide blond hair swaying hypnotically.

She stops just a few feet away. Her skin is unblemished, smooth and pale as alabaster. She stands stock-still, watching me, her amber eyes calculating like a panther's.

"What *am* I going to do with you, JB?" she purrs.

She spins on her heels and perches opposite me, on the edge of the coffee table.

This has to be a booty call. I need to set this woman straight, and fast, before the situation gets any more complicated.

"I'm sorry, but I don't know who you are," I say.

She folds her arms and leans toward me. I smell a waft of her perfume, sweet and rich with musky undertones. "What are you talking about?" she says.

"I have amnesia. I fell off my mountain bike and hit my head, and I've forgotten the last twenty years. I can remember my family, but that's about it."

She considers this for a few seconds, tilting her head to the side. Then a low, salacious laugh ripples up from her belly. "Role play!" she squeals. "You naughty boy."

That wasn't the reaction I was hoping for. "No, this isn't role play. I'm serious. I honestly don't know who you are."

"I think you do!" she trills. She giggles again, but with less certainty this time. She places a manicured finger on my chest and gently pushes me, her pretty face very close to mine now. My pulse races, and I realize how vulnerable I am. I'm drunk, tired, stressed, and lonely. But this is wrong. I can't do it.

I'm in love with Alexia, and although she doesn't remember our time together, that doesn't change the way I feel. I'm a one-woman man. And this woman thinks I'm Other Joe. That wouldn't be fair to her. But even if I *were* tempted, and the sort of person who would hop into bed with another man's stunning girlfriend, there's the not inconsequential fact that I may time travel at any moment. I visited 1963 in my pajamas last time, which was bad enough. I'm not going to risk going with my trousers down.

"What's your name?" I ask her calmly, trying to modulate my tone so she can hear that I'm not joking around. I was really upset when I found out Alexia didn't remember our relationship, so I know how hurtful this might be. I have to let this woman down, but I need to do it kindly. "I'd really like to know."

Abruptly, she gets up, walks over to a control panel on the wall, and stops the music. She turns back to me and leans against the wall, folding her arms. "What's actually going on, Joe? Why are you being like this?"

"I'm not being like anything," I say. "I honestly don't remember you. I'm sorry if it's hurtful." I feel horrible. She's an innocent victim of the New Joe Road Show.

Her lip wobbles. "You really don't remember?" she says. "I'm Chloe, baby. Your little Chloe-Cute-Boot." She undoes the belt on her raincoat. "Does this jog your memory?" She starts to slip the top half of her coat off one of her shoulders, and I can see she's only wearing underwear beneath.

"No!" I say urgently. "Please, don't do that." Tears well up in Chloe's eyes as she pulls her coat back loosely over her shoulder. "I'm really sorry, Chloe. You're lovely and everything, but I'm not the same as I was, and this doesn't feel right."

"If you've changed your mind, you could just be a man about it and break up with me like a normal person," she protests, her voice rising.

"I don't want to break up with you," I say. How can I break up with someone I was never together with? "But I think you should probably go."

"You're not breaking up with me, but you want me to go?" she says, sounding angry now. "Make your bloody mind up! It wasn't easy getting here tonight, you know. It took some arranging. If you didn't want to see me, why didn't you cancel?"

"I couldn't cancel, because I didn't know you were coming," I say wearily. I didn't ask for this either. "You don't understand. I'm not the person you think I am."

Chloe becomes serious for a second, long eyelashes fluttering. "JB," she says earnestly, her voice dropping to a lower, smokier register. "Listen to me, baby. You don't have to be anyone except yourself. You know how I feel about you." She walks toward me. "I don't care that you've put on some weight and your hair's a bit scruffy. I love you for who you are."

The L word. I feel worse than ever. She reaches out to cup my face, but hastily I take a couple of steps back. "No, Chloe, I'm sorry. We aren't going to do this. You should go."

Her face shuts down again. "Fine." She does her coat up to the neck and walks primly to the top of the stairs. "I really think you're going to regret this," she says defiantly, a spark in her eyes. She seems energized. I suspect she's all about the drama.

"You'll come crawling back," she says vindictively.

She clatters at top speed down the staircase, despite the height of her heels. I hear the door to the fire escape slam, and then I'm alone again.

I collapse back onto the sofa with my head in my hands. Poor Chloe, poor me. She didn't deserve that. Neither of us did. My heart is just about back to its normal rhythm when my phone rings.

"Hi, Amy," I answer.

"Hi, Joe, are you all right? You sound a bit . . . tired."

"I'm fine," I tell her. I'm not going to tell her about Chloe. Other Joe's beans are not mine to spill. "How are you? It's a bit late, are you OK?"

"I'm fine, but I wanted to let you know as soon as I heard. Mum and Dad are coming home early."

"Early? Why?"

"Martin called them. I'm not exactly sure what he said, but they're really worried about you. I tried to tell them you're OK, but they weren't having any of it."

Martin. I knew that conversation about canceling the property deal would come back to bite me.

"When will they be home?" I ask.

"Late tonight. They've been trying to reach you. They really want to see you." I think back to Mum's voice message. I probably should have called her back. "I told them I'd talk to you."

I think it through. I was hoping I could sort out this blackmail thing before I met them. Everything's crashing together at the same time. "Do you think I could put them off for a few days?"

"I don't think that would be a good idea," she says flatly. "They'll just turn up at the shop and surprise you."

That's one scenario I definitely want to avoid. I need to see them in a controlled environment, away from other people. "Will you come with me?" I ask Amy. I feel like a five-year-old facing his first day at school.

"I don't know. I'm happy to walk you there, fill you in on some history, but Dad said . . . well, I think it might be better if you see them without me."

"Why?"

"If I'm there, they'll keep asking me stuff, rake me over the coals for not telling them about your accident sooner, you know." She sounds harassed. "Can you go? Mum said to tell you around eleven o'clock tomorrow morning, coffee time."

I check the pocket watch of doom. There's no change, but who knows when it might go off. I'm so nervous about seeing my parents that half of me hopes it'll start its countdown.

"Amy, there's a chance I might not be around tomorrow morning."

"What? Why, where are you going?"

"I don't know yet. It might not happen, but if it does, I'll go and see them afterward."

She's quiet for a moment. "Fine," she says, sounding deflated. "Let me know if you're not coming by half past nine. If you can still go, I'll call for you at ten."

"Thank you," I say gratefully. "You're the best. See you tomorrow."

I hang up and lean back on the sofa. What a night. Chloe, Amy, Mum, and Dad all flicker through my head in rapid succession, one after the other, making me feel nauseous. I focus on one of the spotlights in the ceiling and steady my breathing. My brain relaxes, I'm finally hit by a tidal wave of exhaustion, and I slip into a deep sleep.

14

At first, I think I'm dreaming, but I find myself high above Bridgeman Antiques, hovering over the entrance to the shop like a silent drone. Around me, the dark night howls and swells, the sky swollen with icy rain. Then, just like the viewing I had with Lucy, I'm descending. I glide softly downward through the storm until I'm level with the shop windows, passing straight through the glass and into the building.

To begin with, all I can see is the empty shop, but then tiny shooting stars of light begin to appear and connect to one another, creating lines on my retinas like sparklers in the darkness. A hooded figure materializes before me. The figure is dressed top to toe in black and carrying a small rucksack over one shoulder. I float closer, wrap myself around their shoulders like a ghostly shawl, and connect. Immediately I tense up, breath constricted as the figure listens intently for sounds above the din of the storm.

Eventually, the figure lays the rucksack on the floor and removes their gloves, stuffing them quickly into the bag. The hands are small with painted nails, a woman's hands. On the back of her right hand, near the base of the thumb is a small birthmark shaped like a star. She turns around and notices the thin line of light spilling beneath the door that leads to my apartment. She knows I'm up there.

She moves to the cabinets closest to the desk, looking back at the door to my apartment. She selects the cabinet nearest the desk, opens it, clears some space on one of the shelves, crouches down, and draws the rucksack toward her.

She lifts the top flap and pulls out a compact case. Carefully, she lays it on the floor. She fumbles with the metal clasps and curses quietly under her breath, tucking a strand of hair back into her hood. She's nervous—this is important. I relax into the viewing a little more, to let more of her emotions bleed through me, and get another flash of insight: this is all part of a bigger plan, and she doesn't want to mess it up.

She opens the flight case with ease and lifts out the red Roberts radio. It's just like any other radio, and she feels nothing from it, no indication that it will send me back to 1963.

A huge flash of lightning precedes an immediate, massive crash of thunder. The streetlamps snuff out like candles, and the light under the doorway at the back of the shop goes out. It takes her a moment to adjust to the darkness, and then she hears beeping, probably some kind of alert that the power's gone out.

She tries not to panic, lifting her chin and relaxing her shoulders. She turns toward the back of the shop to locate the source of the beeping, but as she does, she hears a sound from upstairs, then the radio lights up. Static crackles, and it starts to tune itself, snatches of music and voices cutting through the darkness.

Taken unawares, she drops the radio, and it clatters to the floor. She curses to herself, because she doesn't want to be found here. Hastily, she picks it up again and turns the volume dial down. She places it carefully on the cabinet shelf, leaving the door open. She feels proud that she's done what she was asked to do, but her pride is tinged with something else, something bitter.

She hears a creak from the staircase, and she knows she needs to go. Now. As she scrabbles around in the darkness to gather up the flight case and her rucksack, the radio crackles and squeals, harmonizing eerily with the howling of the wind. She's just shoving the flight case back into the rucksack when she hears a sound at the back of the shop.

Her heart sinks. Slowly, she turns and sees a man in the doorway, his skin pale in the reflected glow of the radio. It's Joseph Bridgeman.

"Is there someone there?" he calls out, his voice strong, confident.

Another fork of lightning rips the sky in two, bathing the shop in bright light. The woman just stares at him, frozen in shock. Then she seems to find her wits again, and she grabs the bag, unlocks the door, and runs into the night.

15

I wake to the alarm with a grimace. The ringing thrashes through my skull. I'm horribly hungover. Vinny drank twice as much as I did, but I know he'll be fine. I've always envied his ability to process alcohol—he takes in beer and turns it all into fun. I just get nausea and headaches.

Groaning, I comb back through the viewing. Trying to read the feelings of my host is like trying to eat soup with a fork, and I bite back frustration as I grasp at the wisps of emotion she left behind in me. Who is this woman with the star-shaped birthmark?

And more worryingly, this seems to have been another viewing without an object. At least I know now that the radio was deliberately planted. W. P. Brown didn't do it himself, but there's nothing to say the woman isn't working for him.

I sit up in bed, turn the light on, and reach for the hunter pocket watch. It's 8 a.m., and it still says, *Calibrating*. What is it actually calibrating against, and how long does it take?

I haul myself out of bed and into the shower. My stomach is full of butterflies. Today I meet my parents. I cycle through several wardrobe malfunctions before settling on a plain blue shirt, dark trousers, and black suede shoes. I don't know how Other Joe would dress to see his parents, but I decide smart is the safest option.

Other Joe has a drawer for his socks, belts, ties, and watches. Very posh.

I'm going to struggle to keep it tidy. As I pick out a pair of dark-gray socks and a faux leather belt, a single earring catches my eye. Elegant. Waiting to be found. It has a tiny aquamarine hemisphere, with a miniature sterling-silver butterfly alighting on the edge, as if it's just about to take flight. It's beautiful. I wonder who left it here. One of his previous conquests, maybe. I almost pick it up, but then I pull my hand away. It has energy. It wants me to listen.

"Not now," I say, bargaining with it like a total mad man. "Today, I have more important things to worry about."

I shave and tame my unkempt hair with some weird product I discover on one of the bathroom shelves. I'm about to search for my dress watch, Dad's old Rado, when I realize that he left it to me when he died. I imagine it on his wrist now and get a rush of nervous excitement. All these huge changes and it's sometimes the smallest details that are the hardest to get your head around.

Amy arrives just after ten o'clock, dressed in a long green coat, woolen hat, and leather boots. "I thought we'd walk," she says. "It's such a beautiful morning." She seems tired and distracted, but she brushes away my inquiry with a flick of her hand. "I'm fine!" she insists. "I've just had a few bad nights in a row, but it'll pass. Come on, let's go!"

Cheltenham is cold today, and the grass is a sparkling icy carpet, crisp against a faultless cyan sky. We stroll along the street together, brother and sister, as though we've done it a thousand times.

"How are you feeling?" Amy asks.

"Nervous," I say. "Excited. Freaked out. I think my brain's struggling to reconcile this life with the one I was living last week."

"Of course it is," she says. "We're not wired to handle situations like this. It must be super hard for you." She takes my arm. "Do you still want the basics on Mum and Dad? Can you handle it?"

"Go for it," I say, faking enthusiasm. "The sooner we start, the sooner I can get my head around everything."

"Well, I still don't know exactly how things were for you," she says carefully. "I don't want to put my foot in it, open old wounds, you know?"

"It doesn't matter," I reassure her. "None of that happened now, it's just in my head. Let's assume I know nothing and start from there."

Amy gives me a summary. Our parents have been happily married for thirty-eight years. When Amy and Other Joe were young, Mum worked as a freelance bookkeeper, and Dad managed a warehouse. Then Dad inherited some money and set up Bridgeman Commercial Properties. When the business began to make proper cash, Mum gave up paid work and started volunteering for the local wildlife trust.

"What about you?" I ask. "I've been so focused on my own life, I haven't asked yet what you do."

She squeezes my arm. "I went to art school at eighteen. When I graduated, I got a job at a photographer's studio and painted in my spare time. I started my own online art business five years ago, with a grant from the local chamber of commerce."

"Art online? That sounds cool."

"I like it well enough," she says, "but it's not much to write home about." Amy's dismissive, almost like she's embarrassed.

"What kind of things do you paint?"

She looks shocked. "Oh, I don't sell any of *my* stuff. Gosh, I wouldn't let anyone see that."

"Why not? I remember you were really talented."

"There are so many artists that are way better than I will ever be. And it turns out my biggest talent is spotting what will sell."

That makes two of us then. "You said you got a grant. Didn't Mum and Dad help you out?"

"I didn't ask." She shrugs. "I wanted to be self-sufficient. They aren't really arty people. I suppose I wanted to prove I could do it without them."

"I can understand that. Do you have a shop?"

"No, just a website. I have a storage unit over by the railway station, where I keep most of my stock. I supply a few local galleries, but mostly people order off the website, and I pack up the canvases and dispatch them from there."

"I would love to see it."

"There's not much to see."

"Maybe, but it's your business," I say. "I'm interested."

She lets go of me and stops. "Do you mean that?" she asks. "Are you genuinely interested?"

"Yes!" I assure her. "Why wouldn't I be?"

We continue walking, and Amy takes my arm again. "I have some deliveries to make later. Maybe you could join me, after you've seen Mum and Dad?"

"Sure," I say. "Let's do that."

"Plus, I need to talk to you about something," she says thoughtfully.

"We can talk now, if you like."

"It can wait. You've got enough to think about. And anyway, we'll be there soon. We can chat later."

We'll be there soon. I can't separate the nervous apprehension from the excitement skittering around in my belly. Mum was in such a bad way the last time I saw her. She's bound to be in better health, but Dad . . . I don't know how it's going to feel seeing him again. I'm overjoyed to have him back, but I know he won't look the same as I remember him. He's nearly twenty years older now. I distract myself with more questions.

"When did Other Joe join Dad's business?" I ask.

"Dad took him on as a director in 2011, with the intention of handing the reins over when he retired. Joe kept the antiques shop going, popping in a couple days a week, because he enjoyed it so much. But he was really good at his job, according to Dad."

"So this hotel development, then," I say.

"I don't know the ins and outs, but Dad and Other Joe spent a lot of time talking about it recently."

"Martin wasn't happy when I told him I was reconsidering."

"Don't be too hard on Martin," Amy says. "I think he's only trying to help. Other Joe found him hard work sometimes, but he did respect his decision-making." She glances at me thoughtfully. "Why do you want to cancel the deal?"

"Because Alexia rents an office in that building."

"Alexia . . ." Amy says, thinking. "She's the therapist who helped you to save me, right?"

"Yes. She's the one I called from your flat when we got back. But she didn't remember . . . what we'd started."

"Oh, Joe." Amy's voice softens. "She means a lot to you, doesn't she?"

I nod. "And it appears she's planning to leave Cheltenham altogether. But I'm hoping that if I cancel the contract, she'll stay. Do you think I'm mad?"

"I think you're following your heart."

We turn the corner onto Mum and Dad's road, and Amy stops. "I'll leave you here, then."

I swallow. "Amy, will you come in with me?"

"I don't know, Joe," she says. "I really think it might be better for you to have some time on your own with them."

"I'm just so horribly nervous," I say. "It'll make it easier if you're there. And you can help smooth things over if I say something stupid."

"You won't say anything stupid," she says. "They love you. You'll be fine. And anyway, Dad and I . . ." She pauses.

"Dad and you what?"

"We've had a few problems. It's a long story." She considers me for a moment, chewing the inside of her cheek. "OK, fine. I'll come in. But I can't stay long."

"Thanks," I say. "I owe you."

We walk along the street toward the house. "Joe, you said you might not have been able to make it here today? Where were you planning to go?"

"Nowhere," I say quickly. "I might have been going to an auction, but it didn't happen."

She looks doubtful. "And you thought that was more important than coming here?"

I don't know what to say, so I don't say anything. Amy sticks her hands in her pockets and seems to shrink a little.

We walk the last few yards to the front gate of the house. Amy reaches out her hand to open the gate, but I stop her. "Just give me a minute, would you?"

I pore over the house, the place I once called home. It's a terraced, four-bedroom property in a wide, pleasant street. After we lost Dad, Mum and I lived here until she eventually went into care. After that it was just me, rattling my ghostly chains in the dark while the place crumbled around me. I let it go to ruin. I might have been embarrassed if I'd been more aware. Now, as I peruse the frontage, I can finally put that guilt behind me.

It's cared for, impressive—magnificent even. The brickwork has been restored in the last few years, and the wooden sash windows are beautifully maintained. The small garden has tidy flower beds, swollen with dark soil, just the tips of bulbs visible, poised, waiting to explode with color in the spring.

"Do you remember this house?" Amy asks.

"I do," I say. "I lived here my whole life. I never left."

"Well, you'll know your way around then," she says brightly. "Come on."

She opens the gate, and we walk the short pathway to the front door. I peer through the stained glass at the familiar corridor, filtered through new colors. Only now does it finally sink in. In the same hallway, in a different world, Amy and Dad are gone, and Mum and I are adrift. Here though, beyond this door, my parents await, a chasm of unfamiliar history and knowledge between us.

I look down at the expensive clothes I'm wearing, reminding myself that I need to try and play the part of a confident, successful son. I don't know how I'm going to feel when I see them, but there's only one way to find out. I take the final step onto the doormat and press the doorbell.

We wait. There's no sound from within.

"Do you think they might be out?" I ask Amy. Before she can answer, my heart swells as I see a figure in the hallway, and before I can think or plan or worry any more, the front door swings open and my mother comes bursting back into my life in a welcome cloud of floral colors and perfume.

Amy shared some recent pictures of her, but nothing could have prepared me for this. Her hair is full again, her eyes vibrant and alive, and she's wearing a little makeup too. She looks amazing, healthy, more like the mum I remember from my teens.

"Hello, you two! Joe, darling, I've been so worried about you. How are you feeling?"

"Hi, Mum," I say, my voice sounding like it's coming from somewhere else, and then before I can properly think it through, I hug her. She stiffens in a way that makes me suspect that Other Joe didn't do this, but after a few seconds, she hugs me back, and when we part, she seems happy, if a little confused.

"What was that for?" she asks.

"I've just missed you," I say. "A lot. You can't imagine."

"We've only been gone a week, you funny boy! Anyway, don't just stand there." She steps back and opens the door wide. "Come in out of the cold. How are you, Amy?" she says, kissing her on the cheek. "You look exhausted."

"Thanks, Mum!" Amy replies. "I'm fine. I'll put more makeup on next time."

I follow Amy over the threshold. The corridor is bright, freshly decorated. A chandelier sparkles above us, the familiar grandfather clock echoing through the halls of my memory. When I lived here, I spent most of my time in my study and my bedroom. The curtains were always drawn, the heating off. Now, this home is filled with light, the warm aroma of baking, and the mumble of a distant radio.

Mum takes our coats and hangs them on a row of hooks with other jackets and scarves, all neatly positioned. "Come through. I'll put the kettle on," she says.

Amy and I follow her into the kitchen. They've knocked through the wall into the dining room and made a large airy dining area with pale-green furniture and a tiled floor. The wall behind the dining-room table is decorated with pretty wallpaper scattered with birds and foliage.

The oven is on, and a loaf of freshly baked bread cools on a rack. The radio's playing classical music, and two pairs of outdoor shoes are neatly arranged near the door, a large gray pair and a smaller light-blue pair beside them.

Home. Finally.

"Amy told us what happened," Mum says as she fills the kettle. "She said you fell off that ridiculous bike I didn't want you to buy. How are you feeling? How's your head?"

My head's fine, I want to tell her, *don't worry about me*. The last time I saw her, my mum was in a home for elderly people, devastated by the loss of Amy, heartbroken over my dad's suicide, her memories ripped away by dementia.

"Joe?" Amy and Mum are looking at me.

I pull myself together, wipe my eyes, and clear my throat. "Sorry, I'm just feeling a bit wobbly. I'm really sorry you had to cut your holiday short, Mum."

"We were eating too much. You've probably saved us both from putting on a few pounds," she replies. "But of course we came home. We were worried about you."

"I'm feeling much better now." I feel a flash of guilt for making her worry.

"Amnesia, though." She says the word as though it's catching. "That's a serious mental condition, darling."

"It's temporary. I'll get over it."

I glance around the room. The majority of my memories of this house are painful, some decades old, but I can discern a lightness in this place now, like a song. I can feel the joy and love this house has witnessed. It radiates from the walls like the stored warmth of the sun.

Mum clears a couple of magazines and a dirty mug off the kitchen table, then wipes it down with a cloth, even though it's already spotlessly clean. "Sit down then, you two," she says. She makes three cups of tea and places them on the table. "Here you go," she says. "These'll warm you up. It's so chilly outside!"

I pull out a chair and sit casually, leaning back, hands in my pockets, smiling up at Mum in what I hope is a reassuring manner.

"You don't look right," she says. "Have you seen a specialist yet?"

"Yes, of course," I lie.

"Which specialist did you see?" she asks.

I really should have thought about this before I got here. I grab the first name that pops into my head. "I went to see Dr. Hyde."

"Who?" she asks dubiously.

"He's a specialist in amnesia. He said my memories will come back eventually. The more that people talk normally about the past, the faster my recovery will be. The best approach is to just keep telling me things, remind me if I seem confused." Which will be most of the time.

"Is that so." Mum considers this, clearly unconvinced. "What's the last thing you remember?"

I swallow. "Try not to worry too much, but I've mislaid about twenty years."

"Twenty years?" she exclaims, holding onto the table with both hands as if trying to keep her balance. "For goodness' sake." She shakes her head and presses her lips into a thin line. "It makes a mockery of that clever suspension you were so *pleased* with. What's the point in spending all that money on a mountain bike if it's going to throw you off and destroy your memory? How on earth are you going to cope?"

"Mum, seriously, don't worry," Amy insists. "He's going to be fine. I went with him to see Dr. Hyde. Like Joe said, we just need to be patient, remind him of things when they come up, and in time he's expected to make a full recovery," she says confidently. "You'll be good as new, won't you, Joe? Maybe even better. Right?"

"Right." I smile warmly, sending her invisible thanks for backing me up.

"Well, if you're sure," Mum says doubtfully, as though we've both suffered head injuries. The oven beeps. She dons the oven gloves and pulls out a tray of scones. She sets down the tray and examines them with a critical eye.

"Wow, they look lush," says Amy, standing up. "Are they for general consumption?" She walks over to the tray and goes to pick a corner off of one.

Mum guides her hand away. "Just wait a few minutes till they've cooled down."

"OK, I'm not ten," says Amy good-naturedly. She sits back down at the table and yawns. "Sorry," she says, rubbing her eyes. "No offense to either of you. I'm not bored, just bushed."

"Amy, sweetheart," Mum says with concern. "Are you having trouble sleeping again?"

"A bit, I suppose," she says, picking imaginary lint off the front of her cardigan.

Mum reaches into one of the kitchen cupboards and pulls out a small bottle of pills. "I want you to give these a go."

"But, Mum—"

"They're herbal, darling," she says. "They won't do you any harm. You need your sleep. You know what a tangle you get into when you don't." She walks over and puts the tablets straight into Amy's handbag. "Take two an hour before bedtime."

Amy grimaces. Mum notices and shakes her head.

"You may think I'm being bossy, but you'll miss me when I'm gone," she says. Seeing Mum like this—sharp, confident, and full of life—suddenly fills me with immense joy. Her time at Beech Trees Nursing Home no longer happened. It's like a fading bad dream now, and my eyes fill with tears. People often spend many years—sometimes their entire lives—seeking happiness and fulfillment. They climb mountains, travel the world, study philosophy, strive for wealth, spend a fortune on material things. But I'm starting to realize that maybe sitting in a warm kitchen with your family is about as good as it gets.

"Are you all right, Joe?" Mum asks me. "Are you *crying*?"

I take a deep breath and clear my throat. "I'm fine. Just happy to be here with you both."

Mum looks slightly surprised again, like she did when I hugged her at the door. "Well, that's lovely to hear, darling," she says, glancing up at the clock. "Now then. Your Dad'll be ready for a cup of tea soon." She takes the kettle to the sink and refills it.

I swallow. I was half hoping he would be out, so I could just deal with meeting one parent at a time.

"What's Dad up to?" asks Amy.

"He was getting under my feet, so I banished him to the garage. God only knows how I'm going to cope when he retires. We'll probably end up killing each other! In the meantime, though, I wanted to talk to you both about his birthday party."

"But that's months away!" Amy says.

"It'll be here before you know it," Mum says. "Dad wants to have the party at the golf club, but that's not going to happen. I've picked up a menu from La Saveur Folle. They've got the most wonderful chef. Most of their food is local, and it's all organic. I want to reserve the party date sooner rather than later. Have a look and let me know what you think." She pushes the menu across the table toward me.

Obediently, I pick it up.

"Right. I'll just go and see if Dad's ready for his tea." Mum leaves the kitchen, and I hear the internal door to the garage squeak as she goes through it.

"What do you think of this place?" I ask Amy.

She smirks and shakes her head. "I don't know anything about it, but it doesn't matter. Mum's already decided."

"Why's she asking for my opinion then?"

"It's what she does," Amy says wryly. "She's trying to make you feel included, but don't be under any illusions. When it comes to family events, we're all just willing pawns in Mum's chess game."

"What chess game?" asks Mum, returning to the kitchen with a blue-and-white-striped shoebox. She doesn't wait for an answer. She lays the box on the table in front of Amy and takes off the lid. "Could you put these on the computer?" she asks. "I want to create a slideshow for Dad's party."

"Sure," says Amy. She picks out a wad of pictures and sifts through them.

"You should look at them too, Joe," Mum says to me. "They might help prompt some memories."

"Ha! Look at this one!" Amy giggles and passes me a photo.

It's me and Dad on the beach. I must be about five or six years old. I'm helping my Spider-Man doll climb up a rock. It's clearly a hot summer day. Dad's sporting bright-red swimming trunks, shades and a quality porkpie sun hat, and he's holding three ice creams.

"That was our first family holiday to Padstow," Mum says, peering over my shoulder. "You absolutely loved it. We couldn't get you off the beach. You used to cry every evening on the way back to the hotel. Do you remember?"

I study my little self—tummy puffed out, legs and arms still pudgy with baby fat—and I laugh. "I do. I loved that Spider-Man!"

I reach into the box and pull out another picture. In this one, Dad and I are standing proudly at the helm of a small riverboat, moored under a large weeping willow tree. It's hard to see how old I am—maybe late twenties. The name *Polly Esther* is emblazoned across the stern of the boat. "I don't remember this," I say. "What were Dad and I doing?"

Amy takes the picture from me and lets out a little laugh. "That was your thirtieth birthday," she says. "You and Dad went boating for the weekend. When I say, 'went boating,' I don't think you ever actually left the mooring. You just stayed at the marina."

We all laugh together, a simple family giggle like we used to share. It feels like a lifetime ago.

Amy pulls more pictures out of the box, and she and Mum chat away. I enjoy the banal chatter. For so long, my emotions about my family were guilt, grief, and loss. Now, I need to let all of that go. I feel a pang of uncertainty, and for a fleeting moment I'm jealous of all the years the rest of my family have shared together and the memories they've created.

"Joe? Are you listening?" Mum's anxious voice interrupts my thoughts. "You seem very distant. Try and concentrate, darling."

"Sorry. I'm listening," I say. Mum is back to her wonderful, insistent, demanding self. I feel like I'm fourteen again, and it feels good.

"Look at this one!" Amy says. "Where was this? You are so stylish, Mum!" Mum's a lot younger, in her twenties, and the colors in the photo have faded a little. She's wearing a short green coat, done up with one large button at the neck. Her eye makeup is thick and black, and her hair is piled up into a huge blond beehive.

Mum's expression softens, and she smiles fondly. "That's from our honeymoon," she says. "We went to Edinburgh. We had such a wonderful time. That was the first time I ever drank whiskey, would you believe? Revolting stuff."

I take the photo from Amy and look closely. In the background I see 1960s cars parked along the side of the road. "When was this, Mum?" I ask her.

"Let me think . . . it must have been April 1964," she says.

I'm shocked. I hadn't really considered that my parents lived through the sixties. What would they say if they knew I'd been there too? "What was it like?" I ask. "Living through the Swinging Sixties, I mean?"

"She probably can't remember," Amy jokes. "She and Dad probably spent the entire decade off their heads on LSD."

Mum raises her eyebrows. "We most certainly did not," she says. "We were perfectly happy in the real world, thank you very much." She sighs. "You know, I never really understood why people called them *swinging*. There were lots of great things, like the fight for equal rights for women, racial equality, and the moon landing. The Beatles and the Beach Boys, of course. And I loved the fashion, those enormous flares and cute little miniskirts! But there were challenges too, like there always are . . . The start of the Troubles in Ireland, the murder of JFK." Mum pours boiling water into the teapot and swirls the leaves around. "We have to be careful not to view the past through rose-tinted spectacles. I'm not saying everything's perfect now. Far from it. The planet's in a bad way, and if we don't prioritize fixing it, nothing else will matter. But modern life is also wonderful. We've got running water, and we're not being shot at. We don't know how lucky we are."

Amy leans back from the table and stretches. "Hear, hear, Mum," she says. "I'm with you on all of that."

Mum takes a fresh mug out of the cupboard. "Time to take your father a cup of tea." She adds a tea bag and fills the mug with hot water. "Anyone else want a top off?"

"Not for me, thanks," Amy says. "I'm going to have to make a move."

Mum puts down the kettle. "Oh, Amy! Your father will be so disappointed not to see you. How often do the four of us all get together these days? Please stay."

"Sorry, Mum." Amy zips up her handbag and walks to the kitchen door. "I've got a ton of deliveries to do today. I'll come and see Dad another day."

"Such a shame," Mum says. "Make sure you do. You two haven't seen each other for a while, you know."

Amy shrugs, then turns to me. "I'll give you a call later, Joe, once I'm out on delivery. We can arrange a time for me to pick you up."

"Sounds good," I say. "See you in a while."

"Bye, Mum," Amy says. "See you soon."

"Bye, sweetheart," Mum replies. "Let me know how you get on with those tablets." We hear Amy open the front door and then pull it shut behind her.

Mum walks over to me and puts her hand on my forehead. "Now then, young man," she says. "How are you really?"

"Doing OK," I assure her. "Honestly. Today's been brilliant. Things are starting to come back to me already."

She doesn't seem to be listening. "I'm not at all sure about this Dr. Hyde of yours," she says. "You must go and see Dr. Sharma. Do you remember him?"

"Er, no, I don't think so."

"He's the consultant who saw your father after his bad turn last year."

"Bad turn?"

"He's absolutely fine now. Right as rain, and just as annoying as ever." She says this with great fondness. "I'll bring Dad's tea through shortly once it's brewed. You go and see him in the garage. He wants to talk to you."

The garage is accessible via a door off the hallway. I pause before I turn the handle, my guts turning over, palms sweaty. This is where I found him, after he gassed himself to death. I push that horrifying memory from my mind, square up my shoulders, and open the door.

16

The garage is immaculate. Tins, jars, tools, and boxes are all neatly stacked, labeled, and in their places. The familiar smells of sawdust, oil, and paint remind me of my childhood, when I used to hang out in here with him, learning the basics of carpentry.

I can't see Dad, and I'm about to call out when I spot his legs sticking out from beneath a car raised up on a ramp. It's a classic silver MGB GT. Not my cup of tea, though I'm not really a car person. I'm just relieved it's not red, like the one I found his lifeless body in before.

"Hi, Dad," I say loudly.

"Joseph?" he calls from beneath the car. "Is that you?"

"Yep, it's me."

"Pass me that hammer, will you?" A strong hand appears, just like I remember. Dad used to sand wood smooth by rubbing it with his fingers.

I hand him the hammer. His grasps it and continues working on the car. I work on my breathing.

"It's about time you made contact," he says.

"I know, I'm sorry."

Eventually, after some heavy grunting, he rolls out from beneath the car, a satisfied grin on his face. I swallow hard, my eyes burning. Seeing Mum again was incredible, but this is the big one.

Thomas Bridgeman, my father, back from the dead.

He still has most of his hair. It's peppery gray and thick. His skin is etched with lines I never knew, twenty years deep. Are they a map, I wonder, a way for me to find him again?

Dad hauls himself up, frowns at his dirty hands, and walks over to his workbench. His oily blue overalls do little to hide a modest paunch. He moves awkwardly, as though new knees and hips should have been on his Christmas list. But like Mum, he looks good, healthy. He pumps some gel onto his hands and works at them with a towel.

When you lose someone early, darkness often tarnishes the good memories, sometimes even buries them completely. But now a rush of fond memories floods my mind: Dad's guiding hand on my back as I rode my bike for the first time. Camping on Snowdon, washing our faces in an icy stream one foggy morning. Fishing off the harbor in Padstow. Clear and happy memories, the foundations upon which families are built.

I've been back just a few days, but I feel the first tendrils of connection reaching across time. All these memories from before Amy's disappearance were suffocated by grief, but they're starting to breathe again. He and I both remember all of this. I have a chance here, a unique opportunity, and I'm going to take it.

"It's good to see you, Dad," I say, my voice strained with emotion.

He pulls a pair of red-framed glasses from his top pocket, pops them on, and smiles. "There! It's good to see you too, son." He studies me, his brown eyes shaded beneath heavy, dark eyebrows. "Why didn't you answer any of our calls?"

"I didn't mean to ignore you. It was just . . . a really busy weekend."

He tips his head forward and holds up a finger in gentle warning. "Your mother and I have been worried."

"You don't need to be. I'm fine. And I'm really sorry about the holiday."

He brushes it off. "You know me. I love Cornwall, love the sea air, but four days is enough. I was more than happy to come home and get on with things." He puts down the towel and leans back against the workbench. "Right then. Tell me exactly what happened."

I fill him in on my increasingly stupid-sounding accident, and I'm honest about the memory gap. Unlike Mum, he takes it well. He listens, quiet, brow furrowed, making imperceptible connections, like he's planning his next move. I wait, feeling vulnerable.

"You can't remember anything after you were about fourteen?"

"Not really."

"That must be quite strange."

"It is." *You have no idea.*

"I'm sorry you're suffering, son, but I have to ask—why do you want to stop the George Street hotel deal? You've been working on it for months. If you've forgotten everything, why not leave well enough alone and let Martin take care of business until you're feeling better?"

He has a point. If I actually had amnesia, that's exactly what I would do. But my memories of Alexia are vivid and recent—it's been less than a week since we kissed—and I don't want to let her go.

I scrabble around for plausible reasons to cancel the deal. "The thing is, I found out the design firm on the top floor recently decorated, put new carpets in, and hired a load of new people. I really don't think we should throw them out. We ought to be supporting small businesses in Cheltenham, don't you think?"

Dad doesn't seem impressed. "The contract had a break clause. Everyone knew what they were into. Those guys can find another premises. This kind of situation happens all the time."

"I know, but I've been reading the newspapers this weekend," I counter, "and with the economy the way it is, I think we might be better off waiting a year or two."

"The economy?" Dad studies me as though I've lost my marbles. "I'm worried this fall has affected more than just your memory, son." He walks over and puts his hands on my shoulders, as though he wants to shake some sense into me. "You wanted this! You were excited about what you might do with the cash." He lets go of me, walks across to the workbench, and picks up his phone. "I'm getting you in with Dr. Sharma tomorrow—"

"Mum mentioned him too," I interject, "but it won't make any difference, Dad. Not now. The damage is done. Dr. Hyde said this is just going to take time. Keep telling me things, and it'll all come back eventually."

"Who's Dr. Hyde?" His fingers pause on the phone screen.

"The consultant I saw over the weekend. He's the one who diagnosed amnesia." Dad puts down his phone. "Look, this is my deal, so it's my decision, isn't it?"

He sighs. "Yes, in theory, but you're clearly unwell, son. I can't let you destroy all your hard work. You'll thank me once your memory comes back. I think I'm going to have to talk to Martin."

"Please don't do that, Dad. Let's just keep talking, OK? It'll help me get better faster."

He rubs his temples. "Honestly, I was worried about your sister . . . now, I'm more worried about you."

"Why were you worried about Amy?"

"Oh, you know, the usual reason. I'm concerned that all this stress might trigger another one of her episodes."

"Episodes?"

"You saw her this weekend, didn't you? Did she tell you if she's seeing things again?"

"She didn't mention anything." I start to worry. She did seem tired this morning. "What kinds of things does she see?"

My father frowns, deep concern shadowing his face. "I can't believe you don't remember any of this. This is madness, Joseph."

On that we can agree.

Dad walks back over to the car, stands beneath an overhead light with his hands on his hips, and regards his project lovingly. Eventually, he turns back to me. "Maybe you've forgotten, but last week, you were so excited about this deal, you could barely sleep." He throws his cleaning rag onto the bench. "I'll hold off talking to Martin, son, but don't do anything rash. We've got a few days in hand before we have to send the countersigned contracts back to the developers. Hopefully, your memory will start coming back to you and we can get everything nailed by Friday."

Mum appears at the door with two steaming mugs. "Tea?"

17

Amy glances in the rearview mirror, signals, and pulls away from the curb into the afternoon traffic. Sheryl Crow is blasting out of the speakers, the music raw and uplifting.

"Just let me get out of the rush-hour traffic, then we can chat properly," Amy says, weaving expertly between buses, vans, and family tanks driven by harassed parents on the school run. Amy navigates through the center of town, and I watch unfamiliar shops and strangers flit past, replaying my visit with Mum and Dad in my head. Gradually the traffic thins out, and we turn onto a wide road lined with trees. Amy leans back in the seat and loosens her grip on the steering wheel.

"Sorry about that," she says. "I can't drive and talk when it's that busy. Multitasking is a myth created to make normal people feel inadequate."

I chuckle. "It's fine. I'd rather you concentrated on the road than on me."

She turns the radio down. "Tell me, how did it go with Dad after I left?"

"To be honest, there were a few awkward moments. His son's been replaced, and there's no return policy. It was never going to be smooth."

"Mum texted me, you know, after you left. She said you hardly ate any lunch and she was worried about you, but that you weren't as bad as she expected overall."

"That's a result," I say. "Although I'm not sure Dad would agree. He was desperate to get me in with some head doctor called Sharma. They both were, actually." I try to put myself in their shoes. "I can't blame them. I'd send me for treatment too, if I were them."

Amy sighs. "I don't know. They have a tendency to throw money and experts at everything. I sometimes wish they'd just chill a bit, let time do the healing. Sometimes, the best thing to do is nothing, I've found."

"That's a very Buddhist approach."

"I suppose it is. I think the Buddhists have got a lot of things right."

We turn onto a fast road, and the van growls as she shifts into top gear.

"Where are we headed, by the way?" I ask, glancing at the back seat, which is stuffed with brown cardboard boxes. "Have we got a lot of deliveries?" I'm going to wish I'd eaten more lunch. Mum gave me a huge Tupperware container with enough leftovers to feed a family of four, but it's in the fridge at home.

"Don't worry," Amy says. "We've just got one drop-off, to a new gallery in Coleford. They've agreed to stock some of my prints on sale or return."

"That's brilliant!" I say. "How's your business going at the moment?"

"Fine," she says. "Ooh look, Joe, there's the turning to Puzzlewood!" She waves her hand in front of my nose, pointing out of the left side of the car. I crane my neck, but all I see is the gray back of a metal road sign whizzing past.

Amy's eyes shine. "Do you remember it?" I shake my head. "We went there together once, I must've been five and you'd have been about twelve. We took all your *Star Wars* toys."

I chuckle at how just like me that sounds. "Remind me. What did we do?"

"It was freezing cold, November maybe. We built a den for all the toys inside a cave, and we made them a pretend campfire out of autumn leaves."

Distant memories rush into my mind, of deep-green tree canopies, bridges to nowhere built from skeleton branches and damp, mossy paths. "Hang on, it's coming back to me . . . Didn't we find an animal skull? And we put it at the cave entrance to scare the baddies away!"

"Oh yes, we did! I'd forgotten that." Amy smiles.

"Did you go there again? With Other Joe, I mean?"

"Yes," she says. "We used to go there quite often as a family, a couple of times a year." I feel a shameful jab of jealousy. "But the *Star Wars* trip is the one I always remember. Do you remember how I always used to get the *Star Wars* saying wrong?"

I think for a second, then my face clears.

"May the forks be with you!" we both say in unison and burst out laughing.

"I still say that sometimes when I'm out for food with friends." Amy giggles. "Way more practical than *Bon appétit*, don't you think?"

Twenty minutes later we arrive at Shadow Lane Gallery. Amy skillfully maneuvers through a narrow gap between the gallery and the deli next door. We park in the back and get out of the van. A small wooden door opens in the back of the gallery, and a slight young man, with bleach-blond hair and dressed entirely in black, jogs out to greet us, hunching his shoulders and rubbing his hands in the cold.

"Hey, Amy!" he says, reaching to give her a hug. "Good to see you. I hear you've got a new artist for us this time."

"Hi, Henry. I have indeed! Just wait till you see. The colors are stunning."

Amy lifts one of the boxes out of the back of the van and passes it to Henry. He staggers back to the door with it and disappears inside. "Give me a hand with one of these, would you, Joe?" Amy says, handing me another of the boxes.

I'm prepared for it to be heavy, but it's just awkward. I follow Amy into the building, a large room with a concrete floor and matte black walls.

"Pop them on the floor over here guys, would you?" Henry says, pointing to an area strewn with half-open boxes and piles of cardboard.

A navy silk curtain rustles in the corner, and a short round-faced woman wearing a purple headscarf sticks her head around it. She pulls her glasses down onto her nose and breaks into a beaming smile.

"Fabulous to see you, Amy!" she says. "Unpack a couple of those new canvases and bring them through to the light. Henry, I need you in here with me."

"But I'm just helping—"

"Now." Her head disappears. Henry trots after her like a scolded puppy.

"That's Maude," says Amy.

"She seems a character," I note.

"Heart of gold," Amy responds, unpacking a box, "and the most amazing eye. I love what she does here. She held an exhibition last year where all the artwork hung just three feet above the floor, so that kids and people in wheelchairs could get up close. She's always coming up with fresh ideas. Here." She hands me one of the canvases. "Come on."

We pass through the silk curtain into the main gallery. The walls are painted white, and the windows onto the street go from floor to ceiling. With its subtle lighting, the space feels almost luminous.

Maude transports herself smoothly across the room to us, her lemon-and-lime dress sweeping the floor. "How are you, Amy my darling?" she asks, reaching up and cupping Amy's cheek with a small cherubic hand. "How are you feeling? Energy good?"

"Energy good," Amy confirms. "Maude, this is my brother, Joe."

Maude holds out her hand, and we shake politely. Her skin is very soft and reassuringly warm. "Pleased to meet you, Joe," she says. "Glad to see you're looking after your sister. Now, let me see my new babies."

Amy lifts up a canvas, and Maude considers it in silence. It's a harbor scene, with fishing boats and pleasure yachts, but the color palette is an autumnal burst of orange, ochre, and chestnut brown, with highlights picked out in turquoise and an occasional splash of red.

"The artist works in mixed media," Amy says. "If you look closely, you can see where he's used bits of newsprint. And if you look at the one Joe's holding, you can see he's used pieces of wallpaper and fabric too."

I look down at the picture in my arms. Even upside down, I like it. This one's a seascape, with tall ships and clouds scudding across an angry sky.

"I adore them!" Maude proclaims. "I have the perfect spot in mind. Henry!" She snaps her fingers and Henry comes trotting over. "Clear the west wall, please. We have new works to display!"

After a cup of tea and a slice of Maude's homemade carrot cake, we're back on the road again.

"I bet you could sell your paintings to Maude, if you wanted to."

Amy offers me a wry, sideways look. "You haven't seen them."

"I'm sure they're good."

She shrugs. "I don't want people to see them. I don't really enjoy paint-ing like I used to. It's more therapeutic than anything."

"You used to love painting when you were little."

"Doesn't every child?" she says dismissively.

"Not necessarily."

We roll on in silence for a few minutes.

"Amy, can I ask you something?"

"Of course," she says. "Fire away."

"Dad asked me if you were seeing things again. Will you tell me what he means?"

"He asked you that? Why?"

"It came up in conversation. He's just concerned about you, I think."

Amy harrumphs and stares doggedly ahead at the road. "Look, Joe, I have to be honest. Dad and I have never really had much of a connection. He tried, I suppose, when I was younger, in his own way. But he and Other Joe had so much more in common. They had the business, golf . . . boy stuff, you know. I don't think he's ever quite been sure what to say to me."

There's a sudden, insistent pinging; a red light flashing on the dash-board, just beneath the speedometer.

"Oh no," she says. "Not that bloody warning light again! I had the oil changed last week." A few hundred yards up the road, there's a small park-ing area, and she pulls in.

"I'd offer to check the engine," I say, "but to be honest I wouldn't have a clue what I'm looking at." I wish I could be a better brother.

"Don't worry, I know a local mechanic. I'll give him a call." She climbs out of the van and walks off a little. Through the rearview mirror, I watch her on the phone, hunched over, staring at the ground, and consider what she said about Dad. It's like the world's been flipped on its head. In this timeline she's the black sheep, and I'm some kind of golden boy? It doesn't feel good.

Amy hangs up and walks back to my side of the van. She opens the door. "He's on his way, but he's going to be about an hour."

I consider this and a plan takes shape. "How far are we from Puzzle-wood?"

Amy shrugs. "As the crow flies, probably fifteen minutes' walk."

"Let's go," I suggest. I'm hoping that if we walk, Amy will talk to me more. "It might be fun. And it's got to beat sitting around in a freezing van by the side of the road."

She yawns and stretches her arms above her head, and I hear her shoulders click. "We might as well," she agrees. She sets Puzzlewood as our destination on her phone, then we climb over the fence and set out across a muddy field. "We're going to get pretty mucky," she remarks, shaking clods of earth off her boots.

"At least it's clean dirt," I reply, another of Grandma Bridgeman's favorite sayings.

As we walk, I feel the tension ebb away, and Amy's mood seems to lift.

"I'm sorry if I touched on a sore spot earlier, about Dad," I begin. "I didn't mean to."

"I know," Amy says. "It's not your fault. I do want to explain." She holds open a five-bar gate for me, and we pass through into a field full of sheep and slowly make our way up a hill. "I need to go right back to the beginning," Amy says. "Where it all started."

"I'm listening," I say, panting slightly as the slope gets steeper.

"After you saved me, I traveled again a few times, just short jumps. I knew you'd told me not to, but I didn't know how to stop. I didn't tell anyone about it."

"Weren't you afraid, after what happened in the lake?"

"Of course. I always held my breath after you saved me, just in case I landed in water again."

I imagine little Amy screwing up her eyes and pinching her nose, waiting for time to take her someplace unknown, and it breaks my heart. "I'm sad that no one helped you," I say.

Amy shrugs. "It all stopped suddenly when I was nine, but it started again when I was around fifteen. And then it got really bad."

"What kind of bad?"

"Lots of traveling, often to very confusing and faraway places. Mostly I didn't know where I was, or what year it was. It scared the absolute hell out of me." Amy looks away for a second, remembering. "It was hard on Mum and Dad too, and Other Joe. I see that now. I tried to block it out, pretend

none of it was happening. Mum and Dad thought there was something seriously wrong with me. They presumed I was mentally ill and needed fixing.
They threw everything at it, like they do. Therapists, drugs, the works. It
didn't help though. It made it worse. I actually left home for a while."

"Really?"

"I had to. I didn't come back until I learned to control it. You were
right. In the end, I managed to stop it."

"How?"

"Long story," she says. "Not for today."

"When was the last time you traveled?"

"Years ago now, but Dad still worries."

We reach the top of the hill and stop to catch our breath. Ahead of us,
the valley stretches away, the dark mass of Puzzlewood like a giant green
sponge. The view reminds me of Leckhampton Hill and I get an unexpected pang of grief.

"What is it?" Amy asks me. "You look sad."

"I'm just missing Alexia," I say.

She puts her arm through mine. "Tell me a bit more about her. What's
she like?"

I ponder the question. "She's really cool. One of those people who
exudes positive energy, you know?"

Amy offers me a gentle, understanding smile. "How long had you two
been an item? When you . . . left, I mean?"

"Only a few weeks. But it felt longer than that somehow. In a good way."

"It sounds like the real thing. I can understand why you're trying to cancel
that hotel deal, so she'll stick around." Amy sighs. "But I'm worried you might
be trying to change too much, too fast."

"But you told me I should do things my way, and you were right. I
can't live the rest of my life in Other Joe's shadow, Amy."

"I know," she says patiently, "it's your life. But maybe it's a case of
balancing that with the life he created too. It needs to be a team effort. Do
you know what I mean?"

"I think I do."

We stride down the slope toward the wood, and the daylight fades to green as we pass beneath the trees. There's an otherworldly feel about this place, magical and ancient.

Amy says, "You know, I can't help but think I got your homecoming all wrong."

"Don't be silly!" I protest. "What more could you have done?"

"Hang on, let me finish," Amy says. "I was so focused on fitting you back into Other Joe's life as seamlessly as possible, I completely forgot about celebrating what you did." She jumps up onto a nearby rock and stands with her legs and arms outstretched. "You saved my life," she says. "YOU SAVED MY LIFE!" she yells again at the top of her voice, throwing her head toward the canopy above. She laughs, then climbs back down and takes my hand. "I'm only here, Joe, because you came back to get me. Everything I have, I have because of you. I'll never forget that."

We explore the wood for a little longer and then loop back on ourselves, wending our way back toward the van. "You know what?" I say. "I'm actually really pleased we broke down. Spending time with you like this—just you and me—it's what I used to dream about." I hold open the gate to the muddy field. "Maybe we can think of this as a new start?"

"I'd like that," she says, but she sounds distant.

"What is it?"

She clears her throat. "I need to ask you a question, and I want you to be honest with me, even if it's hard."

"Of course," I say easily.

"I want to know where you've been."

"At Mum and Dad's, you know I have." And I also know that's not what she means.

"Not today," she says. "Yesterday and last night. I couldn't reach you."

"I lost my phone," I tell her honestly, pulling out my new one and waving it at her.

She shoves both of her hands in her pockets. "Joe, I realize you've only been back a few days, but I need to know. Have you time traveled again, since you got back on Saturday?"

The question hits me like a punch in the solar plexus. I consider just telling her the truth, but then what? She'll want to know everything. How can I tell her that if I fail this mission, I'll be condemning her to death and destroying my family again? What good would that do?

"I'm only just back from saving you. I can't tell you how happy I am that you're OK. I wouldn't want to change a thing, and I never, ever want to time travel again."

I'm able to answer without actually telling any lies, but inside me, anger wells up, anger directed fully at W. P. Brown. If I tell Amy about my mission in London, she'll either try and persuade me to stop, or demand to come with me. Either way, I can't win.

My resentment bubbles just under the surface. I clench my teeth to keep it from escaping. Amy searches my face. The seconds stretch out. My pocket watch hangs heavy against my chest. *If you're listening*, I silently tell it, *now would be a very bad time to send me back to 1963.*

"I'm afraid." Amy's trying to sound cool, but her voice catches in her throat. "I'm frightened of losing you. Terrified, actually."

"What do you mean? Why would you think you're going to lose me?"

"When you came back and replaced Other Joe, I think it might've triggered something in me." She swallows. "My visions have started again."

"Visions? Is that what Dad was referring to?"

She rubs her forehead. "Promise me you won't talk to Mum and Dad about this," she says wearily. "Please?"

"I promise," I say. "I get them too, you know. Viewings, I call them. When I hold objects, I see replays of the past. And sometimes I connect to the past through people too."

"Really?" The relief is visible on her face. "I can't tell you how good it is to be able to talk to someone who understands."

"I feel the same," I say. "So how does it work for you?"

"I used to get visions all the time when I was a teenager," she says. "It's a bit like having a waking dream. I see possible futures playing out, the potential in a person or a situation. The things I see don't always come to pass, but I know that they *could*. It feels as though time hasn't decided yet."

"What triggers them?"

"They seem to happen when emotions are running high. When things are unsettled."

"No wonder you're getting them again now," I say. "You've just had your world turned on its head, with me coming back."

"It's different though," she says. "What I saw last night was in the past . . ." She puffs out her cheeks and glances at me. "It was quite foggy, but it was London, and it was clearly the sixties. There was this old-fashioned vibe about everything: the clothes people were wearing, the energy . . . Which is weird because up until now, I've *always* seen the future." She shrugs. "I've been seeing a church too. It's pretty creepy, to be honest."

Visions of 1960s London? My face flushes with guilt. This has to be because of me. I didn't see any churches, though . . . Then something more worrying occurs to me.

"Amy, do you think this means you're going to time travel to London?"

"I haven't traveled in years," she says firmly. "I learned to shut it all down. We talked about this."

"I know, but how can you be sure, if you've been getting visions again?"

"When I was a teenager, I'd see the future, and then at some point over the next few days, I'd travel. I would feel it building. But this is different. The pull isn't anywhere near strong enough. When I'm going to travel, it's like a riptide dragging me out to sea."

"You're sure?"

"Absolutely." Her mouth forms into a smile but it doesn't last. "It's you I'm worried about. I want you to promise me that you aren't traveling."

I look at my sister, the fall of her hair and the uptilt of her nose, and for a second I catch a glimpse of seven-year-old Amy again. There's fear in her eyes. The trees around us creak, as though leaning in to listen. I almost say, "Pinkie swear"—our infallible promise—but I can't bring myself to do it. Instead, I give her hand a squeeze and tell her what she wants to hear, all the while trying to assure myself that it's for the best.

18

Amy drops me off at home. Turns out the only problem with the van was a faulty sensor. We didn't care. We agreed that our impromptu walk in the woods was exactly what we needed. Time together. Connection.

I'm only just through the front door when Vinny calls.

"Yo!" he says jocularly. "Just checking in to make sure you hadn't gone without me. Any news?"

A lot has happened since I last saw him. I tell him I've been with Amy, skip the embarrassing Chloe debacle, and fill him in on my parents and undoing Other Joe's business ventures.

Vinny chuckles. "That reminds me of an episode of *Family Guy*, when Peter Griffin took over his father-in-law's company."

"Never seen it. What happened?"

"It was hilarious," Vinny says. "He destroyed the entire family business. Everything, gone."

"You're not helping, mate," I say.

"Yeah, sorry," he says cheerfully. "I'm sure you'll do fine. How's things with Amy?"

"She's suspicious," I admit. "She asked if I'd been time traveling again."

"You didn't tell her?"

"No. I don't want her to worry, and I don't want her to try and stop me either. Best she doesn't know. It'll all be over soon, and then we can move on. She will never know what happened." I say this confidently, but I'm crossing my fingers.

"What made her suspect?" asks Vinny.

"She told me her visions had started up again, for the first time in years."

"Sorry. Did you just say Amy gets *visions*?"

"Yeah. I see the past. She sees the future."

"Hang on. Are you saying *you* get visions as well?"

It hadn't occurred to me until now. In this timeline Vinny doesn't know anything about my weird and wonderful psychometric gifts. As I explain my viewings, Vinny listens in silence, accepting my explanation as though it were normal.

"Amazing," he says, buzzing with excitement.

I tell him about my viewing of the break-in at the shop and the mysterious woman. "We need to find out who she is and what she's up to."

Vinny does his best Sean Connery impression. "Yesh, Mishter Bond. We do." I laugh. "So your superpower is to see the past." He says this without any apparent sense of how crazy and melodramatic it sounds. "Amy sees stuff like this too?"

"Apparently, yes, but she sees the future—well, possible futures."

"That's so cool. Did she tell you what she's been seeing?"

I've been waiting for this. I decide not to worry Vinny unnecessarily, so just tell him the basics. "She had some visions of London in the sixties."

Vinny scratches his head. "But hang on, I thought you said she sees the future?"

"She does. She's seeing my future."

"Because your future lies in the past! That's awesome."

I'm not surprised Vinny's worked this out so fast. He's well-versed in the tropes of science fiction. "It is pretty incredible," I admit. "And her visions were enough to make her ask me whether I'd been traveling again."

"Well, let's just hope you get this all sorted out before she sees anything else."

"Exactly. That's the plan."

"Talking of plans, I'm working on some cool stuff here," Vinny says excitedly. "I want it to be a surprise though. You like surprises, don't you?"

I hate them, actually, but I decide not to burst Vinny's bubble. We make arrangements to meet up later. He bids me *adios* and hangs up.

My thoughts turn to Alexia. I have to make sure she remains in Cheltenham. The hotel deal goes through in just a few days. I know everyone wants me to leave well alone, but it's only money. And if there's one thing I know—wisdom gleaned from the best band that ever was—it's that money can't buy you love.

I decide to call her, but her phone just rings repeatedly. I'm about to hang up when there's a click, then a rustling sound.

Alexia answers. "I'm busy, Joe." She sounds decidedly frosty. "What do you want?"

No time for niceties. "I'm stopping the whole development," I say. "You don't need to move your business." I cross my fingers, hoping that she'll want to stay.

"Why would you do that?" Her voice is guarded.

"Because it's the right thing to do. For you, and all the other leaseholders. Some of you have been residents for years. I can't throw you all out on the street."

"Have you honestly changed your mind, just like that?" She sounds exasperated. "Joseph, I don't know what your plans are, I never have. But if you're serious about this, you'd better come to the residents' meeting next week so you can tell all of us about this sudden, and frankly inexplicable, U-turn."

"No. It's you that matters."

"Me? Why?"

"Can I come and see you? I'd like to explain, face-to-face."

"I don't think that's a good idea."

"Please, Alexia. I just need your signature by the end of the day, then I can block the sale." There's a pause. I can sense her chewing it over. "Please. Just meet me and look through the lease. It'll only take a few minutes. Fifteen minutes, tops."

She exhales, clearly frustrated. "Where are you now?"

"At my shop."

"You've got the lease printed and ready for me to sign?"

Actual paperwork. I hadn't really thought that through. "Yes. Right here," I assure her.

"I've got a couple of things to tie up first," she says. "I'll be there in half an hour."

The line goes dead. Butterflies flitter around in my stomach.

Shifting into practical mode, I scour the internet for customizable lease templates and download a free one from a website that appears to be marginally more trustworthy than the others. Hastily, I type in Alexia's name, Google her business address and add that, and then set the lease period for five years. I try to print it out on my flashy printer, but it's one of those minimalist devices with no obvious buttons—to be honest I'm not even sure it's a printer—so I give up and head down to the shop with my laptop in hand.

Molly left a while ago, and everything is tidy. The diary is laid out on the desk, ready for tomorrow, and the cabinets are all gleaming. The place smells of polish. Molly is a godsend. I unlock the front door, then sit at the desk and wait.

Twenty minutes later Alexia walks in, the bell jangling her arrival. I jump up to greet her. She's wearing a thick blue sweater and jeans—casual, simple, and thoroughly lovely. Her hair is pulled up into a neat ponytail.

Our eyes meet, and her expression flattens. That does my confidence the world of good.

"Thanks for coming over," I say warmly.

"I almost didn't," she replies, "but this is about my business, and my business is important to me."

I know it is. I've been in her office, seen the books on her shelf, heard her talking about techniques and approaches to helping people.

"Would you like tea?" I ask. "I've got herbal."

"No, thank you." She folds her arms. "Have you got the lease?"

"It's here on my laptop," I say, "but unfortunately, I couldn't print it out."

"You're joking."

"Sorry," I say, feeling genuinely foolish.

I push the laptop toward her. She reaches into her handbag, grabs her glasses, and pops them on. She scans quickly through the pages. I long to reach out and stroke the clear, soft skin of her cheek. She peers at me over her glasses, smoky eyes glistening suspiciously.

"You've just downloaded this off one of those generic law websites, haven't you?" she says dryly. "It's watermarked 'The Law Shack.' Classy." She pushes the laptop back toward me and lifts her glasses onto her head. "Why don't you just tell the people you're selling to that you've changed your mind? Why all this ridiculous song and dance? Or are you just not man enough to stand up and tell them how you really feel?"

My cheeks flush. "I was told the only way to stop the sale was to set up a new tenant's lease, so that's what I'm doing."

"Last year you came to the residents' meeting and said you were committed to the building and the tenants. I believed you."

"I *am* committed," I say earnestly.

She ignores me. "Then in that 'Dear Residents' letter you sent us a couple of months ago, out of the blue, you evoked a small-print break clause and gave us all notice. No explanation, no warning. I know it's business, it happens, but there are ways of doing these things. You don't have to be an—" She stops herself.

"I'm sorry," I say. "I don't remember any of that, but if you sign this, it won't matter."

"It matters to me," she bites back. "I'm trying to understand how you could change tack so suddenly. This changes the lives of all the residents in that building. Four separate businesses, with owners who have lives and families. But you said this was about me. You need to explain what you meant by that."

She looks so angry and confused, I decide the only way forward is to tell her some of the truth. There's nothing to lose anymore.

"I don't want you to leave Cheltenham."

She shakes her head. "You are a piece of work, you really are. When you announced the sale, I couldn't help but feel it was deliberately to spite me, that it had something to do with . . ." She stops again.

"With what?"

"That you did it because of what happened between us." She shifts slightly, the tiniest hint of color in her cheeks.

"Wait, are you saying you and I had a thing?"

She scoffs at me, infuriated. "You know we did! My goodness, Joseph, how long are you going to keep this up? What do you have to gain by pretending like this?"

I am slow. Especially when it comes to women. The signs were all there, for someone more tuned in to this sort of thing. But it's so weird. Other Joe and Alexia. Me and Alexia. Maybe this *was* all meant to be. My shoulders drop cautiously.

"Sorry, Alexia, I truly don't remember. Can you tell me what happened?" I ask her. "Were we an item?"

"Well, I suppose I thought we were heading that way . . ."

"So why did we break up?" I ask her. "Please, Alexia."

There's a subtle shift in her frosty exterior, a crack in her armor. "Level with me, Joe. Just for once, be totally honest. Is your amnesia real?"

"It is." I tell her again about the mountain-bike accident, about how I can remember who people are, but can't recall specific events or experiences. "Sometimes it's embarrassing, sometimes it's painful, occasionally it's almost funny. People find it hard to adjust to the fact that although I look and sound the same, I'm not the same on the inside. I'm like the twin of the other Joe you knew."

She's silent, sizing me up. Then her face softens, and I see a familiar expression, one I haven't seen since we were together on Leckhampton Hill. "You never talked like this before."

"Like what?"

"How you feel about things. I always felt like we were skating over the surface. You wouldn't let me in. I wasn't even sure there were any depths to reach."

"Like I say. I'm not the man you knew."

Alexia raises her eyebrows. "I kind of wonder—"

She's interrupted by a loud jangling. The shop door opens and a man walks in. I don't know him. He's well-built and well-groomed, and a waft of sharp citrus aftershave hits my nose as the door swings shut behind him.

"Are you Joseph Bridgeman?" he says gruffly, his bloodshot eyes locked onto me.

"Er, yes," I confirm. "The shop's closed though. Could I ask you to come back tomorrow?"

"I'm Chloe's boyfriend," he announces. He looks young and strong, and suddenly very dangerous.

Oh, no. I'd almost forgotten about Chloe. I had a hunch that she might cause trouble. God knows what she's said to her boyfriend. He has a fire in his eyes that suggests he might like to choke me to death. I know *I'm* innocent, but I now have very good reason to suspect that Other Joe was dipping his pen in other people's ink.

Alexia glowers at me. "I was just about to leave, anyway," she says to the man, although he's blocking her path to the exit.

"You might want to hear this," he says. "Just so you know who you're involved with."

Alexia looks at me, then back at him. "I can assure you, we aren't involved." She says it as though the very idea repulses her.

The man takes another step toward me. I move behind the desk.

"I've got news for you, Posh Boy," he growls. "Me and Chloe, we're back together, and we're stronger than ever."

"That's great," I say. "Listen, Chloe and I—nothing happened." I'm painfully aware of Alexia's icy glare as I plead my innocence.

"Shut up," he barks. "She told me everything. How you met. All your little rendezvous. Treating me like an idiot, the both of you." He clenches his fists. "She's my girl, and she's done with you. This thing is *over*. Got it?"

Silently, I berate Other Joe for his choice of lady friend. There's clearly no point in arguing with this guy. "Got it. I'm very sorry." I don't know exactly what I'm apologizing for, but I can imagine.

"Find someone single, you sad bastard, and stop stealing other people's girls." He clenches his fist into a ball, then relaxes it again. "I'm going to leave, before I do you some serious damage."

He exits the shop and strides away down the street. I smooth my shirt and try to regain my composure.

"That was awful," Alexia says.

"I know, but it's not what it looked like."

"You haven't changed at all," she growls. "You're still just a player. And to think you almost had me."

Brilliant. I *almost* persuade the love of my life that I'm not a lunatic, then a man I don't know bursts into my shop and nearly beats me up for an affair I didn't have. Can today get any worse?

A harsh vibrating buzz snaps my mind into focus. I fumble for my pocket watch and flip open the fascia.

0 Days 0 Hours 27 Minutes

Seriously?

"Somewhere you need to be?" Alexia taunts me. "Another girl on the hook?"

"Yes . . . No . . . I'm really sorry, Alexia, but I need to go."

"Don't be," she says, with the most demeaning look imaginable. "I'm relieved, to be honest."

She marches to the door, but I call to her, "You'll stay though? In Cheltenham?"

She shakes her head. "You're one of those pathetic men who always wants what they can't have."

"That's not it at all," I counter. "Alexia, I don't know how to make you see."

"Don't bother." She jabs a finger at me. "I'm not for sale, and I'm not some bloody trophy to be pursued." Her expression flattens to cold determination. "For the last time, do whatever you need to do, but leave me out of it!"

She yanks open the door and stalks out of the shop.

I'm almost grateful that I don't have time to wallow in self-pity. I now have twenty-six minutes before I jump back to the 1960s again. I hadn't planned to take him with me, but Vinny wants to help, and now I'm facing imminent departure, I realize I really want him to come. He even called himself my sidekick. I could do with one now. I dial his number.

"Yo, Doctor," he answers cheerily. "What's up? Missing me already?"

"I'm going again."

"Cool." I hear him swallow. "When?"

"Twenty-five minutes," I tell him, already running for the door, "and counting. Vinny, will you come with me?"

"You betcha," he says. The line crackles. "Can you get to me in time?"

"I think so. Be ready."

I make sure I have the money W. P. Brown gave me, then put my head down and run.

Am I being selfish to bring Vinny? Maybe, but he wanted this. He said so himself. As I weave through pedestrians along the streets of Cheltenham, I try to convince myself that's the whole truth, but who am I kidding? I don't want to face this alone. If I mess this up, who knows, Amy might not be here when I return. I consider calling her, but what would I say?

Twenty minutes later I bound up the steps of Vinny's flat. He's like an excited little boy on Christmas morning as he ushers me into the lounge. "I'm so glad I'm coming with you!"

I gasp for breath. My mouth feels like I've just eaten five crackers at once. I check the watch again. Four minutes, twenty-three seconds.

"Are you absolutely sure you're up for this?"

"Totally." He throws his head back and laughs. "It's the Swinging Sixties, man. It's where I belong, baby!"

Laid out on a table is what can only be described as a time traveler's survival kit. Snacks, drinks, a first-aid kit, a couple of guidebooks to the sixties, what looks like an emergency flare, and one of those foil blankets they hand out at the end of marathons. He starts shoving it all into a rucksack.

"No," I say impatiently. "Ditch everything, it's too dangerous."

He looks hurt.

"Sorry, Vin, but the books, your phone, we can't take any of it. We can't risk losing stuff like that in the past."

"OK, Cash," he says, using my nickname for the first time, "you're the boss."

The air feels charged. The hairs on my arms and the nape of my neck stand on end.

Vinny whistles. "Wow! This feels like when I stuck my finger in a plug socket for a dare!"

I smell phosphor, as though someone has just blown out a match. The air pressure increases, and the colors in the room shimmer. It's actually quite beautiful.

"How does it work then?" Vinny asks. "Do we actually have to jump?"

I take his hand and offer a lopsided grin. "It works like this."

And quick as a soap bubble bursting, the present disappears.

PART 4

19

My stomach lurches at the sudden shift in location. We've landed outside. The day is painfully bright, and the shrill sunlight doesn't do anything for my hangover. I shield my eyes against the sudden onslaught of light. In front of us is a dark-bronze statue of a winged man holding a bow. Traffic streams by: taxi cabs, flatbed trucks, buses, and cool-looking classic cars that I recognize. Acrid exhaust fumes mix with cigarette smoke and the odd whiff of food and perfume. There are people everywhere—men in sober suits, women wearing smart coats and short dresses. London is buzzing, vibrant, and instantly familiar.

"Piccadilly Circus," I murmur. I hold up the silver watch. Vinny and I wait as the three dials rotate independently and eventually settle.

Calibrating

4:33 p.m.

September 1, 1962

"Whoa," Vinny gasps, "I can't believe this is 1962! This is . . . this is . . . unreal." He spins like an excited puppy. "Look at that man in the bowler hat! Those taxi cabs are familiar, but those cars . . . Look at what everyone's *wearing* . . . And the shops! Ooh, do you think that's a snack bar?" He settles his attention back on me. "You actually *are* a time traveler." Incredulity dawns across his face. "And so am I."

"Breathe, Vin," I tell him, "nice and deep."

He leans his hands on his knees, inhaling and exhaling aggressively, as though he's trying to hyperventilate. "Gotcha. So what happens next?"

"According to Brown, my watch is like a GPS. It's going to guide us to something he called a waypoint."

"What's that?"

I try to remember what my blackmailer said. "I think it's either something we need to see, or something we need to change, to help solve the mission."

"So which way do we go?"

I check the watch. "I don't know yet. It just says *calibrating*. I guess we have to wait."

I let our new reality soak in. There is an undeniable wonder in standing smack bang in the middle of 1962, especially now that I know I can get home again. But then I remember what happened to Lucy Romano, and the risk to Amy and my family if I don't fix it.

"What's the date again?" asks Vinny, interrupting my thoughts.

"September 1, 1962."

He laughs, shaking his head. "You know what? The Beatles are about to record 'Love Me Do' at Abbey Road." He screws up his face. "It's unbelievable, flipping unbelievable."

"And it's nine months *before* my first jump, when Lucy got shot."

"It's a bit like vinyl, isn't it?" Vinny says. "You've got the whole album, and you can skip around on the tracks. It's like you landed on track three last time, and now we're on track one. Does that make sense?"

I think about it. "Actually, it makes total sense."

"It means she's alive now," Vinny says. "And we've got plenty of time—we're almost a whole year early!"

The watch beeps. Its face updates to *Jump Time Remaining* and begins counting down immediately.

"It's nine months before she was shot," I clarify, "but we're only here for two hours, seventeen minutes."

"Fair enough. So what do we do?" Vinny thinks this is an adventure, that I know what I'm doing. He looks at me expectantly.

A little nibble of panic sets in. "I'm sorry, mate, but I don't actually know what to do."

"That's OK," he replies, still giddy. "I do." He strides away.

"Vinny, wait!" I jog after him. "Where are you going?"

"If we're going to complete this mission of yours, then we need to blend in," he says. "We need clothes, Cash, and I know just the place. It's literally five minutes away."

"But it could be in the wrong direction, Vinny. Every minute counts!"

He stops and gestures as if presenting himself on a London stage. "Maybe you haven't noticed, but people are staring at us."

I glance around. People cover their mouths, whispering, and on the other side of the street, a group of young girls is pointing and giggling. In all the panic, I hadn't thought about it. I'm wearing jeans, a checked shirt, and canvas shoes. Vinny is wearing a Metallica T-shirt, ripped black jeans, and Doc Martens. We stick out like proverbial sore thumbs.

I didn't travel back to the 1960s to go shopping for clothes, but Vinny has a point. "OK, but we need to be quick."

We make our way along crowded streets that feel like the most elaborate and expensive movie set ever constructed. We cross a busy intersection and find ourselves at one end of a narrow road, flanked on either side with shops and thronging with cool-looking young people.

Vinny beams. "Here we are, the fashion hub of London." He hits me softly on the shoulder. "I still can't believe we're here."

Carnaby Street.

I've seen pictures, of course, but nothing could have prepared me for such a vibrant blaze of color. The shops are all perfectly presented in neat rows, painted in rich reds, royal blues, and pale creams. Union Jack flags hang across the street, and the signage of boutique fashion brands bursts from the brick walls.

Groups of people laugh, admiring each other's outfits, comparing purchases as they spill out of one shop and dive into the next. There's a reason it was called the Swinging Sixties, and I can feel the optimism and confidence. The seeds of flower power are being watered here; the youth are about to bloom into an era of joy, peace, and love.

Vinny strides ahead. We pass shops with gleaming window displays that look like museum pieces to me. I don't recognize any of the brands, but

Vinny's in his element. "Look, Cash! Irvine Sellars Menswear! And there's Mates. Oh, and there's His 'n' Hers! Man alive!" We reach a building with a tall exterior, decorated with a rainbow of color tapering down to polka dots that spill joyfully over the pavement.

"Lord John," Vinny announces with quiet reverence. He rubs his chin. "I can't quite believe it. This is the one. Come on."

The shop is spacious, the clientele ultrafashionable. Long display racks are lined with suits, shirts, trousers, dresses, and coats. A stand displays necklaces, belts, caps, and berets. Eye-catching outfits hang from the rails. A couple of young lads earnestly discuss the cut of a jacket with a sales assistant, and a group of young women admire themselves in a mirror, their headwear at rakish angles. Even the mannequins have attitude.

As Vinny and I survey the shop in silent awe, a short, confident young man approaches us. He wears a cream suit, white shirt, and polka-dot tie, and his hair is bleached blond and styled like Andy Warhol's. "Hmmm," he says, stroking his chin, "we need to get you boys decked out."

"Absolutely," Vinny says.

"Where are you from?" he asks.

"Out of town," I reply quickly before Vinny can. "And we're in a bit of a hurry, I'm afraid."

"Well!" He claps his hands excitedly and looks me up and down. "Let's see . . . Your destiny, sir, is *that* suit." He points at a rich-purple velvet suit with flamboyant lapels, positively glowing against a wall of deep magenta.

I turn to Vinny. "I'm not sure that's exactly blending in . . ."

The man frowns at me. "Why would you want to blend in?"

"He'll take it," Vinny announces. "Do you have anything for a larger gentleman?"

Our Andy Warhol look-alike practically glows with excitement. "I have just the thing."

We spend nine more minutes of precious time getting trussed up like extras in *Austin Powers*. I'm starting to worry that bringing Vinny along might have been a bad idea. Time traveling is not supposed to be fun.

Finally, we're kitted out. I hand Andy Warhol a few of the old bank notes. He takes them reverently and salutes us. I guess we've spent a ton, but W. P. Brown was generous. I could probably buy a house with what I have in my pocket.

We emerge from the shop and check our reflections in the shop window.

"Vinny," I moan, "I look completely ridiculous."

The purple suit hugs my body and flares out toward my feet. The cream shirt is all right, and I'm usually OK with a striped tie, but these stripes are in all the colors of the rainbow and swirl around crazily like oil patterns on water. It makes me feel sick. I try to loosen the knot.

Vinny laughs. "Leave it alone, Cash. It's perfect. No one's even giving you a second glance!"

He's right. In the maddest, most revolting suit I've ever had the misfortune to wear, I've become invisible.

And so has Vinny. He's sporting a dark-gray pinstriped suit, a purple-and-yellow floral cravat, and a trilby-style hat. He looks magnificent.

"Right," he says. "Disguised and ready for action."

"You cats look very groovy," a sultry voice purrs.

I turn and see a woman in a dazzling tangerine dress and knee-high white leather boots. She has pixie-like features, sharply bobbed hair, and dark eyes thick with makeup. She works her gaze over us approvingly, long eyelashes flickering, and offers us a toothpaste smile. Then, she turns and walks down the street, bag swinging over her shoulder, hips swaying.

Vinny punches the air in delight. "She called us groovy cats!" He starts jigging up and down on the spot. "This is the sixties, Cash, we're in the freaking *sixties*, and now we look like we belong!"

I check my silver hunter again. One hour, fifty-eight minutes. And still no waypoint. I shake the watch in frustration, like a toddler with a snow globe, silently cursing W. P. Brown. What am I supposed to do?

Suddenly, I feel a tingling sensation travel from my fingertips to my elbow, like a nascent spark of electricity. "Something's happening, Vinny. Look!"

Although the watch face looks analog, it's actually a super-high-definition digital display, and the three-dimensional hands marking the hours and minutes are a clever illusion. The fascia of the pocket watch shimmers and fades. For a second I see the time crystals glowing and sparkling beneath the display. Then, it solidifies into a solid panel and an alert appears across the watch face.

Waypoint

To the left of the alert, the watch displays *558 meters*. To the right, it says *19 minutes*. An arrow appears, its fulcrum hidden behind the waypoint alert. As I move the watch, it spins like a compass needle. I rotate the watch until the needle lines up with the waypoint notification.

Vinny leans in. "Yes! So now we know where to go!"

We head off, following the compass like kids on a treasure hunt. No one here could guess how common it will be in the future to see people staring at a device as they navigate the streets. We pass a blue police box and Vinny chuckles, his eyes sparkling. "Well, at least we have our ride home." He hums the *Doctor Who* theme. I laugh and regret feeling annoyed with Vinny earlier. Even if he does slow me down a bit, having him along definitely makes things better.

We continue through a sea of fashionable people. Gradually, the needle on the watch becomes more responsive. A second pulsing vibration travels through me, and I get the strangest sensation. The world seems to sharpen, colors grow even brighter, sounds louder and crisper.

"I think we're close," I tell Vinny. "Some kind of connection with the watch, I think. I'm seeing things differently, louder somehow." I feel like I'm tuning in to a frequency I didn't even know was there. "Up to the end of the street, then left."

We reach a palatial art deco building, three stories high, with a majestic entrance into a high-ceilinged foyer. Hundreds of people mill around it. Halfway up the building, a neon sign reads: Dancing! The Royal.

"Is this the place?" Vinny asks eagerly.

I rotate the watch, but the compass needle remains locked on the building. "This is the place, but I don't know what we're supposed to do or how this links to the murder."

"There's only one way to find out!" Vinny exclaims.

We cross the street, past a group of Elvis and James Dean wannabes on motorcycles. Vinny and I join a short queue, which moves quickly. We pass a poster.

THE ROYAL HALL
September 1, 1962
Swing, Twist, Stomp!
Featuring the sensational Peter Green and Friends!
Dancing till Midnight

We try to be as unobtrusive as possible, but we're twice the age of most of the kids in the queue. Two girls in front of us—a blond and a brunette, their outfits inspired by Dusty Springfield and Jackie Onassis—keep turning around and giggling. I shove my hands in my pockets and stare at the ground, feeling like a dad at the school disco.

Vinny taps Dusty on the shoulder. "You think we're a bit old for this, don't you?"

"No, not at all!" She shares a mischievous giggle with her friend.

"As far as I'm concerned," Vinny says with a huge smile, "if you're still alive, then you can jive."

For a moment they aren't sure what to say, then they burst into delighted laughter. "You're such a gas!" says the one who looks like Jackie.

Everyone loves Vinny. It's a universal law. We engage in friendly banter about music, and they tell us their favorite bands.

"Who do you like?" Dusty asks Vinny.

He glances at the poster. "Peter and the Spirits."

"How about you?" she asks me.

"Er—the Beatles."

"The who?" They both look bemused.

"You'll hear about them soon," I say. "They're pretty good, you know. I think they're going to be huge."

We reach the door. The girls hand in their tickets, give us a wave, and flutter inside. The bouncer, a tall, solid column of a man with voluminous black hair, crosses his arms. "Tickets," he demands.

"Can we pay cash?" I ask.

"Tickets only. If you haven't got a ticket, you can't come in."

I shove a ten-pound note into his hand. "Here are our tickets," I say confidently, standing tall.

The bouncer looks at the money and then back at me. "Are you serious?"

Vinny nods enthusiastically. "He loves Peter Green."

"And I love you." The bouncer grins, pockets the cash, and waves us inside.

We follow a herd of eager youngsters up a wide set of stairs and into a cavernous, wood-paneled ballroom. Four massive light fittings hang from a ceiling that must be a hundred feet above us. Multicolored crepe-paper streamers hang from it like a psychedelic spiderweb. The hall is thrumming with teenagers—the boys old before their years in well-cut suits, the girls in starched petticoats and cardigans, their hair up in beehives, their eyes catlike with thick black eyeliner—all mingling and excited.

Vinny beams at me. "Apart from this being absolutely bloody mental, this is a dream come true for me, Cash. Thank you for letting me come along."

W. P. Brown may have blackmailed me to get me here, but there's no denying it, time travel is incredibly, mind-blowingly cool. "I'm glad you're here, Vin."

"Me too," says Vinny, rubbing his hands together. "So. What's the plan?"

"I'm not sure," I say. "There's got to be something we need to do here. Let's check the place out."

At the far end of the hall is a stage, where a young lad with spiky hair and dark glasses is dwarfed behind a record deck covered in sparkling silver paper. He rifles through a box of records and selects one with a flamboyant spin. Ritchie Valens's "La Bamba" fills the ballroom, setting the whole place abuzz. The boys spin the girls in a series of seemingly well-practiced moves. A lot of girls dance with other girls, determined to have fun even if the boys won't ask them to dance.

Rock 'n' roll is about to explode. You can feel it, like compressed air desperate to blow. These kids want to scream, to rise above the humdrum and the controlled lives of their parents. They want to go crazy, to let rip. They're searching for meaning. When the Beatles come along, they will welcome this hysteria with open arms. As John Lennon said, the sixties weren't the answer, but it did give us a glimpse of the possibilities.

I check my watch again. The waypoint notification has filled the watch face, pulsing gently. I scan the hall, more slowly this time, working method-ically, hoping something will jump out at me. Just as I think we're out of luck, I spot a woman with dark bobbed hair, big brown eyes, and olive skin.

Lucy Romano.

Alive and well.

20

I catch my breath. Seeing Lucy alive, in this innocent environment, is a shock, but I do my best to pull myself together.

"There's Lucy, over there in the corner," I say to Vinny.

He follows my gaze. "Well done, Cash!" he says. "She must be the reason your watch brought us here tonight."

Lucy is petite, but sinewy and strong-looking as she stands behind a makeshift bar, a fold-up table with a red cloth thrown over it. A poster propped up on an easel advertises sparkling Corona and sarsaparilla. A young man hauls wooden crates of clacking bottles onto the table and begins cracking the tops open. Lucy takes money from the eager kids in the queue. She inserts straws into the bottles and hands them out.

"Are you going to go and talk to her?" Vinny asks.

"Yes," I say, massaging the back of my neck, "but I don't know where to start."

"Didn't Billy Blackmailer Brown tell you what to say?"

"No. He hardly told me anything. He just told me to save her."

Vinny rubs his chin, thoughtfully. "Lucy doesn't get shot in that alleyway until June of next year. That's plenty of time for you to make sure it doesn't happen."

I feel a flutter of excitement at the opportunity to influence a pivotal moment in Lucy's life. She's acting confident, but even from this distance, I can see that she's nervous.

"Tommy Shaw was attacked on August nineteenth," I tell Vinny. "That's only a couple of weeks ago."

"You're right," Vinny says. "So Tommy's in a coma."

"And that means Frankie Shaw must be on high alert."

"No wonder Lucy's on edge. Do you think she's involved?" The doubt in Vinny's voice is obvious.

"I don't think so, but she's scared."

"I guess anyone with connections to Frankie is scared at this point in time." Vinny draws in a breath and places his hand on my shoulder. "Well, if anyone can talk her around, it's you."

"I appreciate the vote of confidence, but I need to be careful. I don't want her to think I'm some kind of psychic weirdo. 'Hello, Lucy, my name's Nostradoomus, and I'm here to help you avoid your own murder.' She'd run a mile."

Vinny chuckles. "You don't need to tell her what's going to happen. You just need to persuade her to stay away from Frankie."

"You're right. But there's a massive queue at the bar. How am I going to get her on her own?"

"I've got an idea," Vinny announces. "I'll cause a diversion, and then you go and talk to Lucy."

"A diversion?"

He winks at me. "You're the hero, and I'm your wingman, Cash."

He's got a point, I suppose. "But what if we get split up? You could get stuck here!"

Vinny raises a hand. "I'm not going to leave this room. Just concentrate on getting to Lucy, and leave the rest to me." He weaves his way into the crowd of dancing kids.

I'm halfway to the bar when a gentle cheer ripples through the crowd. I glance back and see Vinny in the center of the hall, head bowed, one arm pointing to the ceiling. He's already caught the attention of a small group, but I know that's nothing compared to what's coming. I've seen Vinny dance. It's transcendent, fluidity with total abandon. He doesn't care a jot what anyone thinks of him, and the wild freedom and pure joy of his physical expression can be mesmerizing.

The chorus of the song kicks in, and Vinny begins his routine, an improvised mix of rock 'n' roll, the twist, the jive, and a kind of break-dance to the sounds of "The Wanderer." Fascinated onlookers gather around him, clapping in time, awestruck. More and more people throng around Vinny, until nearly the whole room is cheering him on.

The queue at the bar has dwindled to two shy-looking lads. Lucy serves them, then leans back against the wall to watch. I approach, and when she notices me, I feel an intense wave of relief, a deep gratitude that today at least—and for the next six months—this woman is alive.

I smile, and she returns the gesture fleetingly before picking up a cloth and wiping down a spill on the table between us. "Would you like a drink?" she asks loudly over the music.

"No, I'm OK, thanks." I notice dark patches under her eyes, her stooped shoulders.

"Can I help you with something?" she asks, frowning.

Here goes. "This is going to sound crazy," I begin, "but I'm here because I think you're in trouble, and I want to help."

Lucy puts down the cloth and folds her arms. "Who are you? Are you a copper?"

"No, I'm just a normal guy—er, person—but I'm worried about you."

She shakes her head. "Why would you be worried about me? I don't even know you." She turns and starts to unpack a new box.

I try a different tack. "Lucy?"

She turns, her brow narrowed in suspicion. "How do you know my name?"

"Listen, I've been sent to help you. You need to get out of London as soon as you can."

"What are you talking about?"

"Something really bad is going to happen to you . . . I think. Frankie's going to go crazy. He's going to hurt you. Probably." I stumble over my words, trying not to sound like a fortune-telling mentalist, desperate to convey how much danger she's in.

"Are you one of those hippie types?" Lucy asks, bemused. "You're saying it like it's already happened."

I try again. "I know I sound mad, but things aren't going to work out for you here in London."

"Are you threatening me?" she says, her eyes darkening.

"I'm trying to warn you," I say helplessly. I pull the envelope of cash out of my pocket. "Look, I have money. Plenty. You can have it all. It's enough to get away and start again. Just promise me you'll get out of London and away from Frankie Shaw. Just leave and don't come back!"

She peers into the envelope and raises her eyebrows. "Is this real? Why would you do this?"

"I don't want Frankie to hurt you," I plead. "Just take Gus and go."

At the mention of Gus, she shrinks back. I'm losing her again.

"How come you know so much about me?" She shakes her head defiantly. "This isn't right. You need to leave me alone."

"Not until you take this and promise you'll leave town," I say.

"For goodness' sake," she says impatiently, glancing over to the corner of the room. "Even if I wanted to leave, I can't accept this."

I follow her gaze and see the stocky man who will become her executioner in a few short months. My ears ring, the music drifts away, and all I can hear is my heartbeat. He starts making his way across the room toward us. I need to wrap this up, fast.

"Lucy, Frankie will kill you if you don't go soon."

Her breath catches. "I can't leave. And even if I did, he'd come after me." She takes a step closer, lowers her voice, and speaks quickly. "Whoever you are, you obviously don't understand who you're dealing with. If you go now, I won't tell anyone about this, but take my advice. After what happened to Tommy, Frankie's suspicious of everyone. Stay away from him, and stay away from me."

The thug is approaching fast. Time's up. I don't feel as though I've made any headway at all. I walk away and don't look back, skirting quickly around the edge of the dance floor, crouching and using the throng of spinning rock 'n' rollers as cover.

Vinny's still strutting his stuff on the dance floor, and someone nearby takes a photograph. The flashbulb illuminates him just as he starts a Michael Jackson moonwalk.

A girl rushes over and grabs Vinny by the arm. "What do you call that?" she squeals.

"The Funky Vincent," he says and winks. Then he notices me. "Cash!" he calls out. "Did you talk to her?"

I rush to him. "Yes, but the guy who kills her turned up. We need to get out of here. Now."

We dodge and weave our way across the dance floor, find an emergency exit, and tumble down the stairs and onto the street. We jog a little way, and once I'm sure we haven't been followed, we stop to catch our breath outside an old redbrick pub.

I check the jump timer on my watch again. Thirty-four minutes left.

Vinny squats, puffing and panting, wiping sweat from his forehead. Once he's caught his breath, he stands up and leans against the wall behind him. "So how did it go with Lucy?"

"I offered her some money to run away, but she wouldn't take it. She's obviously afraid of Frankie. She said she couldn't run because he would come after her."

"How are she and Frankie connected?" asks Vinny.

"I don't know. I didn't have time to ask." I sigh, playing the conversation over again in my head. "It was really hard, Vinny. I don't think I did very well. I mean, how do you tell someone what's going to happen to them without sounding mad?"

"You can't," he shrugs. "I'm sure you did your best." He places a hand on my shoulder. "Who knows, you might have changed things already. Just your suggestion could be the beginning of a decision process that might lead Lucy to safety. You don't know. We might be done."

I appreciate Vinny's argument, but I can't help but feel like I've wasted a valuable opportunity to change things, squandering a chance to save Lucy Romano's life and secure Amy's future. An image of my little sister floating away from me in the lake flashes into my mind, and my stomach spasms. "It doesn't feel like it's over, Vinny, and I don't know how many more chances we're going to get."

He smiles warmly. "We'll figure it out."

We wander through the streets of London, the September sky beginning to darken. Vinny suggests we find a place to eat and hole up till we go home again, but I'm keen to keep moving in case Lucy's killer is still on the hunt for us. The seconds tick down on the jump timer, and with each one, my heart sinks lower. The waypoint notification has disappeared.

A car edges out from an alleyway just in front of us, blocking the way ahead. A fresh ball of dread punches me in the throat, and the metallic taste of adrenaline fills my mouth. I'd recognize that Rolls-Royce anywhere.

"Get ready to run, mate," I tell Vinny.

"Why?" he says.

I hear heavy footsteps on the pavement behind us, and Lucy's killer suddenly looms from the shadows, grabs our shoulders, and pins us against him. The rear window of the Rolls glides down, revealing the smiling face of Frankie Shaw.

He leans forward. "If you two rather fashionable gentlemen aren't too busy, I'd like a little chat."

The rear door opens, and the thug shoves us roughly toward the car. I consider running, but what am I going to do? I can't leave Vinny, and he's already worn out from all the dancing. Reluctantly, we enter the car, which smells of leather and soap with a hint of whiskey. Frankie's goon manhandles us onto two small seats that face the rear of the car, then sinks down opposite us, leather groaning under his muscle-packed weight.

Frankie sits opposite us, dressed in a pale-blue shirt, cream trousers, and matching tie, held in position with a chrome pin. His red hair is cropped and swept neatly to one side. He gives the impression of a smart, wealthy businessman, but I know better than to judge this particular book by its cover. A gold cross hangs around his neck. He toys with it, rotating it absently. He's still smiling, his lips stretched thin, bending the deeply carved lines that run down his cheeks.

"Do you know who I am?" he asks me.

Vinny clears his throat. "You're Frankie Shaw," he says proudly, sounding like a little boy who's just given his teacher the right answer to a tricky question. "And you're Harry Hurst," he says to the thug. He's sitting bolt upright, cheeks pink, his eyes bright and excited. His lack of fear terrifies me.

Frankie grins, his gaze fixed on me. "That's right," he says calmly. "And I'm going to ask you some questions. I would advise you to answer them very carefully. Ask anyone, I'm honest and decent as they come, but there's one thing I can't stand, and that's a liar."

He twists his head and tugs at his collar, a gesture I recognize from the alleyway. I notice the sleeves of his cotton shirt are stained with patches of what looks like drying blood. Still red, not that old. He slowly unbuttons the cuffs, methodically folding the sleeves of his shirt back. His pale forearms are raked with fresh scratches, some fairly deep, like he just had an argument with a dog in a thorn bush.

He gently strokes the gold cross pendant like a pet. "Harry here tells me you were talking to one of my employees, Miss Romano."

"Miss Romano?" I say, faking confusion.

"Don't mess with me." His voice is sharp as a scalpel.

"You mean the woman serving drinks?" I ask, trying to control my fear.

"You like her, don't you?"

This is one of those trick gangster questions, like, "Are you looking at my girlfriend?" Whichever answer you go for, you lose. If you tell them that you *were* looking at the girl, you get smacked in the mouth. If you say you *weren't*, they ask you why not and suggest you think their girlfriend is ugly. Loop until punched.

Vinny steps in. "Joe wanted to talk to her, and I persuaded him to, but we didn't know that she was taken, honest we didn't."

"Let's cut to the chase. Do you two work for Don Dickerson?"

"Your archrival," Vinny says, his voice laced with nostalgia.

Frankie sneers. "I wouldn't call him that."

"We don't work for the Dickersons. We were here to see the band, have a dance, you know . . ." Vinny carries on digging a hole, his words tumbling out way too fast, but I'm not listening. I'm watching Frankie Shaw. The gangster nods patiently, processing, calculating. On first impression, you might describe him as good-looking, charming even. But he has the appearance and air of a man who has spent years in the shadows. Even his freckles are gray. And I can feel the dark energy that surrounds him.

I've spent my life trying to control fear, especially with bullies like this, but the more Vinny talks, the more Frankie smiles, and the more trouble I know we're in. Frankie rubs at his arm, causing fresh blood to ooze from one of the scratches.

"Shut up!" he barks suddenly at Vinny.

Shocked into silence, Vinny shrinks back into his tiny seat like a scolded puppy.

Frankie trains his eyes back to me. "You always let Sunny Jim here do all the talking?" His gaze remains glacial. "I'm right then, Joe, aren't I? You fancy her, don't you?" He taps his fingers impatiently on his thigh.

"I didn't realize she was with someone," I say, wishing Vinny hadn't given my name away. "I'm sorry. I wouldn't have talked to her if I'd known."

He stares at me for a long time. "OK," he says eventually. "Because I haven't seen you boys before, I'm going to give you the benefit of the doubt." He glances at Harry. "That's rare, ain't it, Harry?"

Harry nods.

Frankie leans close to me, and I smell whiskey on his breath. "But if we bump into each other again, you'll both be going home with a few less digits." His gaze flicks between us, like a lion deciding which gazelle to attack first. "And I don't muck about, fellas. I mean it."

"OK," I reply. "Understood."

I hear a click in Vinny's throat. It's a relief, because I think he's starting to appreciate the danger we're in. But I'm also reassured because Frankie is giving us a warning. You don't warn people you're going to murder. All we need to do is stay calm and placate him.

The silence is suddenly broken by an innocent little buzz, and I instinctively grab my silver hunter under my jacket.

Frankie's eyes glint. "What was that?"

"What was what?" I say.

Frankie laughs, small at first, but it builds to a disturbing belly laugh.

Vinny clearly doesn't understand the trouble we're in because he starts to chuckle along.

"You think this is funny?" Frankie asks.

Ah. Another one of those gangster questions.

Bzzzt . . .

"I think it's his pocket watch," Harry says. "He was checking it earlier."

"Oh, yeah?" Frankie says. "Expecting someone, are you? Got a little something up your sleeve?" I see the slightest flicker of what could be nervousness. I guess a gangster is always watching his back.

"Not at all," I say. "We just want to—"

"Hand it over." Frankie leans forward and holds out his hand. "*Now.*"

W. P. Brown told me not to lose the watch. If he didn't want me to lose the bloody thing, why didn't he show me how to switch it to silent?

"I can't give it to you," I say, my voice wavering.

"Boss?" Harry pulls a knuckle-duster out of his pocket and looks questioningly at Frankie.

"Last chance. Give me the watch," Frankie says, indicating Vinny with a nod of his head, "or Sunny Jim here's gonna see stars."

I have no choice. I lift the chain over my head and hand Frankie my precious timepiece, noticing as I do that the countdown timer is now at 29 minutes and the text has turned red. How the hell am I going to explain this futuristic digital piece of technology? As Frankie's fingers make contact with the casing, though, the watch face transforms seamlessly; the countdown timer disappears, and it looks just like an antique pocket watch again.

He presses the dial, releasing both the front and rear protective casings. He glances up at me. "This is one nice kettle," he says admiringly. He snaps it closed and places it on the armrest beside him. "I'll keep this, I think. Little souvenir."

I feel small beads of sweat on my forehead. W. P. Brown called it my homing beacon, and we're supposed to be going home soon, but I'm worried that without the watch, Vinny and I might get stuck here.

"That watch means a lot to me," I say. "Do you think I could have it back?"

"Don't push your luck, Sunshine," Frankie growls. He claps his hands together and clears his throat. "Right, I can't sit and chat with you idiots all day. I've got places to go, people to intimidate." His voice drops, and his mood shifts with chilling speed. "Consider this a fair warning, unless you want to get a shirt off Harry. Understand?"

I have no idea what *getting a shirt* from Harry might mean, but we both nod mutely.

Frankie glares at me. "There's something about you," he says. "I can't put my finger on it, but if I find out you're connected to the Dickersons, I'll kill you. Both of you."

Vinny and I are dragged out of the car, and Harry pushes us both to the ground.

"So long," Frankie says, his crystal-blue eyes shimmering. "I'm watching you."

Vinny hoists me up and we watch, helpless, as the car pulls away and into a sea of traffic. "Does it matter that we lost the watch?" Vinny asks.

"Yes," I say hopelessly. "W. P. Brown said it was a kind of homing beacon for getting safely back to the present."

"But you got back without it when you traveled the first time, didn't you?" he says. "I was there, remember?"

"I know, but it's not just about getting home. Without the watch we won't have any information about waypoints or how to solve the mission. We won't know when we're going home, or when our next jump is, or how long we have when we travel. Without it, we don't have a cat in hell's chance of completing the mission."

"OK then, Cash. We have to get it back," Vinny says matter-of-factly.

My legs are shaking with adrenaline. I feel queasy and light-headed. The street is suddenly loud, hot, and unfriendly. I slip to my knees and breathe, desperately trying not to pass out, the world pulsing in and out with my breath.

"You're right," I say, once my heart has stopped hammering. "Let's make a plan."

I stand up, look around, and realize Vinny's gone.

21

First I lose the watch, and now Vinny's gone too. Seconds tick by. I'm just starting to panic when my thoughts are interrupted by a deafening roar behind me. I spin around to see Vinny pulling up on a beautiful racing-green motorcycle. Its chrome bars and exhaust pipe gleam in the last of the sunlight.

"Ain't she a beaut?" he asks.

"Yeah," I murmur, mouth hanging open, "but where did you find . . . a motorbike?"

"Some bloke just left the keys in her." Vinny wipes sweat from his glistening brow and points. "He was distracted, so I just wheeled it away."

Across the street stands a row of bikes. I make eye contact with a man.

"Hey!" he yells. "That's my bike. Stop, thief!"

"Come on," Vinny shouts, revving the engine again, "hop on! Let's go get your watch!"

That snaps me out of my daze. I shield my eyes and catch a brief glimpse of the Rolls-Royce turning a corner up ahead. Hesitate, and we lose.

I squeeze myself onto the back of the bike and grab hold of Vinny. He twists the throttle, the engine growls, and we accelerate rapidly, weaving and bobbing through traffic. We pass a green two-tone Triumph Herald and a blue Ford Anglia 105, just like my granddad used to own. A horn blares behind us. I would raise a hand to apologize, but I'm too busy trying to keep a firm grip on Vinny.

I glance around him, wind blurring my vision, trying to see the Rolls. Vinny suddenly veers sharply to the left, leaving Oxford Street to join Tottenham Court Road. The bike leans alarmingly to the side, so I try to lean back toward the center.

"No!" Vinny cries. "You need to lean *with* me when I turn!"

I'm rigid, jaw clenched and hardly breathing. "OK!" I shout back. I try not to imagine what the speeding tarmac would feel like against my elbows, knees, and face.

Squinting against the wind, I see the car enter a tunnel up ahead. "There!" I point past Vinny's face toward the tunnel.

"I see him," Vinny yells, but we're a long way behind, with at least twenty cars between us.

We enter the tunnel, weaving in and out of traffic. Car horns wail, and the sound of our engine bounces back at us from the tunnel walls like angry fire from the belly of a jet engine.

Vinny slows down. I peer over his shoulder and see the problem. Up ahead a policeman waves pedestrians across the street. Frankie's car is still too far away for my liking, but luckily, they are caught up too. In the rear window of the Rolls, I can just make out the back of Frankie Shaw's head. He hasn't spotted us. Yet.

We pull to a stop and wait. The evening sunlight dazzles, bouncing off the cars like a shower of diamonds. Car horns wail, and a couple of drivers wind down their windows and yell. The policeman ignores them.

The lights change, but we don't move. The bike wobbles, weaves, and then stalls, the engine cutting out with a sputter. Instinctively my feet hit the road, and the bike suddenly feels way too heavy to keep upright.

"Come on, come on!" Vinny cries, frantically kick-starting the bike. There's a pop, followed by a large black plume of smoke as the engine catches and explodes back to life. Vinny twists the throttle, and we pull away.

The policeman stops traffic again, waving a fresh crowd of people across the street. I watch, helpless, as the Rolls gets smaller and smaller.

"We have to go!" I shout at Vinny.

"Roger, Cash. Hold tight!"

The bike's horn wails like a demented banshee. Vinny accelerates, and the policeman's eyes widen as he realizes we're coming through. He blows his whistle, and the pedestrians scatter as we hurtle toward them.

Except for one elderly lady with a shopping cart.

Vinny swerves, pushing our center of gravity horribly close to the brink. Luckily, our forward momentum is sufficient to snap us upright, and though we miss the lady, we can't avoid her cart. We clip it, sending groceries exploding everywhere. Angry pedestrians yell as we tear past them.

We fly through the intersection. Traffic from our right nearly blindsides us, one car so close I can't believe it misses. My stomach fills with a rush of acid.

The windows of the Rolls-Royce flash gold in the sun as the car takes a right. We haven't lost them. The road narrows, and we turn right.

"Where did they go?" Vinny yells, slowing.

I lean out, eyes streaming, but I don't see them either. A double-decker bus cuts us off as we approach a roundabout, forcing Vinny to jam on the brakes. The bike kicks sideways a little, but he manages to keep us upright. The bus completely blocks our view. Vinny bangs the handlebars in frustration.

Four roads, all the same. I know I should be panicking, but instead I feel a warm rush of calm certainty. My heart rate settles and my hearing sharpens, as one of the four options glows with extra color, as though someone has turned up the saturation.

I point. "That way, Vinny. I know it."

He revs the bike and swings us around. The acrid smell of burning rubber fills my nostrils. I hug Vinny tightly as we accelerate, and we soon catch up.

"There!" Vinny cries.

The narrow street flashes by. People stare, and I see a couple point back toward the roundabout. I risk a look behind us and see a police car closing in, blue lights flashing.

"We've got company," I cry.

"I see them!" Vinny calls back. "I'm going to try to lose them." He jams the brakes, and we take a hard left. Vinny accelerates, and we squeeze between a truck and a row of parked cars. Metal squeals and sparks fly as we scrape thin lines of paint from the sides of the vehicles. I glance back and see the police car skidding to a stop.

Slowly, it fades from view.

"How about that?" Vinny hollers, jubilant.

"Amazing." I pat him on the back. I'm going to have a heart attack soon.

We rejoin the main road, speeding past the Royal Opera House, and catch up with the Rolls-Royce. They are cruising, unaware of our insane attempt to tail them. With about a dozen cars between us, Vinny suddenly weaves and turns left down a side street.

"What are you doing?" I shout.

"If we get snarled up on the Strand, we'll lose them, but I know where they're heading."

"You do?"

"Yep, Waterloo Bridge."

"How can you be sure?"

"Trust me, I was a cabbie for ten years. 'Waterloo Sunset,' here we come, baby!" He guffaws with glee. I'm not sure all this adrenaline is good for him.

We round a corner and enter a wide market filled with people, stalls, and canopies.

"Weird, I don't remember this." Vinny shakes his head then accelerates again, beeping the horn.

We weave through the stalls, clipping tables, smashing things, and picking up a long stream of garments. I can't see a thing, and I'm pretty sure Vinny can't either.

I pluck a silk blouse from my head and crane my neck to see a fresh police car weaving its way through the gathered crowd behind us. It picks up the chase again.

We zoom onto a narrow side street with tall buildings on either side. Vinny jams the brakes, and we slide to a juddering halt in front of a construction site.

Vinny laughs.

"What's so funny?"

Piled up against a wooden billboard, I see a heap of mud and sand.

Planks lie along it, and a workman descends with a wheelbarrow. The mound is about six feet high, the same as the fence.

Now, I've known Vinny for quite a few years. I love him for many reasons, but the main one is his eternal optimism. He believes anything is possible, and I usually adore that. Today, not so much.

"Vinny," I say, my voice cracking. "If you're planning to—"

"Hold on tight, Cash. Get ready to bite the wind."

The engine roars, the tires howl in protest, and the bike lurches forward, accelerating like a rocket. The street blurs. Workmen scatter. As the front wheel lifts off the ground, I have visions of us flipping back and splatting against the billboard.

But Vinny keeps us straight and true.

I peer over Vinny's shoulder at the tachometer, watching the needle shake into the red. We hit the ramp, and the tires compress beneath our considerable combined weight. My gut drops. We travel the length of the wooden plank and launch into the air, weightless, the engine whining.

Time slows, and my life flashes before me. Technically, I haven't even been born yet.

You know what they say: it isn't the jump that will kill you, it's the landing.

My entire body clenches. I clutch Vinny like he's a life raft. All I can see is sky, handlebars, and the front wheel.

We seem to be falling forever. I risk a glance down. We are descending a considerable slope and covering way more ground than I had thought.

Now we're both screaming.

Vinny said he had waited his whole life for an adventure like this. It's a shame that the wait was so long and the adventure so short. Our rear wheel finally touches down, then the front wheel bangs down like a hammer, crushing me against Vinny, who takes the brunt of the impact. The wind rushes out of me as I compress him.

The bike bucks and twists like a crazed bull at a rodeo, swerving ferociously. The engine whines as Vinny wrestles with it, twisting the throttle and braking at the same time.

It's all too fast . . . just way too fast.

We crash through something green and spiky, a hedgerow maybe, that thankfully slows us down. Unfortunately, it's not enough, and something solid finishes the job. There's a sickening crunch of metal and glass, and the almightiest smack sends me flipping over Vinny's back and through the air like a rag doll. My brief flight ends abruptly in a white flash of pain, followed by blissful darkness.

A distant voice calls my name.

I'm winded and disorientated. Drawing a breath is a struggle, but at least I'm not dead. I swallow, trying to clear the wool from my ears. A high-pitched sound fills my mind, like a grenade detonation accompanied by a distant siren.

Memory colors in my sketchy reality. Bike. Jump. Police.

Gradually, my senses return. I cough, and that brings the smell of oil, earth, vegetation, and the iron tang of blood. I'm trapped, arms pinned to my sides. I wriggle free, my shoulder screaming and my ribs burning. Turns out, I was embedded like a javelin through a box hedge, the thickness of which probably saved my life.

I pull myself out of the hedge, sit heavily on the ground, and check my undercarriage.

"I'm OK," I mumble, my voice thin and scratchy. "All present and correct." My brain feels too big for my skull. Wincing, I assess the scene.

We've landed on a peaceful, tree-lined street. Vinny is up, gasping and grimacing, walking off the pain. The bike is nearby, on its side, surrounded by broken glass and smoke. Dark liquid pools beneath it. The front wheel spins. I pore over the wreckage with an odd sense of detachment.

My mind slowly pieces together what we were doing. My eyes sting. I wipe them, and my fingers come away covered in fresh blood. Vinny makes his way over, limping. I'm vaguely aware of other people too, gathering around us, distant voices, shapes casting shadows.

"You OK, Cash?" Vinny asks.

Hot pain flares over my shoulder. It might be dislocated. I moan.

"Sorry," Vinny mutters. "That wasn't my best landing."

My mouth is suddenly very dry. My body clenches. Waves of heat and ice dance over me.

Good old shock.

It's designed to protect us, but right now it wants to power down the Bridgeman mainframe. "I can't breathe," I gasp, the edges of my vision darkening. My mouth floods with saliva, and I puke. I hear a distant Vinny.

"Stay with me," he cries.

I don't get a say in this one, I'm afraid. Joseph Bridgeman needs a reboot. I descend into a world of swirling black.

And then the shock triggers a viewing, and I just *know* this one is going to hurt.

22

I brace myself as another viewing consumes me, and I'm powerless to stop it. The gloom clears, and as my vision sharpens, I see a corridor. Scuffed linoleum covered with footprints. Gray walls, pockmarked and shabby. Lucy Romano sits on a plastic chair next to a wooden door with a sign that reads Headmaster. As I float down and my awareness melds with hers, Lucy glances up at the clock on the wall: 4:40 p.m.

"Hurry up," she mutters anxiously. "Some of us have jobs to get to."

The door opens, and an affable man in a brown corduroy jacket pokes his head around the door. "Mrs. Romano?" he says, sweeping his thick dark hair up over his head.

"Miss," she corrects him. "*Miss* Romano."

"My apologies," he says. "I'm Mr. Hobson. Thank you for coming in. Please." He stands back from the door and indicates a chair in front of his desk. "Take a seat."

Lucy sits down and places her handbag on her lap. A desk calendar reads August 19, 1962. The headmaster closes the office door.

"Sorry, but can we make this quick?" Lucy asks. "My shift starts at six, and I need to get back across town."

"I'll try," Mr. Hobson says amiably, as he sinks into his leather chair. "I've invited you here this afternoon to talk about Gus."

She can't imagine what there is to say. "His report last year was excellent. I am very proud of him."

"I'm sure you are." Mr. Hobson leans back in his chair and presses the pads of his fingers together. "Gus is a very intelligent young man," he says. "He has enormous potential. The sky's the limit, really."

"OK," Lucy says. "But . . . ?"

"But I have become increasingly concerned about his behavior recently."

Lucy's heart sinks. Hearing it from someone else confirms her fears. "I have noticed that he is going through a bit of a rebellious phase."

"It's more than that," Mr. Hobson says, offering Lucy a cookie from a dented tin on his desk. She declines. "I've seen this before in exceptionally gifted students. Some of them find the burden of their academic talent too much to bear. They rebel against the constant attention and academic pressure of a school environment, and they can become quite problematic."

"Gus is a problem?" Lucy asks. "Is that what you are saying?"

"He's been getting into a lot of fights."

"I know, of course, the bruises, the ripped shirts . . . He told me he's being bullied, but he didn't want me to talk to the school about it. He said it would make it worse."

Mr. Hobson sighs. "I'm afraid Gus said that to you because he's the one who's starting the fights. He tried to hit another student this morning. The teacher on duty managed to break things up, but Gus's behavior has reached an unacceptable level."

Lucy feels tightness in her stomach, a pain under her ribs. Part of her knew this already, but still it lands like a punch. She takes a deep breath, pressing her fingers into her side.

"I'm sorry if this is difficult to hear, Miss Romano, but I always think it's best to get these things out in the open. That gives us half a chance of sorting them out."

Lucy nods, this new reality whirling in her head, searching for reasons. "I work evening shifts," she says. "Gus is alone a lot in the evenings. I thought at sixteen, he would be all right."

"Evening shifts?" probes the headmaster.

"I'm a waitress. At the Unicorn Bar in Shoreditch." The headmaster swallows, and Lucy wonders if he knows that the Unicorn is run by the Shaws. "But I'm studying too, during the day and on weekends."

"What are you studying?" asks Mr. Hobson.

"Medicine," says Lucy. "I am going to be a doctor."

"Admirable profession," says the headmaster. "Gus must get his brains from you. It sounds like you have your hands full. Does anyone else help you at home?"

Familiar metal shutters come down around Lucy's heart. "Gus's father left when he was two. It's just me and my boy." She has never understood how any parent could abandon their own child. Silently, she renews her vow always to be there for him, come hell or high water.

"Aha," says Mr. Hobson. "I did wonder . . ." He rubs his chin. "Sometimes children in Gus's position can lack a strong male role model. When he told me he'd joined a boxing club, I thought it might help him channel his excess energy, but when I heard it was the Shaws' place . . ." He leans forward. "This is a critical time in any young man's life, Miss Romano. I'm worried that Gus has fallen in with the wrong crowd."

Lucy knows the headmaster is right, but she feels helpless, and it makes her defensive. "What can I do? He is always at the boxing club, every night. I thought it was good for him: the discipline, the training. These men, he thinks they care about him. They are powerful. Gus sees that as strength."

Mr. Hobson presses. "I fear they may be a bad influence. He's taken his foot completely off the pedal, in terms of his academic work. He's falling behind."

Lucy is confused. "That can't be right. He told me he is doing his homework in the library at lunchtime so that he can go to the club in the evenings. He knows he must do well on his exams so that he can go to university."

The headmaster shakes his head. "Gus has made it very clear to us that he has no intention of going to university."

"What are you talking about?"

"He told his teacher he's leaving school in the summer. He said—and I quote—'There are other ways to get an education besides hanging around with a load of squares.'"

"I cannot believe you are talking about my Gus," Lucy says. "I have worked too hard for him to drop out like this."

"I certainly feel it would be a waste," says Mr. Hobson. "His physics teacher told me he couldn't remember ever meeting a student with such natural flair, and he's been teaching for over thirty years." He folds his arms. "I think Gus may be at a crossroads. He could have a magnificent future ahead of him, but only if he applies himself."

Lucy has always been mother and father to Gus, but she's been focused on her own life recently, and Gus's future is slipping through her fingers. It's time to take matters in hand again.

"The school will do what we can to guide him," Mr. Hobson says, "but I think you may need to make some changes at home too."

"OK," says Lucy, standing up, already planning what she will say to Tommy Shaw. "Thank you for asking me to come in."

"Gus is a good boy at heart," says the headmaster. "We can turn him around."

The headmaster's office morphs into a sea of static like an old analog TV, and his voice fades to white noise. I wonder if I'm coming out of the viewing, but then time accelerates. Lucy leaves the school; she's out on the street, taking a bus and then walking. The white noise fades. The clarity and color returns. Time resumes its normal speed.

Lucy walks past a traditional London pub and a row of smart shops. She stops outside a grand terraced house with a pillar-box red front door. When she called the Unicorn to speak to Tommy, they'd told her he was working here, his latest refurbishment project.

She runs up the grand stone steps and raps hard on the brass knocker. The sound of hammers and a pneumatic drill is piercing, even out here. A plaque next to the door reads 108. Lucy raps again on the door. No one answers. Impatiently, she tries the doorknob. It turns easily, and she steps into the hallway.

The flat is empty, just dusty wooden floorboards and bare plaster walls. She hears workmen in the flat below, thuds and bumps and muffled voices.

"Hello?" she calls out. There's no answer. She makes her way along the corridor, peering into empty rooms as she goes. At the end of the hallway, she pushes through a shabby wooden door into the main living area. Tall sash windows let in dramatic light, and there she finds Tommy Shaw, sitting on one of a pair of dining chairs, the only pieces of furniture in the huge room. A toolbox sits on the floor near a stone fireplace. On the window-sill, a bright-red Roberts radio plays popular music.

"Lucy!" Tommy drawls, standing up. "Well now, this is a treat. Couldn't stay away from me, eh?"

She remembers how attractive she thought he was when they first met. There's something of the Dean Martin about him, the jet-black hair; the long, straight nose; that easy smile. But that was before she got to know him.

"What have you been saying to Gus?" she asks accusingly. "I've just been to see his headmaster, and he's in trouble at school. He's been start-ing fights."

Tommy chuckles. "My little warrior," he says proudly. "Gus is going places. He's got a bright future ahead of him."

"He has," says Lucy, "but not the kind of future you have in mind. There's nothing wrong with boxing, I'm glad he's learning to defend himself, but you've been filling his head with nonsense. He's got the brains to actu-ally make something of his life—get a degree, get a proper job—but he's been saying he doesn't want to go to university anymore."

"Too right," Tommy says. "He doesn't want to go and waste time hang-ing around with a load of squares."

"Getting an education isn't a waste of time!" says Lucy, exasperated. "Why are you saying these things to him? What is wrong with you?"

"Let's stick to the facts, shall we?" Tommy says. The smile leaves his face. "Gus is a good lad, but he came to me. He knew he needed to toughen up. He's a fine little boxer, and if he wants to learn how to fight, I'm not going to stop him. You've got to admit, that boy needs a man to look up to. I know what it's like growing up without a dad. He needs a father figure, a role model. He needs guidance."

"Not from you!" As soon as the words are out of her mouth, she regrets them. Tommy's face darkens. Lucy tries to regain her composure. "Gus's headmaster told me he's brilliant at physics, that he could have a magnifi-cent career ahead of him. Gus's headmaster said—"

"*Gus's headmaster said,*" Tommy mocks, flecks of his spittle flying at Lucy. "Listen to yourself. Gus needs a strong man in his life, and he admires me." His expression softens with unnerving speed. "The three of us, we could be a family." He reaches out to touch Lucy's cheek. She flinches, even though she knows it might make things worse. She can't help herself. Those hands have terrible stories to tell. Tommy is unperturbed. "I'm not going with any of the other girls anymore. It's just us."

"Tommy, there is no *us*. There never has been." She's lost count of the number of times they've had this conversation.

Del Shannon's "Runaway" comes on the radio. Tommy half smiles and pushes his hands deep into his pockets. He's very still. She can't read him. It scares her.

"Me and Frankie, we're going to hit the big time soon," he says.

Maybe if he and Frankie make a ton of cash, Tommy will forget about her and leave her and Gus alone. "Good for you."

"No, good for us. You, me, and Gus. We could get our own place together."

He's lost his mind. A pneumatic drill kicks off downstairs. Lucy waits. Tommy seems happy, his eyes glazed over, dreaming some crazy dream. She feels sick.

The drill stops, and the room is quiet again. "Tommy, this is all in your head. It's madness!"

"It's a dream, but I'm going to have enough money soon to make it happen. We can live anywhere you want. I'll take care of you both."

"We don't need looking after," she says. "I'm going to be a doctor, pay my own way."

His eyes glint dangerously. "You left Italy because your fella got himself into a spot of bother, didn't he," he says. "And you got tied up in it too."

"How do you know about that?" she says, derailed.

"No secrets from me." He taps the side of his nose.

"Just leave me alone, Tommy!" She turns and walks back toward the hallway.

"But I love you!" he calls after her. "No one else makes me feel the way you do. Turn around now and tell me you don't love me!"

She turns back to him. "I . . . don't . . . love . . . you," she says, as steadily as she can.

"You don't mean that," he says. "I've seen the way you look at me!"

She turns her palms up in exasperation. "I could never be with a man like you!" she says. "I saw what you did to that man at the club the other day. It was horrible!"

"He deserved it."

"There's always an excuse."

"I'm a businessman."

"And I don't like the business you're in."

"You should be grateful. You're not exactly a catch with a kid in tow. You had nothing when you came here, and I gave you a job. You owe me."

"No. I work, I get paid. It's a transaction. But that's over now, anyway."

"What do you mean?" he says menacingly.

She needs to get out of here right now. "I'm leaving, and I'm not coming back." She turns and walks away quickly.

"No one walks out on me," Tommy growls. He catches her and grabs her arm. He's holding her too hard.

"I asked you nicely," he spits. "But if you won't give it to me, then I'll take it." He presses his mouth against hers, bruising her lips. He smells of sweat, old cigarettes, something sour.

"Let me go. You're hurting me." She struggles, and he loosens his grip. "If you don't let me leave, I'll scream," she says.

He leers at her. "No one will hear. The walls are three feet thick, and the workmen downstairs won't hear you. Even if they did, they're not going to mess with me."

Terror grips Lucy's heart. She makes a run for the door. Tommy grabs her coat, and she kicks him in the shin. He groans, and as he leans down to hold his leg, she shoves him hard. He falls backward and hits his head on the toolbox.

He doesn't move.

Lucy takes a cautious step toward him. His eyes are closed. His face is pale. Blood seeps from the back of his skull.

What has she done?

She stumbles back from Tommy, runs to the front door, and lets herself out.

She doesn't look back.

23

I'm being shaken by the paws of a giant bear. It growls. It grunts. Words. A talking bear?

"Wake up, Cash! Come back to me."

I crack open one eye. Where am I? My mind feels like a smashed jigsaw puzzle. Slowly pieces click into place, my poor brain rebooting. I'm away from Tommy Shaw, but pain reverberates throughout my body. My head pounds, my leg screams, my arm aches. My eyes are streaming.

Through the teary haze, I recognize the reassuring bulk of my best friend.

"Vinny," I exhale, my relief palpable. "Thank goodness."

"I wish they all said that when they woke up next to me." Vinny's trying to stay cheerful, but I can hear the pain in his voice. "We're in trouble," he says. "The police are waiting outside. They want a statement."

I painstakingly hoist myself up onto my elbows. We're in the back of an ambulance. I'm on one of those roller beds, with a green blanket over my legs. Outside, a small crowd has gathered, their faces reflected in blue flashing lights.

Perched on a stool next to me, Vinny groans loudly.

"Are you all right?" I ask him.

"Twisted my knee pretty badly, but I'm OK otherwise." He flinches suddenly. "Ow!" he yelps. "My head! It's killing me!" He looks at me alarmed. "That's weird. I didn't bang my head in the accident. D'you think I'm having a stroke?" Nervously, he rubs the back of his neck.

"I'm sure you're not," I say. "Probably just whiplash."

I shut my eyes again, trying to get a grip on the pain.

Then, with a jolt, I ascertain what's going on.

"It's brain freeze! Vinny, I've got it too."

"Brain freeze?" He looks confused.

"It's one of the symptoms of time travel. It means we're going home soon," I explain. "It feels a bit like when you've eaten too much ice cream all at once. Don't worry. It passes. Try to relax."

"Too much ice cream?" Vinny says dubiously. "I didn't think that was a thing. Anyway, I suppose it's fair enough. We've been messing about with time, now time's messing about with us."

"That's one way of looking at it," I agree.

My throat constricts. This jump has been a complete waste of time. And the watch is gone. Without it, I don't even know if we're going to get home safely. Vinny's relying on me, and we're both injured. I get flashbacks of the zoetrope, the dangers of navigating my way home. How am I going to do this?

There's a vibration in my chest, and for one horrible moment, I think I'm having a heart attack.

"Hang on, was that what I think it was?" Vinny says.

"You heard that?" I say. There's another vibration, softer this time. I reach inside my shirt, grab the chain around my neck, and pull out a silver pocket watch.

"Is it yours?" Vinny asks.

My hands tremble as I check it over. There's no question. It's the same watch Frankie just stole from me.

"It's mine," I say. "It's definitely mine."

I kiss the little silver orb. When W. P. Brown said it was bonded to me, he was right. I send him a silent thanks, check the jump dials, and grab Vinny's hand.

"What's going on, Cash?"

"Hold on to me! There's just under twenty seconds before we travel home."

Vinny grabs my other hand too. "Anything I need to know before we go?"

I recall hovering thirty feet in the air, arms flapping. "Just pray for a soft landing."

"I'm good at those," Vinny says, without an ounce of irony. He licks his lips. I think this might be the first time I've ever seen him nervous.

The watch beeps as it counts down. We chant the numbers together.

"Five."

Someone outside rattles the door. Vinny squeezes his eyes tight shut.

"Four."

"We've secured the suspects for safekeeping, sir. Here's the key." A man's voice, but with a Doppler effect to it.

"Three."

The key rattles in the lock. Vinny is translucent now, glimmering.

"Two."

The interior of the ambulance swims with color, like a deep-blue waterfall in sunlight. The rear door unlocks.

"One!"

The ambulance is instantaneously replaced by the interior of Bridgeman Antiques.

W. P. Brown described my watch as a homing beacon. He said it would add stability and safety. He was right. There is no transition, no zoetropes, no collapsing scenery or emerging details. The jump was instant, more than fifty years, quick as a blink, our landing smooth. Compared to my previous landings, that was an upgrade to business class, the only way to time travel.

The shop is eerily quiet. I check the watch. The jump dials roll and then settle back to zero. "Welcome back to the present, Vinny. Local time is six fifteen p.m."

Vinny whistles. "Blimey, that was intense!"

He begins to chuckle and soon, despite our injuries, we're both laughing. I'm exhausted, but I feel a colossal wave of relief to be home and alive. Vinny, my self-appointed sidekick, made all the difference.

Someone clears their throat behind us, making us both jump. It's Molly. She's standing at the rear of the shop, her reading glasses perched on top of her head. "Hello, Vincent," she says formally, like a schoolteacher.

Vinny is sheepish. "Hello, Molly."

"Hello, Mr. Bridgeman." She raises an eyebrow.

"Hello, Molly!" I attempt a reassuring smile, but instead, I wince. Everything hurts.

"You look like you've been dragged through a hedge backward!" She glowers at me. "You really ought to be more careful, after that head injury of yours. You're supposed to be recuperating. And what an interesting choice of attire."

I'd forgotten all about my sixties gear.

"We've been to a sixties party, Molly," I say, "and we got into a spot of bother with some troublemakers. We got beaten up, and we came back here . . . er . . ."

"I don't need to hear any more," she says. "I'm taking you to hospital. You both need proper medical care."

There is no point arguing. I grab my phone and wallet and change into a sweater and jeans. Molly gives us a ride to the hospital. There isn't a lot of chatting in the car. I imagine she's missing her old boss.

She leaves us at the door to the emergency room.

"Give me a ring when you need picking up," she says curtly. "You'll forgive me for not waiting with you."

"Thank you, Molly," I say gratefully.

I load Vinny into a wheelchair and push him into the waiting room, leaning heavily on the handles as I hobble along.

After three hours in line, Vinny and I are called through for treatment. My wounds, though painful, are superficial, and I'm soon cleaned and stitched up by a deft-fingered nurse. Vinny's injuries are more serious, and he gets carted off for an X-ray. When I find him afterward, propped up in bed in a far corner of the trauma ward, his knee is packed in ice and heavily bandaged. He appears to be asleep, and he's got a line in his arm, presumably painkillers. As I approach, I see his sixties clothes are folded neatly over the back of the regulation hospital chair beside his bed.

I sit quietly on the chair, shocked by the state of him. "Sorry, mate," I whisper.

He opens his eyes. They roll a little. "I hoped that was you," he slurs. "I'm sorry, Cash. I royally messed up."

"Vinny, you chump, you were amazing. It's me who cocked everything up by getting my watch stolen. I'm sorry it was such a horrible trip."

"Are you kidding? It was mega!" He lowers his voice. "I can't believe we were threatened by Mad Harry Hurst." He prods my shoulder and giggles like a schoolboy. "Mad Harry Hurst, Cash! He's a nasty piece of work, but what a privilege! He's gotta be one of the most famous thugs in recent history."

I can't agree that being threatened by anyone is a privilege, but I'm glad he's taken everything in his stride. I fill him in on the viewing I had while I was lying unconscious after the motorcycle crash. He listens intently, occasionally raising an eyebrow or grunting quietly in acknowledgment.

"So this means Tommy Shaw wasn't killed by the Dickersons!" Vinny exclaims.

"Correct. It was all an accident. Lucy thought she'd killed Tommy, so she probably planned to run away. Thing is, Tommy wasn't dead. Eventually he woke up, probably tried to get back to the club, collapsed in the street on the way, and fell into a coma. Word gets out, and everyone immediately presumes it was the Dickersons, so Lucy thinks she's safe and sits tight."

"Hang on," Vinny says, scratching his head, "when we saw Lucy at the dance, Tommy was still alive, right?"

"Right," I confirm. "On my first jump, I went back to June 6, 1963. Tommy died in the morning, and Lucy was shot by Harry Hurst a few hours later. Today we jumped all the way back to September 1, 1962. Tommy had only been in a coma for a couple of weeks."

"No wonder Lucy was so worn out and nervous at the dance," says Vinny.

"She must have been feeling the pressure, hiding in plain sight like that," I agree. "Think about it from her perspective: If she runs, she implicates herself. If she waits, she knows that when Tommy wakes up, he will tell Frankie everything. The fact that we know he never recovers is irrelevant. Lucy doesn't know what's going to happen."

Vinny frowns, deep in thought. "I'm thinking this could all be avoided if we could just arrive before Lucy meets Tommy at that house. Then we could stop it all."

I smirk at him. "Spoken like a true time traveler."

Vinny's thinking is sound, but it raises fresh questions. What does success mean? Could I save Lucy and stop Frankie Shaw's reign of terror? And if so, should I? Could I make things worse?

A nurse arrives. "How are you feeling?" he asks.

"Hungry," Vinny replies with a comedic growl. "All these drugs give me the munchies. What've you got for me there then?" The nurse places a tray down in front of him. "Never mind about the savory stuff, pass me the pudding!" Vinny picks up his spoon and attacks a slice of cheesecake, groaning with pleasure.

I rub my hands over my face. I can't remember the last time I felt so tired.

"You go, Cash," Vinny says. "I'll be fine. I'm in safe hands. Don't be traveling without me now."

"I'll try not to," I say, smiling wanly. I stand up and stretch, my back sore from my heavy landing earlier. "I'll come and see you again tomorrow." As I turn to go, I notice Vinny's clothes have disappeared from the back of the chair. They must have gone back to the sixties while we were chatting. "I'll bring you some jeans and a T-shirt too," I say. "Your fancy Lord John's gear has gone back to where it came from."

Vinny looks at the back of the chair. "Is that how it works?"

"That's how it works."

"Cool," he says. "See ya."

As I leave the hospital, I pass a sign leading to intensive care. It might as well read *intensive guilt*. It's my fault Vinny's here. But we were lucky. How would I have felt if Vinny had been really badly hurt, or worse? How would I have lived with myself? He thinks this is all cool and exciting, but it isn't TV, it's real life. With real stakes. In some ways, I'm glad Vinny's been temporarily taken out of the equation, because it means I don't have to tell him that he can't come with me next time.

I pass through a glass corridor between buildings. It looks freezing cold outside. Bare trees sway in the wind under yellow streetlamps. I turn on my mobile phone and dozens of messages come flooding in: emails, texts, and voicemail. I skim a few and stop when I spot Amy's name. I open up the conversation.

2 p.m.:

> I stopped by the shop to say hi, but Molly said you were out. Are you OK?

5:15 p.m.:

> Please ping me so I know you're all right.

8:30 p.m.:

> I'm properly worried now. Call me as soon as you get this.

I text her back:

> I'm fine. Sorry. Been sleeping a lot. Chat later.

That lie works for about ten seconds, because around the corner ahead of me, Amy appears. I freeze, and she spots me.

She shakes her head and strides in my direction, her expression shifting from anger to concern. "Joe, I've been so worried!" she says. "You look terrible! What happened?"

I feel light-headed and stumble. Amy takes my arm and guides me to the hospital café. Which bright spark decided that acid yellow was a soothing color? We sit next to each other on a bench. I avoid her gaze.

"How did you know I was here?" I ask.

"Molly called," she replies. "She said you'd run into some trouble at a party." She doesn't quite manage to keep all the sarcasm out of her voice. "Is Vinny OK? Molly said he could hardly walk."

"He's hurt his knee pretty badly, but he'll be OK."

"Good." We sit quietly for a while, just the sound of distant phones and footfalls. I glance at Amy. Her brow is narrowed, her lips set in a thin line.

"What?" I say.

"I'm waiting for you to tell me the truth," she says.

"What do you mean?" I protest, although I know it's pointless.

She clenches her jaw. "You *promised* me you weren't traveling. You said you'd talk to me if things got difficult. Why did you lie?"

For a moment, I consider adding another story to my house of cards. But then I reconsider. I thought I was protecting Amy by hiding things from her, but it's clear that I'm damaging our relationship and giving her reasons not to trust me. If I start to tell Amy what's going on, she will want to know everything, but I simply can't lie anymore. I got hurt this time, and next time, I might not be so lucky. I'm not going to die in the past, without a trace in the present, and leave my sister wondering what happened to me for the rest of her life. To hell with W. P. Brown and his stupid rules. It's time to start telling the truth and dealing with the consequences.

I turn to Amy and take her hand. "I'm being blackmailed," I tell her. "I'm being forced to time travel."

"Oh my God, Joe," she says, tears in her eyes. I can't tell if they're tears of anger or relief. Maybe both. "I knew you were traveling. To London, right? Quite a long time ago?"

I nod. "I've been going back to the 1960s."

"Who's blackmailing you?"

"A man called W. P. Brown."

"W. P. Brown? Who is he?"

"He's a time traveler too, an older guy. He said he works for some kind of organization, a group of time travelers."

"But why's he blackmailing you?" she asks. "What does he want? What do they want?"

"A woman was murdered in 1963, but she's innocent. Her name is Lucy Romano. I don't know much about her, but Brown says saving her is important. She got caught up in a bad situation. She made a mistake, but she's innocent. I've seen it."

"And what happens if you don't do what he says?"

There's no way to avoid this, no way to soften the blow. "He said he'd put things back to how they were—with you, I mean. He took me back to the fair again, to the night you went missing, and told me I had to do as he said. It was horrific."

"Oh, Joe. This is awful. Why didn't you tell me?"

"He told me not to, but that's not the reason. I thought if I could fix it all, then you would never need to know. I didn't want you to worry."

"But if you'd told me the truth sooner, I wouldn't have been so worried. I told you I was having visions of London. It was hard for me to open up like that. I've been going out of my mind trying to make sense of what I've been seeing. And then that day we walked to Puzzlewood, you told me that you had viewings, that you saw the past, and it was a relief because I felt like I wasn't alone." She stands up and paces back and forth.

"I'm sorry," I say, knowing how lame I sound.

"The visions of London haven't stopped. If anything, they've become stronger." Amy is talking loudly, and people are beginning to stare. "I've seen worrying things, Joe. It's like a nightmare."

"Why don't you sit down and tell me what you saw," I suggest.

She sits back down and works her hands on her lap. "In the visions I've had, it's foggy, and you're in a car, being driven to a church. You're in a group. The men are bad people." She takes a deep, shuddering breath. "The church has a broken stained glass window. Something happens here that is transformative." Amy looks drained. "There are powerful forces at work. They're buried deep. I can't see them, but I can feel them. I feel anger, a deep sense of sacrifice, and the weight of a terrible burden."

"The emotions you're feeling make sense to me," I say, trying to reassure her. "The woman I'm trying to save made a mistake. I think the burden you're feeling is her guilt."

Amy's heavy gaze settles on me. "And what about the sacrifice?"

I shrug. "I don't know. Maybe that's connected to her as well."

"Or it could be you, Joe, sacrificing yourself to save her." She leans forward and takes my hand. "Every time I get this vision, someone dies, and last time it was you."

That sends gooseflesh dancing over me. I try to keep my voice calm.

"When you told me about your visions, you said that what you see are only *possible* futures. So everything you're seeing can be changed. I'm not going to die. It's not going to happen."

"How can you be so sure after what I've just told you?"

"Well, you've warned me, for a start. I'll be extra careful. I'm going to save Lucy, and then everything will be all right. You will be safe."

We sit in silence for a few moments, both lost in thought.

Amy turns to me. "You're being blackmailed, but you'd do this even if you weren't, wouldn't you?"

I peer directly into my lovely, grown-up sister's troubled eyes. "Yes, I think I would." She nods. "Amy, that day we broke down in the van, you said that when you were little, you used to have visions and then travel into the future. I know you said you didn't think you were going to travel again, but with all these visions you've been having, how can you be sure?"

"The pull just isn't there," she says with a shrug. "And anyway, I'm not seeing *my* future. I'm seeing yours." She strokes her hair back from her face. "When are you planning to go back?"

"I don't get to choose. It's not like before. This watch tells me when I'm due to leave." I show her my silver hunter. She turns it curiously in her fingers, then lets it go. As I lay it back against my chest, it feels heavier than ever. "W. P. Brown gave it to me. When I'm in the past, it tells me how long I have till I return to the present. It's like a homing beacon too. It gets me back safely."

Amy seems smaller, resigned to the fact that I'm hooked into this mission till the bitter end. "I can't believe this is happening," she says. "I thought we were done with all of this. You saved me, and I will always love you for that, but I'm not sure I'll ever forgive you for risking your life like this, without trusting me." She shakes her head, then regards me, her eyes welling with unshed tears. "Do you understand?"

"Yes," I say, because I want her to feel heard. I have to live with this guilt. I'm her brother, and it's my job to protect her, no matter what. My future lies in the past, but if I succeed in completing this mission, Amy can be as angry as she likes. At least she will be alive. If I fail, then nothing matters anymore.

She offers me a ride home, but I tell her I want to walk, that I need some air. Reluctantly, she agrees. She doesn't hug me goodbye, and the space between us is palpable.

As I leave the hospital, a thin mist of rain covers Cheltenham. The wind picks up, and the trees hiss Amy's warning. *There are powerful forces at work. I can't see them, but I can feel them*, Amy said. And I believe her because I think I can feel them too.

PART 5

24

I spiral down from a still gray sky. Beneath me a vast inky loch appears, a stain spreading across the silent Highland moors, and as I sink toward the water, craggy mountains loom around me like sentinels. Far below I see a lone figure sitting on a rock near the shore, but then I'm caught in an eddy and flung this way and that, powerless to resist. The figure, a man, has his back to me, hat low over his ears, a black overcoat pulled around him against the cold. I float down between the naked branches of a rowan tree, and as he turns his gaunt face toward me, I realize that the man I'm about to inhabit is W. P. Brown.

I drift down and settle like a layer of snow into his consciousness. He's speaking, intoning a poem:

> *"Snow underfoot,*
> *icy winter losing its grip;*
> *fresh shoots, poised beneath,*
> *wait blindly.*
> *Who would be afraid of spring?"*

The question hanging unanswered in the air. W. P. Brown catches his breath, his jaw clenched. His attention is drawn toward a path, where a woman in furs and snow boots draws near.

She walks hesitantly, as though unsure how she'll be received. "I thought I would find you here." Her voice is calm and measured.

"Iris," W. P. Brown says tightly. He's happy to see her, but his heart remains troubled.

Iris surveys the loch. "Flat as a millpond today," she remarks. "Not a breath of air."

He turns to her. "Are you here as my friend or as my colleague?"

"Both," she says. "Why did you leave the meeting like that?"

"I'm struggling," he says simply. "I miss him. I hoped if I came here, I might find some answers. We used to come here a lot to talk. He always knew what to do."

A lone white bird flies over the loch.

"And?"

"I fear this may be asking too much of me," Brown says. He feels like a bear in a pit. Whichever way he turns, there's darkness. "You should have seen his face, Iris, when I took him back to the fair."

"We discussed all the options," Iris says dispassionately. "This is the only way."

He closes his eyes. "I feel like this could be a terrible mistake. What if it goes wrong?"

Iris sits beside him. "Don't you remember, all those years ago, when I was new to all of this, and you told me that it is the struggle that shapes who we become?"

He shakes his head. "But that's just it, Iris. I'm *ashamed* of the man I've become."

"You always told me that we all must play our part in this great story," she says, "that we must do what has to be done, and I have seen that to be true."

"But I've threatened Amy Bridgeman's life, Iris!"

"We must stay focused on the goal," Iris replies. "If we succeed in changing the direction of Gus Romano's life, he will go on to do something incredible."

"But that's the thing. We don't even know what he's going to do!"

"We do know that it's to going to affect many lives for the better.

You've seen the potential of Gus Romano's timeline. He will be a genius."
She studies W. P. Brown thoughtfully, her face grave. "We must do what
is right, even when it requires sacrifice."

"I don't want to do it," he says.

"And yet you must," she says softly, taking his hand. "Trust in the Great
Unfolding. Everything is precisely as it should be."

"I know, but that doesn't make it any easier."

She stands up. "Take your time. I'll see you back at the house when
you're ready."

She turns and walks quickly away, back into the forest, her breath
shooting plumes of mist into the freezing air.

The edges of the scene buckle and fade, like film that's caught fire, and
the last thing I see is W. P. Brown with his head in his hands as the world
turns to black around him.

25

I wake confused, uncertain where I am. The viewing fades, and reality settles back around me. Every time I think I have W. P. Brown pinned down, he slides away from me again. Could he have known that I would see his conversation beside the loch? Did he fabricate the whole exchange for my benefit? I wouldn't put it past him.

But if he didn't know, does that mean I should take his doubts at face value? Who is Iris, and was he telling her the truth? I think about Amy's "powerful forces at work," and I wonder about this organization that W. P. Brown talked about. Is Iris part of it? Who's really pulling the strings?

I don't know why I'm having these embodied viewings, and I don't know if I can trust them. But if Brown truly didn't want to force me into this mission, if he blackmailed me under duress, maybe I can appeal to his better nature and persuade him to drop the threat on Amy.

Thursday's quiet in the shop, so I leave Molly to it and hang out at home. Every time I move, a fresh slice of pain reminds me I am not a stunt-bike rider. My battered body is a map of scrapes, cuts, and bruises.

I check the silver hunter almost constantly.

Friday's busy. I start work at 8:45 a.m., and there's so much to learn that my head is spinning by lunchtime. Molly finally sends me upstairs in the afternoon, after things have died down a bit, telling me she'll cash up and get everything ready for tomorrow. I don't argue.

I'm in the kitchen fixing myself a single-shot espresso when Dad calls.

"How are you feeling, son?" he asks.

"Not too bad," I say. "I'm a bit tired. It's hard work trying to remember everything."

"You need to take some time out," he says. "That's the reason I'm calling. I decided to keep our tee time."

"Our what?"

"Our tee time at the golf club!" he says.

"Oh. Right. But I don't know how to play."

"Muscle memory. It will come back to you."

"Maybe, but I don't know where my clubs are," I protest. "Do I even have clubs?"

"You do, but I will bring my spares, just in case. I'm not taking no for an answer. It will be nice to spend some time together."

I recognize that tone. As a kid it usually meant pain or trouble. Now, it makes me glow inside. I feel a lump in my throat at the thought of spending the day together, father and son.

"OK, Dad, let's do it," I say.

"That's my boy," he says, cheerily. "Tee off at two p.m. tomorrow. Broadway Golf Club. Don't be late."

It's hard to equate this positive, energetic person with the man who brought an end to his own life in my prior timeline. I wonder, if he'd stuck around, whether he might eventually have managed to find some joy in his life, even without Amy. Which reminds me that I need to get to the bottom of what he meant when he said Amy might slip into one of her episodes. That's a conversation for when we're face-to-face though.

We say our goodbyes, then I head to the study and sink into my comfortable leather club chair. As often happens when I'm left alone with my own thoughts, Alexia pops into my head. I reflect on my conversation with her the other day in the shop. She dropped the bombshell that she and Other Joe had had some kind of relationship. When we were rudely interrupted by Chloe's bullish boyfriend, I didn't have a chance to find out any more about what went on, but it occurs to me that Facebook might shed some light on things. My old life was too dark to broadcast on Facebook, but that's not why I've avoided logging in so far. I feel like a voyeur, but I can't keep putting it off.

I fire up the laptop, log in with a prefilled password, and get immediate access to Other Joe's online life. I steady myself before scrolling through his timeline. There are messages from friends in the USA, South America, South Africa, and Australia; endless photos of smiling people at festivals and parties; raucous snippets of video shared by members of his rugby team; posh events and awards ceremonies. I can't tell if he's presenting the awards or receiving them, but in every one, he's wearing a dark suit and shiny shoes, with slicked-back hair and a toothpaste smile.

Many people have wished me well after hearing about the accident. Some are genuinely kind, but others—mostly from the rugby gang—are loaded with gleeful schadenfreude, photos of horrific bike accidents down precipitous mountain slopes, alongside laughing emojis. I feel overwhelmed. How does a person handle so much interaction?

Other Joe comes across as a confident, happy, fun-loving person with a great sense of humor. Peering straight into his profile picture's eyes, I try to see into his soul, but he doesn't let me in. Or maybe, on-screen everyone is skin-deep. Alexia implied that he skated across the surface of life, but if there's one thing I know for sure, it's that the easy stuff doesn't shape who we are. It's the hard stuff, the stuff that smashes us into a million pieces, that forces us to dig deep to put ourselves back together.

I scan down his list of friends until I find Alexia. Her profile features various shots of herself, smiling, hanging out with friends, out on dog walks with Jack. One photo from a couple of weeks ago is some kind of social gathering. She's with Gordon, her "knight in shining armor." She thinks he's just helping her out, but I think he's moving in on her.

Then I find the chats between Other Joe and Alexia.

I scan through them. The conversation began about six months ago. Other Joe invited Alexia out for a drink after one of the residents' meetings, and it must have gone well, because over the next few weeks there are regular messages and invitations. I scroll to the last few messages to see if I can shed some light on why things came to an end.

109 days ago:

Hey. Really enjoyed dinner. I've got a charity bash at the town hall next Thursday. Fancy it? 8 p.m., black tie. Let me know.

Thanks, I'd like that. Let me know what time.

I'll pick you up at 7:45 p.m.

92 days ago:

Joseph, I was very clear with you. I don't want to see you again, and I need to ask you to maintain the boundaries we agreed. I know you might find this difficult to hear, but please respect my wishes.

After that, nothing. Why did they split up? I'm the first one to say people shouldn't jump to conclusions, but I think it's pretty obvious from my experience with Chloe and her boyfriend's visit to my shop that Other Joe cheated on Alexia. What a bloody idiot!

Then I see a photograph. Alexia and Other Joe at a wedding. She's wearing some very distinctive earrings. Silver butterflies. I have one of them in my bedroom. It wanted to tell me something, and I ignored it.

Time to find out what it was.

I head to the bedroom and find the earring. I lie back on the bed and close my eyes, the earring in the palm of my left hand. In my mind's eye, the butterfly quivers, then takes off and flutters upward into the evening sky. Mesmerized by its beating wings, I follow it through wispy clouds laced with pink and gold, and then gently down again toward a grand, stately home, straight out of a Jane Austen novel. The facade is designed like a Greek temple, and the butterfly draws me through the air, weaving between the sandstone columns, through huge oak doors, and into a vast entrance hall. The little creature flies on, along airy corridors lined with shields and oil paintings. Distant music and laughter grow louder, until we pass through another doorway into an immense hall.

The butterfly hovers, as if getting its bearings. The room is packed with round tables set with fancy flower arrangements, wine bottles, glasses, cups, and saucers. People drink and talk and laugh. At the far end of the room is a long rectangular table, where a bride and groom sip champagne and laugh.

I scan for people I recognize, and my heart skips a beat when I see Alexia. She's walking purposefully, a silk shawl loose around her shoulders, and as she moves, the subtle sheen of her dark-green dress glimmers in the evening light. The butterfly dips toward her, grazing the top of her head. For one breathtaking moment, I think I'm about to get a viewing from Alexia's point of view, but the butterfly carries on, drawing me toward the bar in the corner. Just as we reach a group of men drinking beer and brandy, the nearest one turns, and I see Other Joe's face staring back at me.

"No! I'm not ready for this!" I shout silently, but I'm powerless to stop it.

The butterfly leads me inexorably on until I am engulfed by Other Joe. His body is taut, energized, like a snake about to bite. He addresses the man next to him, a Prince William look-alike—tall, handsome, balding—in a three-piece brown tweed suit.

"I can't believe he's done it!" Joe says. "I never thought Andy would settle down, the old rogue. The three musketeers are no more, mate. Just you and me now." He rubs the back of his neck, staring at the floor, feeling bereft. Then he finds his mojo again. "You and me can still go out though, right?" He grins and waves his glass. "And we'll get Andy out on the town with us again, once the honeymoon period's over."

Prince William chuckles. "I gather there was a bit of pressure from his parents," he says. "You know what a stuffed shirt his dad is. He insisted Andy got married before he took over the business."

"Really?" Joe whistles and sips his brandy. "My dad would never pull a stunt like that on me. He knows I need my freedom."

"What about Alexia?" asks William. "You guys have been an item for a while now. How's it going with her?"

Joe puts down his glass. A young bridesmaid has caught his eye. She blushes prettily and whispers to one of her friends, then makes her way across the dance floor toward him. He drags his attention back to William.

"Alexia? Yeah, I guess it's been a few months," he says. "We're taking it easy though. It's not serious."

"Fair enough," says William. "By the way, I've been meaning to tell you, me and Daisy are moving in together."

"No way!" Joe claps him on the shoulder, but his stomach contracts. "Good luck! Make sure she knows who's wearing the trousers."

"I think she already knows it's her," William says good-naturedly.

The bridesmaid taps Joe on the shoulder. Her cheeks are pink with prosecco, and she can't be any more than twenty-five. "Hi," she says, twirling her blond hair. "I'm Helen. Do you want to dance?"

"Er, Joe," William murmurs.

Joe ignores him. "Hello, Helen," he says. "That's a very pretty dress." One of the straps has slipped down her arm, and he reaches out and lifts it back onto her shoulder, brushing her skin with his little finger. She giggles, batting her eyelashes.

"Joe?" He turns around. It's Alexia. "We need to talk," she says. "Can we go outside?" She doesn't wait for an answer. Joe follows her across the room toward a huge pair of French windows, planning what he's going to say and admiring the sway of her hips. She leads him through the tall glass doors and out to a large balcony flanked by a low stone wall. It feels like summer, the air warm and humid, but there's a keen breeze and tall billowing clouds on the horizon.

"I was only talking to her," Joe begins, anticipating Alexia's attack.

"Isn't she a bit young for you? But anyway, this isn't about her. You've been ignoring me, Joe. It's not really fair to bring me here and then ditch me."

"I haven't ditched you," he protests. "And you do know people. You know Lola and Mikey. We met them at the golf club. I just didn't think you'd want me hanging around your neck all day, cramping your style."

"Wow." She looks bewildered. "Spending time with each other isn't supposed to feel like that." One of her earrings has worked itself loose, and she pushes it back into her ear.

Joe suspects that whatever he says will be wrong. His shirt feels tight around his chest. He rolls his shoulders.

Alexia walks over to the French doors and closes them, shutting out the noise of the party inside, then turns back toward him. "I really didn't want to have this conversation tonight, Joe, but I can't figure you out. Do you actually want this to work? You and me?"

"Of course," he says. "I love hanging out with you." He rubs his chin. "But . . ."

"But?"

Joe folds his arms. "I feel like we're getting too close."

Alexia raises her eyebrows. "You think we're getting *too close*?" She laughs incredulously. "What's the point of having a relationship if we're not going to get closer?"

Joe leans his arms on the parapet and peruses the lake. Swallows swoop and dive in the evening light. "I feel like you're forever trying to analyze me," he says. "I'm not one of your clients, Alexia."

"I know you're not." She walks over to him and takes one of his hands. "I just want to get to know you properly, Joe. The real you."

He stands up and takes his hand back. "You do know me though," he says. "What you see is what you get. There are no hidden depths. I just want to have a laugh. We have fun together, don't we?" He undoes his tie and shoves it in one of his pockets.

Alexia leans back against the parapet and folds her arms. "Fun?" she says, coolly. "Is that all I am to you?"

"You're gorgeous," he says, "and you're brilliant company. I just don't want anything serious right now."

"Listen to yourself! You sound like a teenager," she says. "We're not kids, Joe! We're in our thirties. You're still going to nightclubs, for goodness' sake!" She takes a deep breath, holds it, and exhales. "Sorry," she says. "But what about all the wining and dining, the midnight calls, the promises? Did you mean any of it? Or was it all just words to get me into bed?"

"Of course I meant it," Joe says uncomfortably. "I'm not saying I don't want to see you."

"What exactly *are* you saying then?"

"We can still date if you want to, Alexia. I just think it's best if we don't get too . . . you know, attached."

Alexia nods. "I see. And while we're 'unattached,' are you planning to date other people?"

"I didn't say that."

"But are you?"

"I guess. I mean, we both could, if that's what you want."

"No. That isn't what I want." Her voice wobbles.

"You're angry," Joe says flatly.

"No, I'm upset! You persuaded me to go out with you in the first place. You showered me with attention, gifts, messages . . . I'm upset because I allowed myself to believe this might be real."

"It is."

"No, Joe. It isn't." She shakes her head. "I would never have started seeing you if I thought this was the plan."

"There you go again," he says.

"What do you mean?"

"You always have to complicate things. Why does there need to be a plan?" His mobile phone starts to ring. He pulls it out and looks at the screen. It's Becky, from the gym. He wants to talk to her, but it'll have to wait.

Alexia senses his guilt. "Oh God, Joe, have you been seeing other people *while* we've been together?"

"Why are you taking this stance?" Joe says, deciding that attack is the best form of defense. "We've been doing just fine, but you're turning into a crazy woman."

A single tear rolls down Alexia's cheek. "I can't believe this. And at a wedding."

"Alexia, come on." Joe feels bad. He didn't mean to hurt her.

She stands up straight and composes herself. "You know what, you're right. I have been trying to make this into something it isn't. I want you to be someone you aren't. I must've been mad." She wraps her shawl tighter around herself. "I'm looking for substance, and it's obvious you can't give that to me. I think we're done."

She turns and walks back toward the French doors.

"So that's that, is it?" Joe calls after her, feeling an unfamiliar fluttering in his chest, like a trapped bird.

Alexia turns back to face him, calm now. "Listen to me very carefully, Joe. This is over. I wish it had never started. I really thought . . ." She shakes her head. "Do not call or email me, and definitely do not come to the office. If you need to get in touch with me about the lease, get one of your staff to do it. Goodbye, Joe. Good luck with the rest of your life."

She stalks through the doorway and back into the dining hall.

Joe turns back to the lake and sighs deeply. He's not sure exactly how he feels. He's sorry, and he'll miss her, but there's also relief. He shrugs. "So bloody dramatic," he says to himself. "I can do without that." As he turns to go, something glints near his foot. He reaches down to pick it up, examines it closely, and when he realizes it's one of Alexia's earrings, he puts it in his pocket and goes back inside.

26

"You idiot!"

I sit bolt upright in bed, trying to work out who's shouting. When I discover it's me, I carry on.

"You blockhead. You imbecile. You utter moron! What were you thinking?"

I stalk around the bedroom, raging at my previous self.

"I hope you realized afterward what a total arse you made of yourself. I've been trying really hard not to judge you for all your womanizing and partying, but I can't forgive you for the way you treated Alexia. Do you have any idea how amazing that woman is?"

The butterfly earring lies near the pillow. I reach over and pick it up, desperate to feel close to Alexia again.

When I've expelled the worst of my anger, I sit back down on the bed. Although Amy insists that Other Joe and I are the same person, it hasn't felt that way to me, and the viewing has made it even more obvious. Other Joe's body felt alien. His thoughts were distorted and unfamiliar. Never mind our identical genes—the things that happened to us after the age of fourteen clearly turned us into different people.

I'd started to form preconceptions about Other Joe, and some of them have been confirmed. He comes across as an enviably popular, confident man with plenty of friends, someone who thrived on social connection. As I recall his playfulness and camaraderie at the wedding, hazy memories push to the surface, scenes from my early teenage years, before we lost Amy. I wasn't that great at school, academically, but I eventually found my place as the class joker. I remember the buzz of being the center of attention, the energy I got from an appreciative audience of giggling faces. That clown died the day we lost Amy, but I don't need to ask, *What if she'd lived?* It's right here in front of me.

Other Joe and I are like an impossible, unethical science experiment. Step one: take an average boy and clone him. Step two: give the first clone a happy, privileged life with plenty of money, and give the other one a shocking tragedy that destroys his family. Step three: watch the first one blossom and the second one shrivel up.

That all sounds very neat, but is it *true*?

I go into the bathroom and stare at myself in the mirror, faced with an uncomfortable reality. Despite the torment, losing Amy also had a beneficial impact on me. Through losing my sister, I learned to dive into my emotions, while my alter ego was still splashing around on the surface.

"I'm starting to understand," I say aloud to the man in the mirror, and I feel genuine compassion for him. "You didn't know what you were missing. You pursued Alexia, you wooed her, you drew her in. But once you had her, you didn't know what to do with her, did you? She was too much for you. And I bet you couldn't cope when she dumped you either. I imagine you continued to chase her, and your other women, and Alexia had to force you to agree that you'd leave her alone.

"But why did you keep the earring?"

My face stares back at me.

"Joe?"

I liked her. I didn't want things to end. I wanted to keep something of her near me.

There he is. There we are. There's the bridge between us.

"I understand," I tell him. "I'm going to try and get her back. For both of us."

I change into what I hope is acceptable attire for golf, but also not a total embarrassment to wear across town. I head down to the shop to let Molly know I'm going to be out for a while.

"Ah, Mr. Bridgeman!" she exclaims as I appear. "Just in time! I wonder if you could help me with this gentleman. He's brought in a box of 'trinkets,' as he says, and I'd like your opinion."

"So sorry, Molly—sir—but I have an urgent appointment. Molly, I'm sure you can handle it." I head for the door.

"Are you coming back?" she asks.

"Not until later on. Hopefully, see you Monday. Enjoy your day off tomorrow."

"Hopefully?" she asks. She doesn't miss a single thing.

"Definitely," I say.

I'm almost out of the shop when my subconscious urges me to stop. I pause and turn back. The customer standing with Molly at the desk is a tall elderly gentleman with a striking head of fine white hair. Older folks in Cheltenham seem to purchase all their clothes from the Beige Shop, but he's wearing an orange sweater and brown corduroy slacks.

He smiles. "Hello, Mr. Bridgeman."

For a second I'm convinced I see recognition in his cool gray eyes, but if it was there, it fades quickly. He does seem familiar, though. I consider telling him about my amnesia and asking how we're acquainted, but he's probably just a regular customer. He regards me with a quizzical expression. I don't want to freak him out, so I just ask, "How are you today?"

"Oh, I'm rather creaky, but I'm still alive," he announces jovially, "and I've made a special trip today to bring you these."

Molly jumps back in. "Mr. Bridgeman, as I was saying, I wonder if you could go through these and see if there's anything you want take in." She indicates two shoeboxes. The smaller one is open and contains books and black-and-white photographs in old frames. The larger one is unopened. On the desk next to it is a collection of keys.

This kind of thing happens more often that you might think. People bring boxes full of old things into the shop and presume we want them just because they're old. Sometimes you find an absolute gem, but if you take something in and it doesn't sell, it becomes junk that you have to get rid of. So you have to be discerning. Today, though, I don't have time, so I decide to make an exception. "Let's take it all. I can go through it later."

Molly looks concerned. "But if you haven't seen it, how will you price it?"

For the hundredth time since my eviction of Other Joe, I feel sorry for Molly. I'm clearly more relaxed about the shop than he was, and she's finding it hard to adjust. I smile at the customer. He has a good energy, and I can't shake the feeling that I've met him before. "Why don't you tell us what you think is reasonable?"

"That sounds more than fair," he says gratefully. "They've been in a box in my spare room for months, but something told me today was the day. Some of the items have sentimental value but . . . we can't take it with us. It's time to let go of the past."

It's a nice idea. I hope that when I head back to the 1960s and my work is done, that I, too, will be able to let go of the past. But for now, my thoughts are well and truly in the present, specifically on a golf date with my dad.

27

An icy wind nips at my neck. I tug at the zipper on my jacket, but it's already done all the way up. I rub my hands, cup them together, and blow, trying to instill life in my frozen digits, hoping that Dad didn't see.

"Do you want to borrow my scarf?" he calls. "That breeze is going to make things interesting this afternoon."

We're at Broadway Golf Club. It's 2:30 p.m., and we're at the first hole. The winter sun casts pale-yellow light, and the view of the distant Welsh mountains is breathtaking.

Dad lines up his shot, takes a few trial swings, and then adjusts his position slightly. I wait a few yards away, leaning back against a dry stone wall. He finally takes the shot, a satisfying *thwack*. I've never played golf in my life, but to me, he looks like a pro.

The ball flies through the air and down the fairway, landing not too far from the green. Dad harrumphs, but it's playful. He's clearly satisfied. "Could be heading for an eagle there, son, what do you reckon?" I don't know what an eagle is, so I just agree with him. He leans down and picks up the tee. "Not a bad way to start. Right, you're up."

"I can't remember how to play, Dad," I remind him, silently thanking the stars that there's no one else out here to watch me screw up.

"It's like riding a bike," he says. "It will come back to you."

"I'm not so sure." I pull a club out of the bag at random, take a ball out of my pocket, and head to the tee.

Dad frowns and hands me a different club with a bigger head. "Use this one," he says. "That one's an iron. You'll need it later."

I take the club and, on the third attempt, balance my golf ball on the tee. Standing up, I try to position myself like Dad did, sideways to the ball with my legs apart.

"Like this?" I ask, trying to recall the handful of times I've seen golf on the news.

"Looks good," Dad reassures me. "Take your time. It's all coming back to you. I'm sure it is."

Just as I'm about to swing, I hear voices behind me, and a group of a dozen or so people appear around the wall, led by a smartly dressed woman in a red sweater, pink trousers, and pristine white lace-up golf shoes. As soon as she sees me, she stops dead and holds out both arms to stop the people behind her.

"Hold up, ladies and gents," she announces. "Just a moment while Tiger here takes his shot." She turns back to me and winks. "Terribly sorry, Joseph. We'll wait here until you're done."

Everyone looks at me expectantly. I imagine Other Joe in a diamond-patterned sweater, spotless slacks, and a golf cap, effortlessly swinging his way around the course. Then I consider throwing the club to the ground and running for it.

Dad's impatient voice interrupts my thoughts. "Come on, son, don't keep everyone waiting. It's not good form."

There's nothing for it. I take a deep breath, raise the club high, and swing it with confidence. My club makes contact, and I feel the power of the follow-through.

I wait for the awestruck gasps and warm applause, but there's silence.

I open my eyes and see that the ball is exactly where I left it. Right next to a brown hole the size of my fist.

I grimace at the lady in red. She shrugs and smiles awkwardly. The gaggle of onlookers appears confused. I adjust my stance, take a second swing, and gouge another clump out of the turf.

Dad clears his throat. "Seems you might need a bit of practice after all," he says gruffly. "How about you caddy for me? We'll just do nine holes, then head to the club."

Just over an hour later, I follow Dad into the warm clubhouse. The foyer is bright and airy, with views over the course. The walls are decorated with photos of club members in action or proudly holding up trophies.

We find a quiet table in the bar and order a couple of pints of real ale. "I've told you before, son, and I'll tell you again," he says, "a lot of business gets done in this place. You ought to think about spending a bit more time here."

I'm suddenly overwhelmed with gratitude for the chance to get to know this happy and fulfilled version of my Dad, to have this extra time with him, however long we get. "I will," I say. "I'll think about it."

He sips his pint. "When's your next checkup?"

"In a couple of weeks," I say vaguely. I give it five seconds until he mentions Dr. Sharma again.

"At first, I thought you'd just had a bit of a knock, and you might be off your game for a week or two, but I realize this is going to take a while. I just want you to know I'll support you in whatever way I can. In fact, I've decided to delay my retirement. Just for a while."

I had guessed this was coming. It upsets me to think that by replacing Other Joe, I'm having a major impact on his life. "Dad. Please don't change your plans just because I've bumped my head. I'm fine, really I am. I can cope."

"This isn't a discussion," he says, gently but firmly. "I've made up my mind. I'm not saying forever, just for a while. And listen, if you still feel you want to cancel that hotel deal, then of course I'll support your decision."

That takes me by surprise. "You will?"

"I'm concerned about your mental health. You've had a nasty accident, and you've got a lot to cope with. The last thing you need is more pressure. I want you to take things at your own pace and get up to speed again slowly. Take your time."

I wonder what's changed. Who's he talked to? What's he planning? I don't ask. "Can you let Martin know I definitely want to cancel then?"

"Of course, if that's what you want." He softens a little. "I know what you're like. You'll try and get through this on your own, but I'm here for you, and I'll do whatever it takes. And I'd happily pay for you to see Dr. Sharma, if you'll just think about it—you know, to help you get back on track." He pauses, waiting for me to respond. When I don't, he says, "I'm only trying to help."

"Thanks, Dad," I say, and I mean it. "You won't forget to talk to Martin?"

"I'm not the one with the head injury, son," he says. "I shan't forget. Also, I was thinking you could maybe spend a bit of time with your sister. I think she might be brewing up for another of her dark episodes." He pauses, picking at his fingernails. "But I don't need to worry you with all this, you've got enough on your plate."

"No, it's OK. I want you to talk to me."

"I'm not sure what you remember, or if I've ever told you this," he muses. "I think you know Amy and I have had our problems over the years. I have some regrets about my behavior toward her at times, but boy, she didn't make it easy." He takes a sip of beer and studies his glass. "I talk to someone now," he says quietly, as though admitting to some shocking crime. "Your mother suggested it. I refused for a long time, but she was right. As always."

"You mean a therapist?"

"Yes." He studies me, trying to assess my reaction.

"That's good, Dad. That's great. Has it helped?"

He considers this. "I didn't think it would, but it has. He is helping me to see that at least I didn't abandon her. Even though things were hard, I tried, and I kept trying. He says that's really what matters. The fact I stuck around."

I feel a flare of anger. In my previous timeline, Dad wasn't there for me. He didn't stick around. I shake it off though, because he's facing his feelings about Amy, and I'm proud of him.

"Your therapist is right, Dad. You just have to be there, even if you get it wrong. You're doing it now, actually."

"How do you mean?"

"For me. With everything else going on, the last thing you need is a son who can't remember most of his life. You can't fix me, but you don't have to. You're here. In the end, that's what matters."

After our beers, Dad offers me a lift home, but I explain that I want to walk. It feels good, and I let my mind wander as I meander my way across Cheltenham.

My thoughts are interrupted by a beep from my pocket watch. I pull it out from my shirt and check the display. The three jump dials spin like some kind of ominous one-armed bandit, then they settle, informing me of my fate.

0 Days 7 Hours 5 Minutes

A single red dot appears at the base of the watch, a ruby crystal glowing like fire. A line of text beneath it reads, *Final Jump*. This will be my last chance to save Lucy, and all I hold dear. Watch out, 1960-something. Here I come.

I call Vinny.

"Yo, Cash!"

"Hi, Vinny. How's the knee?"

"Size of a football and hurts like hell, but I'll live. Hey, any travel news?"

"That's why I'm calling. The watch just updated. I'm off tonight. Final jump."

"What time?"

I do some quick calculations. "I'm heading off just after eleven p.m."

"Right," says Vinny. "So this is it?"

"Yeah. Listen, Vinny, I know you'd come with me if you could, but just knowing you're there means the world to me. Really, I couldn't do this without you."

He sniffs. "Well . . . all right then. But listen, I thought it would save time when you land if we get you kitted out before you travel. I've found just the place."

He tells me where to meet him, and I assure him I'm on my way.

Way Back When is a vintage clothing shop. Vinny tells the owner—a fiftysomething hippie with flowers in her bleach-blond hair—that we're off to a fancy-dress party. "You need some more old-fashioned gear," he says to me. "And I know I'm staying home alone, but I'm going to dress up too."

We get decked out for the sixties.

Vinny squeezes himself into a cream double-breasted suit, blue polka-dot shirt, and suede desert boots. Wendy scans him head to toe, her expression serious, and then adds a matching blue handkerchief. For me, she picks out a black turtleneck, dark-blue velvet jacket, white jeans, and winkle picker boots.

"Well," Wendy says, her voice deepened by years of dedicated smoking, "you two certainly look the part!"

She's right, but it's another reminder I'm traveling solo this time. Wendy bags my clothes. Vinny keeps his on. We pay and head outside. I check the time. It's 6 p.m.

"How long've you got?" Vinny asks.

"Five hours."

"Right, next stop, my place. There's something I want you to see!"

Vinny's house normally looks like a horde of strangers broke in, had a house party, had a change of heart, tidied up for a bit, and then just partied again. This evening it's unrecognizable, organized to the point of immaculate. In the lounge the usual pictures and mirrors have been replaced by four large corkboards displaying photographs, newspaper clippings, and sticky notes. Some are pinned and connected with colored thread. It looks like Vinny is trying to catch a serial killer.

"The way I see it, Cash, we can't plan anything in real detail. But we can do our best to prepare, like good little Boy Scouts." He holds up three fingers in a Scout salute. "I've done a ton of research, laid it all out for you. This is how we work going forward . . . well, back. Anyway, I'll organize things behind the scenes."

"This is amazing, Vin, thanks."

"No problemo." He walks proudly to a shelf crammed with DVD box sets: *The X-Files*, *Star Trek*, *Friends*—all neatly ordered by season. On another row: *Street Hawk*, *The A-Team*, *Knight Rider*, and an extensive *Doctor Who* collection. Vinny glides his finger along them affectionately, then turns to me. "They all have a sidekick, Cash." He taps his chest. "That's me, researching and helping the hero."

The corkboards display numerous photographs of Frankie Shaw throughout his life as a criminal, news articles with titles like "The Rise of the London Gangster," and even a few shots of Frankie in a prison cell. His dead eyes seem to taunt me across time. One photo, a book cover entitled

No Angel, displays Frankie's shaved head. He's lean, with his signature gold cross hanging on his bare chest.

"Mean-looking fella, isn't he? Thought he was special," Vinny says. "Believed he'd been singled out by God to select those who needed 'smiting.'"

"'Smiting?'"

"His word. And one of those people was his old ma," Vinny says gravely.

"His mum? What did he do to her?"

"Killed her."

"What? Why?"

"I watched a documentary about this," he explains. "Rita Shaw, she ran things in the background, a real tough old boot by all accounts." He points to her photograph. He isn't kidding. She looks like a Rottweiler in a blond wig. "Tommy was the head honcho originally, but after he fell into the coma, there was a leadership void. Rita knew Tommy could be out of action for a while and she decided she needed someone to take over the family business in his absence."

"Let me guess, she didn't choose Frankie."

"Right," Vinny says, "and that sent the ginger hand grenade into a frenzy."

"I can imagine. So how did he kill her?"

Vinny swallows loudly, rubbing at his neck. "He choked to her death."

"My God. How could he do that to his own mother?"

Vinny opens his laptop, pulls up a web page, and skims it. "In one of Frankie's confessions he talks about their final conversation. According to him, when he threatened her, she taunted him: 'You haven't got it in you.' I guess he wanted to prove her wrong. He snapped and he killed her."

I whistle through my teeth. "Frankie admitted all this?"

"Yep." Vinny nods. "When he realized he was going to spend the rest of his life behind bars, he doubled down on his religious beliefs and confessed to four murders, including that of his own mother." He winces. "Bit late for redemption though. He hanged himself in prison." He scrolls a bit further down the page and shows me a picture of a Woody Allen look-alike wearing thick glasses that make his eyeballs look huge. "This is a guy called Squint Daley. Squint was an electronics whiz, one of Frankie's regular crew. He's the reason Frankie got caught. A payroll scam got busted and Squint was arrested. He cracked under the pressure, told them everything he knew. Had to spend the rest of his life living under police protection."

Vinny clicks on a link and a photo of a newspaper clipping appears on-screen, with the title "Police Officer Murdered." I recognize the man in the picture. "I've met him. That's DI Price. He interviewed me after Lucy was shot."

Vinny tuts. "Poor old Price was murdered in 1965," he says, with a little too much glee. "People suspected Frankie, but it was never proven. Mr. Bloody Untouchable strikes again."

I stare at the doomed policeman, trying to remember that my one and only job is to save Lucy. That's it.

Suddenly, Vinny goes pale. "Hey, Cash. When we traveled, what was the date of our arrival, the day of that dance?"

"It's burned into my memory. Saturday, September 1, 1962."

"They found Frankie's mum on September third. Coroner said she'd been dead a couple of days."

"Those scratch marks on his forearms, when we were in the car with him," I murmur.

Vinny scrunches up his face. "Frankie must've killed his mum that morning." He gasps. "We were in the car with a murderer! Fresh from the crime scene!"

I recall how Frankie slowly rolled up his sleeves, displaying his wounds like recently won trophies in a cabinet. He scratched them until they bled.

"He's a bad man, all right," I say, feeling a little queasy. "I think I've seen enough now."

"Yeah, me too." Vinny closes the laptop and takes a hefty slug of Coke from a half-empty bottle nearby. I feel sorry for the incredible machine that is Vinny's body. He gives it a lot to do.

I glance up at the cork incident board nearest to me, and one of Vinny's printouts catches my eye. The title reads "Knightsbridge Robbers Still At Large."

"What's that one, mate?" I ask, pointing at it.

"Oh, you can probably ignore that. I was just collating major events and stuff I thought might be useful. That's an article about a massive robbery that was never solved. Why?"

I untack the clipping from the board and scan the text. There's also a map of the location . . . and a photograph of a house with a bright-red door and a brass knocker in the shape of a lion's head. I turn to Vinny. "That looks like the house that Tommy lured Lucy to." I hold up the article, not quite believing it. "This is the house from my viewing, no question."

"Holy cashmolee!" Vinny's face lights up. "That's the Knightsbridge heist. Are you seriously telling me that Frankie Shaw could be behind the biggest unsolved crime in British history?"

"I don't know," I tell him, "but it's too much of a coincidence, isn't it?"

Vinny raises a finger. "Right, hold that thought." He bangs away at an ancient-looking laptop with an alien on the cover. As he surfs through news articles and photographs, I see Barclays Bank, then police officers and cordons around a house, *the* house. "Here," Vinny says, pointing and smudging the screen. "Thieves spent months digging the tunnel across Brompton Road. The tunnel was constructed professionally, stabilized with beams and supports. Forty-five meters long. They blasted through a concrete wall and then hit the vault and security boxes. The heist was legendary, bigger than the Great Train Robbery, and unsolved . . . until now."

A headline jumps out at me: "The Knightsbridge Ghosts." "Why did they call them ghosts?" I ask.

"Because they never caught them," Vinny says. "Didn't even have one single decent lead." He clicks another image: writing sprayed onto a wall next to hundreds of safety deposit boxes, all wrenched open.

YOU WILL NEVER CATCH ME

"He was a cocky so-and-so, wasn't he," Vinny says. "It's claimed that some of the security boxes contained—how should I put this?—*compro-mising* material."

"Photographs?"

"Proper kinky stuff featuring a member of the British royal family, as well as a few politicians." He shrugs. "All rumors of course . . . but clearly true." Vinny attacks the keyboard and brings up a new page. "Four days after the robbery, a D-notice was issued," he reads aloud.

"What's a D-notice?"

Vinny turns around, beaming like a cartoon cat. "I'm glad you asked, Joseph. All media channels, newspapers, and reporters were told to discontinue coverage of the heist." He shakes his head, then fixes me with a serious gaze. "This is government-level stuff. They only pull this kind of thing for reasons of national security."

"So our mate Frankie robbed a bank and got more than he bargained for."

Vinny whistles through his teeth. "This is how he became Mr. Untouchable. Those photos were leverage, and they put Frankie well and truly in charge. He killed his mum and then Lucy, but that was just the beginning. Once he had those photos, he knew the police couldn't touch him. It all makes sense now." He clicks another link. "Oh, and there's this too."

A headline reads "Choking Fog Consumes Britain." Beneath it are images of people in masks and vehicles cloaked in gloom. Another clipping reads "Thick Yellow Smog Brings Capital to a Standstill."

"Smog?"

"Yep. December 4, 1962. The night of the robbery. They reckon this was another reason the robbers got away with it. It says here that coal fires and cold weather created a blanket of dense smog. Visibility was zero. It went on for days."

The hairs on the back of my neck stand up as Amy's prophecy comes back to me. Both times, she mentioned fog, said things were unclear. She also mentioned a church with a broken window. "Can I have a look?" I take the laptop from Vinny and scan the page, clicking on various links. Nowhere do I find mention of a church, but this has got to be the night Amy was talking about. I wonder if I should tell Vinny about Amy's visions, but I know that if I do, I'll end up telling him about her certainty that someone's going to die, and all that will do is worry him. I decide to say nothing and hand back the computer.

Vinny's voice interrupts my thoughts. "I was just thinking, maybe if you land before the robbery, you can tell the police what's going on, and they can catch Frankie red-handed."

"It's a good idea," I agree. "Bad guys get caught, no one dies."

"The future is in the past," Vinny says conspiratorially, "and it's waiting to be rewritten." He says this like it's the last line in a trailer for a movie he's really looking forward to, then belches loudly. "Right then, are you ready?"

"I'm scared," I admit, pushing my hands into my pockets so he doesn't see them shaking. "I think I'm a coward."

He pats my arm. "You're confusing cowardice with fear, Cash. If you're afraid but you do what you have to do anyway, that's courage."

I feel some of the weight lift from my shoulders. "What would I do without you, Vinny?"

I'm about to find out.

28

It's 9 p.m. The sky is totally black. It's cold, but at least it's stopped raining. I head toward home, feeling anxious, carrying my sixties outfit in a paper bag. I check my pocket watch: just over two hours until I leave for the past.

For some reason, instead of heading directly home, I take a slight detour. In the distance I see a golden glow, like Vegas appearing out of the desert. It's a restaurant, its front windows bright like candles inside a doll's house. I feel drawn to it. As I near the entrance, I hear the sounds of glasses clinking and vibrant chatter. The smell of coffee and hot food is a tempting prospect, but I decide against it. I can't shake the feeling it might end up being my last supper. But then, my instincts take over, filling me with primal energy that sets my skin dancing and my head buzzing. I had a similar feeling in London, when Vinny and I lost sight of Frankie's car and I needed to choose which road to take. It isn't déjà vu, although it has a similar intensity. It's more a sense of certainty, of the world being right and the whole game of life being a shoo-in, if only I could just play along.

The feeling fades quickly when I see a man in a long coat and trilby hat standing outside the restaurant. He raises a hand in a relaxed gesture that suggests he is expecting me.

It's W. P. Brown.

In many ways, he's the last person I want to see tonight, so close to my final jump. However, my viewing of his conversation beside the loch means I now have inside knowledge. I know he's ashamed of stooping to blackmail. I know he didn't want to do it. That doesn't mean he's off the hook, but if I can leverage that shame, then I think there's a chance I can persuade him to leave Amy alone, even if I fail the mission. It's worth a shot, but I don't want to reveal my hand too soon. First, I'm going to find out what he has to say.

"Joseph," he calls out.

I walk slowly toward him. "Well, I must say, your timing is impeccable as always."

"I don't have a choice when I am guided to you."

"If you've come here tonight to give me the speech, I don't need it," I tell him. "I'm invested now, OK? Lucy is innocent, and I couldn't turn my back on her even if I wanted to."

"That's good to hear," he says in the tone of a concerned friend. "How are you?"

I scowl at him. "What do you want?"

"I'm here to help you, if I can." He removes his trilby and studies me with thoughtful eyes. "Would you allow me to buy you a drink?"

"I don't think so," I tell him coolly, despite the fact that I have every intention of going into the restaurant with him. I twist the knife. "It wouldn't feel right, drinking with the enemy."

He nods understandingly. "I have some information that may help you when you arrive in London. All I ask is ten minutes of your time."

"*All* you ask?"

He doesn't rise to my attitude. "I can only imagine what you must think of me, but you and I want the same outcome." He gestures to the door of the restaurant. "Shall we?"

I'm tired and the coffee smells good. "OK. Ten minutes, then I'm gone."

The restaurant is Italian, a one-off. It looks expensive. Brown asks to be seated away from the other diners. We follow our waiter to a small table next to a window, where we can talk freely without being overheard. I gaze around at the patrons, living their lives, unaware that a couple of time travelers just walked in. We order double espressos.

I sit opposite W. P. Brown, arms folded, waiting for him to speak. He offers me a faint smile, deepening the crow's feet around his temples. "How have you been?"

His concern feels confusingly genuine, but I need to stay alert. I will not be lulled into small talk. "Well, let's see. Since I saw you last, I've been back to the sixties again. This time I was involved in a motorcycle accident, which put my best friend in the hospital, by the way. There are some seriously nasty people on this mission of yours, and the more I find out about them, the more I dislike you."

"I'm sorry your friend got hurt," he says.

"I'm sorry I ever saw your face," I bite back. He doesn't react. "Anyway, you said you had some information that might help me?"

He clears his throat. "I know you are due to travel again tonight. Our data suggests you will arrive on the evening of December 4, 1962."

After all the research Vinny has done, this particular date is baked into my brain. December 4, 1962, is the evening of the Knightsbridge heist. There is a certain symmetry to the fact this will be the destination of my final jump, but as I imagine London, wrapped in a blanket of smog, I shudder.

My anger simmers just below the surface. "If you knew the date of my arrival, why didn't you tell me before? I could have planned better."

The time traveler nods patiently. "We didn't know. It's the observer's effect. Each time you travel, you disrupt the past, like a pebble on a pond. The ripples give us information, feedback that can be interpreted."

I stare at him, frustrated by the fact that what he says is often interesting. The waiter delivers our coffee. I take a sip, hot and bitter.

W. P. Brown drops a lump of sugar into his cup and stirs. "You already have many of the skills required to complete this mission successfully, but I wanted to give you some advice before you travel."

I place my elbows on the table and interlace my fingers. "I'm sorry, but I'm still finding it hard to take advice from the man who's blackmailing me."

"That's understandable," he says, "but use your gift, trust your instincts. You have powerful intuition, and it will become even more sensitive when you are in the past."

"How can you know that? You don't know me."

"I know that you're a time traveler, and the two go hand in hand. I have never taught anyone that doesn't have this intuition." His watery blue eyes drift away for a moment, then snap back to me. "On your way here, did you sense anything before you arrived at the restaurant?"

I consider the question. I did feel drawn here, but do I tell him? My watch hangs heavy around my neck, reminding me that I will be traveling back in time in less than two hours. I tell my head to be quiet for a moment and listen to my gut. It tells me to go with the conversation. "Actually, I did feel something," I say. "As I was walking through town, I took a detour without a good reason, and when I arrived here, at the restaurant, it felt like I was . . . supposed to be here, I guess."

He nods, as though this is perfectly normal. "That is your intuition at work. My students often ask if this is fate or destiny, but I prefer to describe it as *subtle serendipity*."

He holds my gaze, and I get a strong sense that he's wearing a mask, one that I have seen behind. He continues, "Time is trying to help us. It wants us to do its work and it will often nudge us in the right direction, steer us back on track. As a traveler, it's a case of tuning in and learning to trust your instincts. I have complete faith in your abilities, Joe, but if you are to save Lucy Romano, you must embrace these feelings of intuition. They are critically important. Trust them above all else."

He seems pleased, relieved even, as though this mumbo jumbo was weighing heavy on his mind, and now that it's poured out of him, he feels lighter. He takes a sip of his coffee, and I decide it's time to make my move.

"Actually, I want to talk to you about what happens when this is over." I need to tread carefully here because I know from experience that people don't like it when you know their secrets. If I'm going to get him to agree to leave Amy alone, then I need to appeal to the regretful man I viewed at the loch.

He puts his cup down and sits back in his chair, waiting.

I lean in, unblinking, my voice strong and calm. "If I fail, and I don't make it back, I want you to leave Amy's timeline alone."

He dabs at his mouth with a napkin. "We've talked about this, and I've been very clear. If you fail, your sister's timeline will be reset."

I wait, hoping for a glimmer of the man beneath the mask, but there's nothing. He is resolute. "You *say* that's what you'll do, and you're very convincing, but I don't think you'll go through with it." I offer him a triumphant smile. "In fact, I *know* you won't."

His right eye twitches involuntarily.

"Your heart isn't in this whole blackmail thing," I press, "is it?"

"Joseph, I was clear with you at the fair . . . that unless you—"

"Just stop," I say firmly. "I had a viewing, Mr. Brown. I saw you. The *real* you."

I let that sit between us, forcing myself to embrace the discomfort. I need him to feel threatened. It isn't easy. I don't like to see people suffer. I conjure Amy's face into my mind. It helps.

"Can you tell me what you saw?" he says.

"I saw you sitting on a rock beside a loch. It was winter, snow everywhere. There was a woman there too."

He is silent for a moment. I have him on the ropes, and although my natural tendency is toward empathy, I need to take advantage of my position. "You see? You aren't the only one with secrets."

"I think perhaps you are confusing a dream with reality."

It's a confident move, but I'm prepared. "You said you were ashamed of blackmailing me, of threatening Amy's life. And the woman's name was Iris. She mentioned—what was it? Something about trusting how things are unfolding? I saw it all."

The color drains from Brown's face. It ages him, his cheeks sunken, his eyes hollow. He leans forward, as if to examine me more closely. "How could you *possibly* have seen this?"

"I get viewings often," I tell him.

"Viewings," he says quietly.

"It's what I call them."

"It's what we call them too." The ghost of a smile crosses his lips. "Viewings are always connected to focus objects though . . . Were you channeling through an object when this happened?"

"No, I wasn't," I tell him. "This is a new thing for me, but it seems that if I make an emotional connection with someone, it can spark a viewing. I don't need an object."

"Remarkable," he murmurs, a hint of excitement in his voice. "Truly remarkable." He stares at me in wonder.

I seize the advantage. "Whether I like it or not, you and I are connected now. It's how I know you don't want to do this."

Brown lowers his gaze, staring down at his hands.

"I remember something else about the viewing," I continue. "You said you were missing someone, someone you used to talk to a lot beside the loch. You were hoping for guidance from him. Whoever he was, I think he would tell you to do the right thing. You're not a blackmailer."

"Joseph, I can't promise anything," he insists. "There are powers at work here that are stronger than the will of men."

I feel a sense of mounting desperation. I had hoped he would be easier to persuade. "Look, I'll do whatever it takes to save Lucy and complete this mission. But please, will you leave my family out of this?"

He straightens his back and regains his composure. "If I am to have a hope of doing that, then you need to be completely honest with me."

I swallow my outrage at his hypocrisy. "I will try."

"I explained to you previously that the Romano mission was not destined for you. We would never have sent such an inexperienced traveler on such a challenging job, no matter how talented. My colleagues and I, we're still at a loss as to who might have placed the radio in your shop, and why. We're investigating, but so far we've found nothing conclusive. If you have viewed anything else, anything that you think might help, please tell me. Even if it appears small or inconsequential to you, it could be very important."

I consider my next move. This is my last chance to negotiate for Amy's safety. The more he knows I can see, the more powerful he'll think I am, and the more seriously he'll take me. I hope.

"I had a viewing of the person who planted the radio in my shop," I tell him. His eyes widen. "But it doesn't prove you aren't involved."

"But it's confirmation that we were right. It *was* a deliberate attack, on us and on you." His eyes sparkle, suddenly alive. "Can you describe the person you saw?"

I tell him everything I can remember: the break-in, the woman, the radio. He listens, processing this news, and when I'm done, he asks, "Are you sure it was a woman?"

I replay the scene in my mind, the way she moved, her frame, her hands. "Yes, I'm sure. It was a woman."

"And you say she had a case?"

"She used it to carry the radio."

"Can you describe it to me, please?"

"It was metal," I say. "It looked tough, like a flight case."

He nods. "That radio was in the case when it was stolen from us, from what we thought was a safe location." He takes a sip of coffee. "I appreciate that it was dark, but could you tell if she was wearing gloves?"

A piece of the puzzle drops into place. "She was, but she took them off when she handled the radio. So she can't have been a time traveler, otherwise if she had touched the radio, she would have become bonded instead of me. Right?"

"Very good," he says, with the proud intonation of a teacher. "Did you see anything else? Any other details?"

"I got the impression, when I caught her, that I wasn't supposed to see her," I tell him. "I was just supposed to go downstairs, discover the radio, and travel."

"Yes, that makes sense. She must have known that a primed object would be hard for you to resist. You were like a moth to a flame."

I think back on the radio, gleaming, playing that song. When I reached out to touch it, I thought I was trying to turn the volume down, but I wonder if he's right. I wonder if I really just wanted to connect with it. Another detail flickers up from my memory. "When she removed her gloves, I saw her hands. It might be nothing, but she had a small mark on the right one, a birthmark, I think . . . in the shape of a star."

"Of course! Why didn't I see this coming?" His attention drifts deep into his thoughts. He knits his fingers together and his knuckles whiten. "Her name is Scarlett. She was a time-travel student of mine for a while. I haven't seen or heard from her for some time."

"But you just said she couldn't be a traveler."

"Scarlett is gifted, but she's not like us," Brown clarifies. He frowns as he talks, clearly recalling some painful memory. "She doesn't travel in the same way. Her gifts are unique, but sadly, she couldn't accept the fact she was different."

In some ways, Scarlett feels like a distraction, but I decide to press on. "Why do you think she would do this to me? Did you fall out? Is she trying to get back at you somehow?"

"I don't know. It's a puzzle, but at least we have a lead now." He dabs his mouth with a napkin. "You said that you have viewings of people after you've formed an emotional connection with them. What do you think caused the connection between you and Scarlett?"

I finish my coffee too and lean back. "I've wondered that. I guess because I made eye contact with her in the shop. The situation was quite intense. She was as shocked as I was, I think."

"And that's all it took?" He shakes his head. "Your gift is exceptionally powerful." He pulls his pocket watch from his waistcoat and frowns. "I'm afraid I'm leaving soon."

I panic. He can't leave yet. "I've leveled with you. I've told you everything I know. Just promise me you'll leave Amy alone."

He glances around the restaurant and deftly slips his pocket watch into his waistcoat. "Let's talk outside."

He pays, and we leave. We walk for a few minutes in the chill of the winter night, until we're alone beneath the milky glow of a streetlight. The frigid air works its way into my bones.

W. P. Brown's skin takes on the translucent sheen of impending travel. He places his trilby on his head and adjusts it. "I'm sorry Joseph, about all of this. I wish it could have been different." He checks his watch again. I see a momentary flash of sadness in his eyes. "You will discover that the life of a time traveler is one of half-truths and lies. It seems to be the way of things."

The cold sinks further into me. "What are you saying?"

"It's too late to change the deal. I have no control over the decision to reset your sister's timeline." His voice sounds as though it's already leaving.

"But you said you hoped there would be a way to keep Amy out of this. You lied to me!"

"The organization I work for sees a bigger picture, and those wheels have been in motion since the very beginning. I'm sorry."

My anger threatens to boil over. I want to grab him and scream, but the last thing I need is to be dragged back to wherever this son of a bitch comes from. There are so many things I could say. Instead, I look him up and down, then turn and walk away. I will go into the past on my terms, head held high.

When I look back, he's gone.

29

I arrive home just after 10 p.m., an hour before I'm due to leave. I shower and get dressed in the clothes Vinny picked out for me, adding a thermal base layer and a thick leather jacket, a scarf, and a hat. Thinking about the smog, I rummage around in a few cupboards and find one of those white masks you get in hardware stores, ideal for sanding, DIY projects, and time traveling.

I spend the next hour writing letters: one each for Amy, Vinny, and my parents. I place them in my desk drawer. If I return, I will burn them. If I don't, someone will find them, and at least I will have said the things that matter to the people I love, given them closure. I know how important that can be.

When it comes to Alexia, a letter just isn't going to work. I imagine her thought process: *Fake amnesiac stalker who believed himself a time traveler now dead? Big deal.* She would probably just be relieved.

My phone shrieks, hacking at my already jangling nerves.

"Joe?" It's Amy. She sounds upset.

"What is it, what's wrong?"

She sniffs and clears her throat. "It happened again . . . I saw you."

"Another vision?"

"Yes. I don't know what it all means. It feels like I'm condoning what you're doing if I tell you, but I thought it might help."

"What did you see?"

"The car, the church, the stained glass window . . . but I saw more this time." Her voice takes on the silky quality that it does when she recounts her visions. "There is a beacon of light in the darkness," she says. "Trust it, follow it. It's the key to something important." She sighs. "Does any of that mean anything to you?"

"The night I'm due to land was foggy. Maybe that's why your visions have been unclear. The rest of it doesn't make any sense yet, but it might when I'm there. Thank you for telling me."

She doesn't say anything for a while, but I wait, and it comes. "I'm not sure I will ever forgive you for not being honest with me. This is awful, Joe, I'm worried sick."

"Try not to worry, Amy. I'll be OK."

"Just make sure you come back, so I can be cross with you."

I can't help but smile.

She hangs up, and I think about what she said. *A beacon of light in the darkness, the key to something important.* I sit in silence for a while, nasty ripples of fear flickering around in my stomach. I decide that if this is to be my last day, I deserve a drink, and it might as well be the good stuff.

Other Joe kept a well-stocked wine rack. I blow the dust from a champagne bottle, a Bollinger. "Oh well," I say with fake enthusiasm. "You can't take it with you." I grab it and head upstairs to the terrace, where I pop the cork, pour some fizz, and raise my glass. "To Other Joe," I say. "I'm going to honor your sacrifice and save Lucy so that W. P. Brown doesn't reset the timeline." I take a sip. It's good.

I raise my glass again. "Alexia," I say, "in a different world, you and I were good together." I pause, searching for the right words, but in the end, the simplest are the best. "I miss you," I tell her, "and I love you." I down the glass.

More toasts are in order. I assure Amy that I will do everything I can to keep her here, to continue this timeline. I promise to tell Vinny everything when I get back and to buy him lots of pies. He loves pies.

It seems fitting to include Lucy. "I will do everything in my power to prevent your murder, to give you a chance at life and time to raise your son." And I mean it, not only because I need to keep Amy safe. I *want* to help Lucy and Gus.

My final toast is to my parents. I keep it simple. I just hope to see them again.

I'm a bit drunk now. The Bollinger is *really, really* good.

And yet, this isn't right. I've forgotten something, an idea that has been stealthily circling at the edge of my understanding . . .

"You can't take it with you . . ." I murmur to myself. Where have I heard that recently? I rack my brains. Then I remember. It was that old chap in the shop the other day. He said the same thing when he brought in those boxes. I head downstairs and rummage through them. Among the various things inside is an old, slightly rusted key. It's a simple design, and although I only feel some faint psychometric energy coming from it, I put it in my pocket. W. P. Brown said that I must trust my instincts. I don't trust *him*, but the feeling that I've forgotten something has gone now. I'm ready.

Just then, I feel the watch buzz. It's time.

My destination: 1962, the night of the bank robbery.

My mission: ensure Lucy Romano lives and Amy's timeline remains untouched.

My choice of song: obvious. The Beatles. "Lucy in the Sky with Diamonds."

I blast the song out of the balcony speakers that Vinny installed, and the rich tones of the Fab Four sound better than ever.

I feel strangely calm. Being tipsy probably helps. Colors shimmer as I begin to shift out of the present. The phased vocals of the first verse finish, Ringo hammers his kit, and the chorus kicks in, perfect harmonies soaring. Lucy in the Sky with Diamonds.

I changed the past once. I can do it again.

"Screw you, Death," I say, loud and confident.

My body is weightless for a second, and then I feel the ground again.

I am alone. It's 1962. London is adrift, the night shrouded in a blanket of smog. Beneath my feet there's a rough cobblestone surface. Streetlights glow like silver moons over an enchanted moor. I cover my mouth against the smell of rotten eggs, so powerful I can taste it.

A single disc of light emerges from the gloom, like a huge boat drifting into view, plumes of smoke swelling from its bow. But it isn't a boat,
it's a double-decker bus, gliding through the treacherous smog, accompanied by a deep rumble and the shockingly loud wail of a horn. I dive
to my right as it thunders past, way too close. I land hard, banging my
elbow and shoulder, cursing my sluggish reflexes. I briefly glimpse the
passengers inside, all wearing masks, before the bus is swallowed by a
stinking blanket of fog.

I scramble to my feet and pull my mask over my face. Staring into the
frigid darkness, I gather my thoughts. My watch confirms that I've landed
on the night of the robbery, just as W. P. Brown told me I would. Local
time is 8:55 p.m.

0 Days 11 Hours 25 Minutes

The robbery was estimated to have taken place between 10 p.m. and
midnight, so I have enough time, but I'm not sure what to do next. I
decide I just need to get moving, find help, and somehow find my way
to Frankie Shaw. I work my way between streetlamps. Figures emerge
from the murky gloom, coughing and spluttering, all wearing some kind
of makeshift mask. Despite mine, I wheeze and cough, tasting an acrid
bitterness.

I continue moving, pausing occasionally to lift the mask and eject thick
phlegm that feels like glue. My hand traces along brickwork that feels greasy,
everywhere coated in thick slime. My eyes fill with burning tears. It's like
being stuck inside a house filled with charred plastic. I slide down a wall,
eyeballs on fire, light-headed.

I knew the smog would be bad, but I totally underestimated it. I need
a gas mask. I feel myself sinking deeper into self-pity and resignation,
overwhelmed with the impossibility of my task. Then, within this barren
stillness, I feel a draw, like magnetic attraction. With eyes pinched shut,
I crawl to a nearby bench, haul myself up, and begin to walk the streets
of London half-blind, unsure where to go, proceeding on gut feel alone.
Eventually, through the milky gloom, I see the most beautiful sight: a huge
solid silhouette topped with a pulsing red light that lashes at the smog like
a solar flare.

My salvation. A police box.

I remember Vinny pointing one out on our previous trip. Perhaps he was right after all, perhaps I am the Doctor!

Trust it. Follow it.

I'm coming for you, Frankie Shaw.

I desperately wipe my burning eyes and find a panel that reads For Public Use. I open it and lift the handset to my ear.

Nothing.

I tap the cradle urgently. It's dead . . . and so am I if I don't get out of this poisonous hell. I try the door. It's locked. I smack my palm against the cold police box in frustration. Then, I remember the key in my pocket.

The key to something important, something transformative.

No way.

With trembling hands, I place it against the lock. The key is a perfect fit and slides in easily. I twist, and the door opens. If I weren't nearly choking to death, I would cry out in joy. I step inside, close the door, and give in to a convulsing coughing fit. The air isn't clear in here, but compared to outside it tastes like a forest glade. Eventually, my coughing subsides, and I take in the interior of the police box.

It's well laid out, like the world's neatest miniature office. Every inch is utilized. The walls have mounted cabinets and three clipboards hang neatly in a row. On a wooden table is a rotary telephone, a notepad, and a stack of pencils. There's even a kettle and tea-making supplies. The coppers of the day had their priorities right.

I wipe my nose and eyes, which are still streaming. My fingers are covered in a thin, treacly coating. I grab the phone and hear a dial tone. It connects.

"Hello?" I say, voice desperate. "Can anyone hear me?"

A serious voice with a hint of a northern accent answers. "Limehouse Station. This is DI Price. Who is this?"

Detective Inspector Price, the man who interviews me six months from now. Talk about subtle serendipity.

If I succeed tonight, that interview will never happen.

"Hello?" he growls. "Is there anyone there?"

"I need to report a crime in progress."

"If you want to report a crime, I need a name." He sounds just as angry as the last time I met him.

"My name is Joseph Bridgeman," I say. "Please listen to me. This is urgent. I'm calling to report a bank robbery."

He sighs heavily. "You do understand that if you're wasting police time, it's a serious offense."

"I'm not wasting your time," I plead. "It's happening right now!"

DI Price sucks air through his teeth. "You are going to have to forgive me, but I'm not buying it. Stay indoors and stop wasting police time. I don't know if you've looked outside but—"

"Please," I insist, "you have a chance to catch Frankie Shaw tonight."

There's a long pause, and for a horrible moment, I think he may have hung up. "If I'm going to believe you, I need to know how you came by this information."

Now *that* is a good question.

One of the websites Vinny showed me discussed a known associate of Frankie's, a man who reminded me a bit of Woody Allen. He was famous for snitching on Frankie in a few years' time. He would make an authentic source of information, if I could just remember his name . . .

"Well?" DI Price demands.

I close my eyes and *will* the crook's name to the surface. "Squint Daley!" I exclaim. "He's my source, he's reliable . . . He told me where the robbery is happening. This is the big one, and if you ignore it, you'll wake up tomorrow, see the news, and spend the rest of your life knowing you could have caught Frankie Shaw."

I actually sound pretty convincing, probably because I'm telling the truth. I'm handing Price the potential for fame, respect, and a promotion. I just hope he takes the bait.

"Christ, I can't believe I'm saying this," DI Price says. "Stay there. I will come and pick you up myself."

"Thank you."

"Don't thank me," he growls, "just be right!"

The line dies. I check my watch; it's 9:40 p.m.

0 Days 10 Hours 40 Minutes
Plenty of time to alter history.

Twenty minutes later I hear a car pull up. Covering my mouth, I head back outside. Ghostly shafts of light flash across the gloom and settle on me. Even in this murky hell, I can't help but admire DI Price's car, a Ford Anglia with flared wing mirrors.

DI Price lowers his window and glares up at me, his unruly gray hair ghostly in this light. "Joseph?"

"Yes."

"I can't believe you persuaded me to do this tonight. We're short-staffed as it is." He glances around. "And it's fair to say you've chosen your bloody moment. This fog. I've never seen anything like it." He revs the engine loudly. "Well don't just stand there. Get in."

I do as I'm told. The car is warm and welcoming, the seats like armchairs. Price is wearing a thick sheepskin coat and a frown that owns his entire face. He's a formidable presence.

"Where are the other officers?" I ask him.

He laughs heartily. "Do you really think I'm calling in the troops, based on your flaky excuse of a story?" He shakes his head. "No. We'll go and check this out first, then we'll see." I consider trying to persuade him, but the fact I even got him here feels like a minor miracle.

Like the key that made it through time, opened the police box, and led to the call that brought us here.

"Well?" He glowers at me. "I haven't got all night, sweetheart. Where are we going?"

"Barclays Bank, Brompton Road, Knightsbridge."

"That would usually take about half an hour," he says. "Who knows how long in these conditions." He turns the car around, wrestling the wheel like a captain turning a boat in high winds. He could really use some power steering.

We drive through London streets, deserted like an abandoned battle-field. Visibility is about ten feet, at best. Vinny would probably be bouncing around in the back of the car, cracking jokes. I miss him.

"By the way, fair warning," Price says determinedly, "if you're mucking around, you won't just be arrested. I will throw the bloody book at you, do you understand?"

"I'm not lying," I insist. "You're going to catch Frankie Shaw, but I'm a bit worried it's just the two of us."

"Don't you worry about him," Price says. "If you're right and he is robbing the bank, rest assured, I'll call for backup and we'll nick him like any other criminal."

DI Price is rough around the edges, but he's also a proper, decent copper, and he's giving me the benefit of the doubt.

I swallow, staring at him dubiously. "Have you got a gun?"

Price snorts. "If *we* start carrying guns, then *they*'ll start carrying guns, and then where will we be?" I want to tell him we would be in the present. His hands grip the wheel, and he peers intently into the gloom. "Anyway, before we start arresting anyone and celebrating, let's get there first, shall we?"

Price takes a right and informs me that we are nearly there. The smog is thicker than ever, and there are no other vehicles on the road. The windshield wipers smear sludge over the glass. We are both coughing.

Suddenly, Price spins the car around, headlights flashing across the unmistakable frontage of what will become the most famous bank in history. He kills the engine.

It's 11 p.m.

According to Vinny's research, Frankie and his crew should be in there now, but the time of the robbery was only estimated. All I can do is hope we're not too late, but Price sits motionless next to me.

"Shouldn't we go and see if we can catch them?" I ask.

Price frowns at me with a troubled expression and rubs his chin.

"What is it?"

"Something's been bothering me." He blinks, shaking his head. "Your description matches that of a man we've been keen to talk to for some time. There was a dance at the Royal back in September." While he speaks, I process the chronology. "What were you and that other bloke doing there? Why did you want to talk to Lucy Romano?"

How does Price know I wanted to talk to Lucy? "Listen, I really think we should get in there."

"And what was the story with that pocket watch? How the hell did you get it back again?"

Dread swells in a wave of horrible realization. The only people who knew about the watch were Frankie and his murdering thug, Harry Hurst.

"How do you know about the watch?" I ask, dry mouthed. "You weren't there."

"No, I wasn't." Price smiles and pulls a gun from his jacket. "But I know a man who was."

PART 6

30

Fear. It's a powerful thing. It ices you to the core, and I was pretty frozen already.

I stare down at the pistol, helpless. Price continues to talk, but I can't hear him. Part of me wants to dive out of the car and run screaming into the night, but if I do that, he'll just shoot me.

I try to swallow, but my mouth is dry as sandpaper. I decide my best bet is to keep the conversation going. "Why are you doing this?" I ask, my voice thin and shaking.

He seems to genuinely consider this question. "I didn't much like Tommy," he says, "but Frankie is definitely going places."

Yeah, to prison and then straight to hell. "So you're doing it for the money?"

He scowls at me. "Do you know how hard we work? What we get paid?"

I shake my head. *It's always money.*

Price's expression becomes almost wistful. "It's my missus's fault, really," he tells me. "Retirement's looming, and . . . well, let's just say she has expensive taste."

His gun remains fixed on me.

"Frankie Shaw is a killer," I say, "and if you help him, you're going to have blood on—"

"Shut up," he growls, baring his teeth. "You don't know anything."

"You're wrong about that. I know plenty." I'm goading him, but if I'm going to die, then I'm going down as Captain Confident of the good ship *Know-It-All.*

Price leans in. "You keep popping up like a bad penny," he says, his voice calm and deliberate, "and you're involved now, Sunshine. You're right in the thick of it. You're going to wish you and your chubby mate had stayed at home."

The dashboard radio crackles, sending my heart racing. "Viper to Stingray. Are you here yet?" Despite the poor audio quality, I can tell it's Frankie. Hearing his voice again sends fresh waves of panic through me.

Price grabs the radio. "Stingray receiving. We're outside."

"Is he with you?" Frankie asks.

Price turns to me, gleeful. "Oh yes, he's here."

"Well then," Frankie says cheerfully, "come in and join the party."

Price hauls me out of the car and pushes me down the street, his gun pressed into the small of my back. The smog is so thick, I can't see more than a few feet in front of me.

"Hands where I can see them," Price orders.

I think he may have watched too many Westerns. I raise my hands and keep walking.

We arrive at a familiar pillar-box red front door with a brass knocker shaped like a lion's head. This is 108 Brompton Road. The house where Lucy, defending herself, set all of this in motion. Price taps the door in a deliberate sequence. Two bolts slide, and the door opens.

An undesirable-looking man nods at Price and lets us in. I'm led through a corridor. It's dark, but I recognize it from my viewing. We pass the room where Lucy and Tommy argued and descend stone steps toward the basement. At the bottom of the steps, I am greeted by a scene Vinny and I studied. A black-and-white photograph comes to life in front of me.

The entrance to the tunnel is as wide as a doorway, surrounded by tons of rubble. Price marches me into it, his gun still pressed into my back. The tunnel is supported by a wooden frame and reinforced every ten feet or so. A string of light bulbs snakes into the distance. It's cold and claustrophobic. I feel acutely aware of the immense mass of earth, concrete, and tarmac between me and the London street above. I choose not to think about the scene where the tunnel collapses in *The Great Escape*. That said, I have historical knowledge on my side. I know the tunnel remains intact. As we near its end, I smell a noxious chemical stink that reminds me of Bunsen burners and phosphorus. A set of ladders rest against the end of the tunnel.

"After you, sweetheart," Price says.

I climb. Price follows, his gun trained on me. We emerge directly into the bank's vault.

Scattered around us are leather bags crammed full of money and jewelry. I spot Mad Harry Hurst—all ten tons of him—stuffing one of the bags like he's packing laundry. He is suitably dressed, top to toe in black. He stares at me, smirks, and continues his work. A thickset bearded man drills loudly into a wall of safety deposit boxes. The men work methodically; they seem relaxed.

Frankie Shaw is smiling, his face pale as the moon. He is dressed in a dark-blue shirt, cream trousers, and pointed brown suede shoes. He walks over, exchanges a few muttered words with DI Price, then stops a few feet away from me. He sticks his hands in his pockets and studies me, his blue eyes glowing with amusement. "When I woke up this morning, I had a plan. I've been working on it for a long time." He leans close to my face, and I smell aftershave and mint. His good humor fades. "And then you turn up again."

I don't say anything.

"It's Joe, isn't it?"

I just nod.

"I'm going to ask you a question, Joe." His voice is slow and calm. "All I want you to do is give me an honest answer. OK?"

I nod again.

"How could you possibly know about me hitting this bank tonight?"

It's a good question, one that leaves me tongue-tied. I didn't think twice about telling DI Price that Squint had let slip about the robbery. I was sure he wouldn't actually come to any harm. But there's no way I can tell

Frankie it was Squint who gave the game away. God knows what torture I'll be condemning the poor guy to if I mention his name now.

Frankie tires of waiting for my answer. "Don't tell me: it was a lucky guess!" He glances around at his crew. The men laugh obediently. Harry's smile chills me another couple of degrees. Frankie leans in and whispers to me. "The damage is done. Price just told me all about the mole you mentioned. Little snitch has got it coming."

Suddenly, the drill grinds to a halt and the room falls silent. No one moves, but they all look in the same direction.

Following their gaze, I see a man I hadn't noticed before, a Woody Allen look-alike sitting on a stool, wearing headphones and fiddling with a radio unit. He's holding up a finger. I recognize him. It's Squint Daley. I had no idea he was going to be here tonight, any more than I knew that DI Price was crooked. What the hell have I done?

"We've got a couple of coppers on the beat nearby," Squint whispers. Minutes pass in silence. Eventually, he wipes his brow. "All clear. They're moving on."

Frankie is so close, I can smell his minty breath. "You know, I love this work," he says, gazing around the vault. "I might do more of it, actually. Jock, get that drill going again."

"You aren't going to believe this," the man called Jock replies. He holds up an envelope and then spreads its contents over a nearby table. The crew gathers around it. DI Price keeps the gun on me.

This must be the incriminating photographs of politicians and royals, the ones that Vinny and I read about.

"Blow me," Frankie chuckles delightedly.

"I bet that's what *he's* saying," Jock replies.

Frankie turns to DI Price, a slow smile creasing his lips. "We've just hit the bloody jackpot. No one can touch me now."

He has all the leverage he'll ever need. *Jackpot is right.*

His crew piles bags at the tunnel entrance. Frankie shakes an aerosol can, sprays the wall, and stands back, admiring his work.

YOU WILL NEVER CATCH ME

He turns to me, grinning. "I wasn't supposed to be here, you know." His eyes glaze over for a second, and his jaw flexes as his smile drifts away. "I don't mean here at the bank. I mean I wasn't supposed to *live*. My dear old mum told me once that I was an accident."

The room is silent as Frankie talks, the men quiet and expectant.

"She partied pretty hard, my mum, during the pregnancy . . . thoughtless bitch. I popped out two months early. Doctor said I wasn't going to make it. He doubted I would live through the night. Well, look at me now. Proved him wrong, didn't I? Proved them all wrong. I'm a fighter. I've always been dead keen."

He walks over to me.

"You might be wondering why I'm telling you this," he says in a tone that makes clear I shouldn't answer. "I fought hard to get to where I am now. And no one, especially not a chancer like you, is going to take it from me." He leans closer, his minty breath burning my eyes. "Frankie Shaw is the one who does the taking. Do you understand?"

He's switched to third person. A sure sign of an ego out of control.

"Whatever you thought you were doing tonight, you failed," Frankie says empathically. "No one can stop me, no one." His eyes glow cool blue, like a welder's torch tightening into a white flame. "Now, Detective Inspector Price told me what you said to him on the phone. That's very interesting." He turns to the man wearing the headphones. "Squint, get your sorry arse over here."

Squint clears his throat and steps forward. "What is it, boss?" he says like a frightened mouse.

Frankie gestures toward me. "You know Joe, don't you?"

Squint blinks at me through bottle-thick glasses. "Er, no, don't think I do. Don't think I've met him before."

"You don't *think* you've met him before?"

This is my fault, but how was I supposed to know that Price was playing on the wrong team?

Squint swallows audibly.

"Thing is, Squint," Frankie continues, "you've been seen talking to the coppers. And you knew the date in advance." He glances at me. "And then

Joe turns up tonight and says you told him all about it. I just want you to tell me the truth."

"I don't know this geezer," Squint whispers, tears rolling down his cheeks. "Never seen him, I swear." He wipes his nose with his sleeve.

Frankie stares hard at Squint. "Jock's a demon with the old fizzer, cuts through that concrete no problem," he says, menacingly now. "How about we cut you open, Squint? See if the word *traitor* is written through you."

"Please. I'm not a rat, I would never give you away. You've got it all wrong."

To his credit, Jock steps in. "Boss," he says warily, "I don't think—"

"Shut your mouth!" Frankie growls at him. To Squint, he says, "How else did pretty boy here know all about our plans tonight?"

Squint looks absolutely terrified.

Price sees it too. "Frankie, why don't you calm down, think this through. If Squint is the rat, I would have known about it."

"You *do not* want me to think this through, Detective Inspector," Frankie assures him. "Because this could go either way." He smiles a ghostly grin. "You're not telling me *you're* the rat, are you?"

"Of course not," Price says, indignant.

"What about you, Jock?" Frankie asks.

Jock shakes his head. "You know me, boss, I'm solid."

Frankie closes his eyes and draws in a long breath. "I trusted you, Squint, and I like you, but I can't let you get away with this." He nods to Harry, and the thug passes him a small shotgun. Frankie points it at Squint and slides his finger over the trigger.

Price steps in. "Listen, Frankie," he says carefully. "Why don't we get to the safe house and sort it all out there?" He gazes around the vault. "We're sitting on bloody millions here, not to mention the photographs. We should get moving."

Frankie glares at him, chest rising and falling.

Price continues, "Once we get to the safe house, you can do what you like, for as long as you like. We will have days to kill."

Not my favorite turn of phrase.

Squint lets out a sorrowful gasp, and I notice a dark patch around his crotch.

Frankie sniffs the air. "Oh, Squint, that's disgusting!"

Squint collapses, out cold.

Price glances at me, emotions passing over his face like time-lapse clouds across a landscape. I see fear, defiance, a flicker of acceptance, a shadow of his own greed. He looks lost; he knows he's in deep.

I recall Vinny telling me that Price will be murdered a few years from now. I had plans to warn him, but I suspect it's too late. His fate is already sealed.

Frankie glares at me. "I knew there was something about you," he says. "I can't put my finger on it, but I'll get there . . . I always do." He turns to the crew. "Right, good job, fellas. Let's move out." Then, to Harry, he says, "Tie Squint up and put Joe in the car with me."

"You want me to blindfold him?" Harry asks.

Frankie shakes his head. "Nah, no need."

"Where are you taking me?" I ask.

"Somewhere nice and quiet." Frankie studies me. "I have a surprise for you."

We follow another car out of London, its brake lights barely visible. Mad Harry drives. I'm in the back with Frankie. He's crunching peppermints, humming along to the radio. I peer out into the yellow mist, feeling horribly alone. I miss Vinny, although I'm glad he isn't here, obviously. At least he's safe. I'm beginning to doubt I will ever see the present again. I don't need to check my watch to know that time is running out. I can feel it, like sand through my fingers. When it's gone, it's gone.

And I've seen enough gangster films to know that if they don't blindfold you, it's because they don't care what you see. It isn't going to matter.

31

Houses become fields. The smog thins. Eventually, we turn down a narrow, pot-holed track. The car's headlights move across an old, battered sign draped in ivy. It reads, "St. David's Church. Welcome to All God's Children."

We pull into a derelict garage. Harry kills the engine. According to the clock in the car, the time is just after 6 a.m. Sunrise is still a couple of hours away.

Frankie has been quiet for the last half hour or so. He taps my knee with his shotgun. "Out of the car, nice and slow," he says. "And don't get any funny ideas."

The air is cold and damp. The smog has been replaced by a mist that hangs a few feet from the ground. Mad Harry pulls Squint Daley out of another car. Squint's eyes are wild, like a trapped animal's, his breath shooting out in fearful gasps.

In the distance I see a church, its Gothic spire a black sword against a gray sky. It has fallen into disrepair—windows boarded up, stone crumbling—and is surrounded by a tall chain fence. Ivy covers everything.

Handheld flashlights cut cones of light through the gloom as we walk through the churchyard. The smell of damp earth fills my nostrils. Creatures rustle in the undergrowth, their silvery eyes observing us. Gravestones poke up from the ground like broken teeth.

We pass a sign. Danger: Keep Out. The sense of solitude and decay is all-consuming. I shiver. Amy's visions have been accurate so far. The smog, the beacon of light, and now the church. Everything Amy predicted is coming true. Does that mean someone is going to die here tonight? Will this be where it all ends for me? Is my story already written?

We reach the entrance to the church, a large wooden door. Frankie turns to his crew. "Right, you boys go and get the party started." He looks at Harry. "Tie Squint up and stick him in the vestry. I'll deal with him later."

The crew heads inside, leaving Frankie and me alone. He moves his light slowly over the graveyard like a lighthouse over a calm sea before settling on a solemn-looking stone angel. He moves the light down her body, past a mound of freshly dug earth, and into an open grave.

"It's your choice," he says softly, "whether you end up in there tonight." I look around me, searching for ways to escape, and notice the crescent moon hanging low in the blackened sky, just above the roofline of the church. I'm overcome with sadness. *What if I never get to see another sunrise?*

Frankie leads me into the church. The nave is a high, cavernous space. Portable lamps cast long, untrustworthy shadows across the stone floor. The ornate windows are boarded up, the walls peppered with graffiti. Some pews remain, scattered along the aisles, and the air smells of old wood, dust, and damp stone.

Frankie walks past me, whistling. He switches on another portable lamp, illuminating a patchy ceiling. Ivy has found its way inside, hanging down like braids over the rusting, broken pipes of a huge organ. A rat scurries away, which doesn't do my already banging heart any good.

Frankie heads toward the altar. "This place was bombed pretty badly in World War II, so they boarded her up." He turns to me, lighting his pale face with his flashlight. "I bought it, planned to convert it into a nightclub . . . not that I need to do that now. I'm loaded, got a ton of cash and some nice diamonds too. And those photographs? Well, I gotta say, now the world's my oyster . . ." He chuckles and begins lighting candles. "This place is the perfect little hideaway. No one for miles." He turns to me with expressionless eyes. "The last time I saw you, you and your fat mate were chasing me on a motorbike, a couple of right jokers. Where is he, by the way?"

"He sends his regards."

Frankie eases into a grin. "Send mine back, won't you? I like him."
My silver hunter buzzes.

Frankie grabs my collar and, with a sharp tug, rips open my shirt, sending buttons tumbling. "How . . . *the hell* . . . did you get that bloody watch back?" he seethes. "I had it when we drove off and then I lost it . . . and now it's back around your neck." He scratches his chin. "That's impossible."

Yes, it is.

I watch the cogs in Frankie's brain desperately trying to figure it out.

"Hand it over," he says. I'm not worried this time. I know I can't lose it, but I'm also beginning to think it won't matter. There isn't a single scenario where I see myself getting out of this. I hand it to him. As I do, I notice the waypoint has updated, but just like before, as soon as he touches it, the watch transforms into an ordinary timepiece again.

He snatches it from me and inspects it. "This is mine, and I'm not losing it this time." He cocks the shotgun. "Now, let's get down to business, shall we? You're too smart to work for Don Dickerson. So I want to know two things. Nice and simple. One: how you knew about my plans to hit the bank. And two: I want to know what you want, because everybody wants something." A large wooden door creaks open, interrupting Frankie's monologue. He holds up a finger, grinning maniacally. "But first, I have a little surprise for you. Let's call it a reunion."

Harry appears, pushing a struggling woman ahead of him. My heart sinks like a stone. It's Lucy Romano. She's flustered but defiant. Her dark eyes scan the church. "Let me go! How dare you kidnap me and drag me out here? Who do you think you are?" Her Italian accent is more pronounced, and although she's petite, her attitude takes up space. She pulls her coat up around her ears and then sees me. As far as Lucy's concerned, she met me three months ago at the dance hall. I can tell she recognizes me, but she knows better than to say so. She glowers at Frankie. "What's going on?"

He pulls out his gold cross and rotates it in his fingers. He moves his attention between us, then a familiar smile spreads over his face, touching his eyes momentarily. He claps his hands. "Oh, Lucy, this is quite the performance. Acting like you hardly know each other!"

Lucy looks at me again. "Actually, I do remember him, but I have only seen him once. He was hassling me at the Royal."

"Shall I tell you what I think?" Frankie says, pointing at her. "You're getting paid by Don Dickerson to take me out, and you have your boyfriend here doing all your dirty work."

"What?" Lucy laughs, incredulous. "That's crazy."

Frankie presses a finger to his lips. "Your voice hurts my head. I used to like it, but it grates on me now." He turns to me. "Before this night is done, I will have answers. What do you think of that, pretty boy?"

"She's telling the truth," I reply. "We don't know each other."

"Let's play a game," Frankie suggests, his voice jovial. "Guess where I've been tonight, Lucy."

She curls up her nose. "I have no idea."

"I popped to the bank."

Lucy waits.

"Yeah," Frankie says. "Barclays Bank."

"Right." Lucy shrugs. "So?"

"There's a house right opposite the bank, owned by a company called Ashburn Estates. Anyone heard of them?"

"No," Lucy says.

"*No?*" Frankie mimics. "And what about you, Joe?"

I shake my head.

"That's the beauty of it. Ashburn Estates has nothing to do with me. Completely untraceable." He taps a finger to his temple. "Unfortunately for you, me and my brother own that house."

Frankie places his shotgun against a nearby pew and leans on a stack of tables covered in dust. I stare at the gun, calculating whether I can grab it.

"Now," Frankie resumes, "I'm going to cut a long story short." He drums his fingers on a table, his attention fixed on Lucy. "My brother is in a coma, and it's been driving me insane trying to figure out what happened to him. It's funny, you know. If Joe here hadn't turned up and taken such an interest in you, I don't think I would have noticed how scared you seem all the time."

"What are you talking about?" Lucy protests.

My mind works through the timeline. Before I intervened, Lucy's panic after Tommy's death had made Frankie sure of her involvement. This time, my meddling has brought Frankie's suspicions forward. I've guessed his plans, and I've been seen talking to Lucy. I've handed her to him on a plate, months ahead of schedule. *I've made things worse.*

Frankie shakes his head. "It's time to tell me the truth, Lucy—and don't forget my God-given gift. I *will* know if you're lying."

Lucy's olive skin fades until it almost matches the cold stone floor. She glances at me, a desperate fire in her eyes. She starts to cry, her final shreds of hope draining away. Frankie studies her, motionless, grinding his teeth. Then, his entire persona changes. His shoulders drop, his face smooths over, and he adopts a more empathetic tone. He holds the gold cross still against his chest. "You met him at the house. Something happened there, didn't it? Tommy got hurt, but it was an accident. I'm right, aren't I?"

I'm afraid that once he is satiated with the truth, he will kill us both.

Frankie shouts, "You hit him over the head, didn't you?"

"No," Lucy whispers.

"Tell me what happened then!"

She raises her chin. "He attacked me. It was self-defense." Her voice is racked with guilt. "I told your brother so many times that I wasn't interested. I told you as well, asked you to stop him, but you would not listen. Tommy was delusional. He thought we had something." She begins to sob. "I did not mean to hurt him, honestly I didn't."

Frankie stares at the ground, drawing long shuddering breaths. After a few seconds, he offers Lucy a reluctant smile. "Thank you," he says, almost kindly. "Thank you for telling me the truth."

He picks up the shotgun and walks toward her.

My mind races. *Can I rush him and wrestle the gun away? Force him to shoot me instead?*

"Frankie!" I shout.

He stops, a few feet between him and Lucy.

"Don't kill her, please . . . I'm begging you."

"Because you're working together?" His eyes flash with anger. "Or because you love her?"

Suddenly, it becomes clear. Not only does he want revenge, but he's jealous too. Frankie wanted Lucy too. It's a perfect storm of sibling envy and betrayal.

I take a step toward him. "She was just defending herself," I say. "She had no choice."

He shakes his head in denial. "He might be a cabbage for the rest of his life! And you want me to spare hers?"

"Yes. She told you the truth. She had no choice."

"Wait a minute." He points the shotgun at me, eyes shimmering with rage. "Were you there as well? How are you bloody *everywhere*? Who the *hell* are you? Start talking, or I start shooting."

I have to try and keep him talking. If Frankie shoots me, Lucy will be next.

Frankie's gold cross suddenly appears to glow.

An idea quickly forms, coalescing into a plan. I know that Frankie killed his own mother. It's common knowledge back in the present, documented in numerous books, news stories, and internet interviews. Here and now, though, it's Frankie's deepest, darkest secret, one that I know he will keep to himself for another five years. This is a dangerous game, but I think I know the best angle to play.

Frankie's faith.

I need to offer him an olive branch, a path to forgiveness and redemption.

"I've been sent to guide you, Frankie. To guide you from the path you're on."

"Oh, right . . . you're my bloody guardian angel, are you?" He laughs, but his heart's not really in it. I think Frankie Shaw is afraid.

"Yes," I assure him, as calmly as I can. "We all make mistakes, but if you want forgiveness for the things you've done, all *you* have to do is forgive Lucy." I pause. "She was defending herself, Frankie. You can understand that, can't you?"

"Forgiveness for what *I've* done?" Frankie swallows, lifts his beloved gold cross to his lips, and kisses it. He surveys the church, his eyes desperate, and then, in an almost childlike tone, he says, "I think it's a bit late for that."

I peer at the broken ceiling. "God doesn't see it that way."

Frankie glances back at me suspiciously. "What do you *think* I've done?"

I decide I'm all in. "I know that you killed your mother, Frankie. That's why I'm here."

"What are you *talking* about?"

"You choked her to death," I say, my voice deliberately quiet. "You killed your own flesh and blood."

Lucy is forgotten. Frankie's eyelids flicker, and his lips are fixed in a rigid O. "How do you know this?"

"God moves in mysterious ways," I say, digging deep, trying to channel what I imagine a man of faith might say. "And he sees everything."

"But . . . God and I have an agreement."

I do my best to play along. "You do, but he thinks you went too far this time."

A deep frown etches over Frankie's face. "So God really does see everything," he murmurs.

"He does," I say.

Frankie's demeanor shifts. He smiles. "OK then. What's the last thing my mum said to me?"

I feel like I'm on a quiz show. All the answers have been easy up until now, but this is the final, sudden-death question, and I'm out of lifelines. Frankie told the whole world exactly what his mother said in his tell-all book. I can visualize the words. Vinny even read them to me aloud. But . . . *what did she say?*

Moments tick by.

The gold cross catches the light, a red eye winking at me.

Suddenly, I remember exactly what his mother said. Telling Frankie could fan the flames of his guilt, but I have no choice.

"Just before you killed her, your mother said, '*You haven't got it in you.*'"

Confusion and disbelief flash over him. His lips peel back, and he lowers the gun to his side. He grips his beloved cross. "How could you . . . know that?"

"I told you, I've been sent to help you," I say, cautiously. "God is ready to forgive your sins. All you need to do now is forgive Lucy and let her go."

Frankie is frozen. His blue eyes flick between Lucy, myself, and the divine presence I have desperately conjured above us.

I take a step toward him. "Put the gun down, Frankie."

He looks at me, his soul lost, but then a familiar and terrifying shift occurs in his demeanor. He narrows his gaze, his lips easing into a cruel smile. "If you're an angel," he says slowly, "then I can shoot you and you won't be harmed."

I swallow, my throat clicking. "Why would you do that, after what I just told you?"

"The way I see it, we're testing each other's faith. If you're an angel, you have nothing to worry about. You're immortal."

"It doesn't work like that," I say quickly. "I've come here in . . . human form to help you take the path of forgiveness." My words are weakening. Frankie Shaw is going to kill us, probably Squint Daley too. And he will sleep soundly afterward.

He laughs. "More tricks. I have no idea how you know all these things, but however you do it, it's one hell of a gift. I will give you that. It's a shame, I could have used a good con man like you." He raises the shotgun and points it at me. "Unfortunately, it's time to say goodbye. Say your prayers like a good little angel and give my regards to *Him*, won't you?" He lifts his cross to his lips and kisses it.

A sudden explosion of noise makes me cry out. I think it's the gun going off, but it's not.

It's a genuine miracle.

Somehow, impossibly, there are people here, lots of people.

Whistles scream. A man shouts, "Drop the gun!"

Police swarm into the chapel. One shouts, "Do it, Frankie. Put the gun down!" The voice is loud and aggressive, but it sounds like an angel to me.

A policeman moves between Frankie and Lucy, shielding her.

Even in this commotion and panic, I realize what this means. I might have done it . . . I might have saved her.

Something catches my eye, drawing my gaze up toward the roof. A warm multi-colored glow streams down through a circular rosette-shaped window at least twenty feet wide. Its remaining stained glass is aflame with the first embers of morning light.

Then I see movement—a man peering down from the rafters, his shocked expression clear, even from this distance.

But it's not as shocked as mine. It's W. P. Brown, watching all of this unfold.

My elation is now laced with confusion and a darkening concern. Amy's vision comes back to me again, her words filling my mind. *The church. Something happens here that is transformative. Powerful forces at work.*

I can feel them now, but why? Lucy is safe. I've completed my mission, haven't I?

I look back at Frankie, his eyes reflected red in the dawn's light. His devilish expression says, *If I'm going down, I'm taking you with me.*

He points his gun at me and pulls the trigger.

32

A shadowy figure darts in my peripheral vision. I turn to see a man running across the church at impossible speed.

The shotgun barks a flash of brilliant white.

I cry out in shock as a slash of pain tears at my right ear. I'm injured, but not badly. Frankie intended to shoot me in the chest, but the speeding man took the full force of the blast. He stumbles and collapses in front of me.

I watch all of this, strangely detached.

My ears ring with the sound of the shotgun blast. White and orange shapes dance in my vision. I blink, trying to focus.

Frankie stares at me in disbelief. He raises the shotgun again with a manic grin. Lucy screams. Frankie's crew is shouting. Before Frankie can get another shot off, two burly policemen descend on him. He cries out in protest as they manhandle him to the ground, wrenching the shotgun from his hands.

Moments pass like the flickering pages of a photo album. I see a flash of handcuffs as one of the policemen digs a knee into Frankie's back. The gangster grunts and struggles, but the police drag him away.

"You've done it this time, Frankie," another says. "They'll have you for murder."

Murder. Death came for me . . . but *someone* had other ideas.

I turn my attention back to my savior, lying in the floor, unmoving.

I walk slowly toward him, rubbing my eyes. Part of me expects it to be PC Green; the young enthusiastic copper might just be stupid enough to do this.

Then I wonder if I might see myself, back from the distant future to correct yet another of my mistakes.

As I approach him, I realize that I'm wrong on both counts. It's W. P. Brown.

I collapse to my knees. "Mr. Brown—Bill, what have you done?"

His eyes flicker open, gaze around, and then settle on me. I take his hand. It's cold.

"Robbery . . . and now murder," his voice cracks. "You did it, my boy."

"No, Bill, *you* did it." I glance at his waistcoat, soaked in blood, torn open just below the shoulder.

He smiles fondly. "It's what we do, Joseph . . . We sacrifice."

Lucy is next to me. She scrunches her scarf into a ball and says, "We need to apply pressure to the wound."

She hands it to me, and I tentatively press it against W. P. Brown's shoulder.

"No," Lucy urges me. "Press firmly."

I do, and Bill winces. "You managed to stop Mr. Untouchable before he ever got started, Joseph."

Sounds swirl around me. People. Activity. The criminals shout and swear. Mad Harry doesn't know when to stop. It takes three policemen to wrestle him outside.

Lucy takes Bill's hand. "You brought the police. You saved us. Thank you."

He shakes his head. "No, Lucy. It's Joseph you must thank. He never stopped. He was determined to save you, and Gus too."

"Gus?" Lucy's voice is guarded. "What does this have to do with him?"

"Everything." Bill smiles at her.

A policeman tells us that an ambulance is on the way. He hands Lucy a couple of blankets. She lays one under Bill's head and covers him with the other. Wrapped up like this, it's easy to imagine he's unharmed.

"Thank you, Lucy," he says. "Joseph will explain it all, but I need a few minutes alone with him, if you don't mind."

Lucy holds my gaze. "Keep pressure on the wound," she says. "They won't be long. I will keep an eye out."

Reluctantly, she leaves us. As the commotion subsides, it feels as though it's just Bill and I, alone in the church. His skin is clammy and horribly pale, but he appears calm, almost peaceful, as though a good day's work has been done. I need to keep him talking.

"You're going to be all right," I tell him, my voice deliberately loud.

His eyelids flicker. "Would you check your pocket watch?"

I'm relieved to feel the weight of my silver hunter around my neck where it belongs. I check the jump dials.

Waypoint

I frown at the display. "I don't understand. Is the mission complete or not?"

"This can happen sometimes," he says, wincing a little. "The waypoint itself can shift as we alter time."

"Shift? Where?"

He glances at Lucy, who is standing near the entrance. "You did well. Lucy is safe, but you aren't done yet." He squeezes my hand. "There are loose ends. You must set her on her path, push her in the right direction. You must ensure Lucy is there for her son."

"And if I do that, Amy will be OK?"

"Yes, Joseph. Everything is connected. You save Lucy, and Amy will be left alone."

"And the organization you work for, will they know too?"

"Yes." He shifts his weight. "Now, there are things I need to tell you." He studies me, and although it's clearly an effort, he manages a smile. "I'm dying, Joseph."

"No, you aren't."

"I'm not afraid," he says, "but please, listen to me. You saw me at the loch. You know I didn't want to blackmail you. I'm sorry." His brow narrows, as if he's drifting in deep reflection. "You're very special to me."

"But you barely know me."

"I haven't been honest with you," he says, "from the very beginning." He swallows, licking his lips. "When I came into the shop, it wasn't the first time we had met. The first for you, but not for me." He sighs. "Continuity. One of the hardest things for a time traveler to contend with. It's like acting, playing a part, blending in . . . This one though . . . the hardest of all."

I have questions. But I don't want to interrupt him.

"I can't complain, Joseph," he continues. "How could I? The things I've seen . . . the winds of time in my hair . . . shining light into the shadows, putting things right. Wonderful . . . a life beyond what most people can imagine."

Sunlight casts a gentle warm glow through the stained glass window. I'm struck with a sense of inevitability. Amy's vision. The church, the window, this moment. I gaze down at my blackmailer, now also my savior. I don't know how to feel about him, but I don't want him to die.

"This can't be right," I say. My words tumble out. "I'm just getting to know you. I've only just begun to believe that you might not be the bad guy."

He forces a smile, and when he speaks, his voice is a rattling whisper. "Will you do something for me?"

I nod, my throat so tight I can't speak.

"You and I are going to have such adventures together," he says. "Remember them for me."

Cold adrenaline courses over me. "Don't talk like this, Bill. You're going to be OK."

"I'm glad it was you," he says.

"What do you mean?"

He draws in a long, jagged breath. "Haven't you figured it out yet?" he asks. "My final mission was *you*, Joseph."

He exhales, and his sparkling blue eyes, so full of mischief and wonder, fade and close. His face slackens, and he is gone.

Slowly, I lift the blanket over his head. My hands are stained in his blood.

My awareness of the world around me begins to resurface. My head pounds, my ear burns. I guess I got hit after all. Adrenaline is a wonderful thing.

I work my gaze over the now-shrouded W. P. Brown. I don't know how to feel, what to make of all this. But I need to act now and feel later.

Bill said I wasn't done yet. I take one look at Lucy's expression and I think I understand what he meant.

I check the jump dials.

18 Minutes

Enough time to finish this properly.

Lucy takes a step toward me, her expression respectful. "I am sorry about your friend," she says. "Who was he?"

I wonder what to say. All I know is that he just gave his life to save mine. Why? Well, that's a question for later. Lucy waits patiently for my answer. I'm about to leave her time for good, and whatever I say will define how she feels about W. P. Brown for the rest of her life.

"His name was Bill," I tell her. "He was one of the good guys."

PC Green arrives. I expect him to recognize me, but when I think it through, I realize he hasn't met me yet. We won't meet until June next year. No, wait. That won't happen now. Frankie will be in jail. Lucy won't be on the run.

PC Green glances at Bill's shrouded body and suggests we get some fresh air. We follow him outside.

The morning sun smudges the horizon, the remaining mist a pale-yellow glow. Numerous police cars and vans are parked at jaunty angles, bathing the scene in blue flashing lights. A kind-looking policewoman hands us cups of sweet tea and more blankets.

Squint Daley is being questioned nearby. He survived the night. Then again, the only reason he *almost* died was because of me. Frankie is in the back of a police van with DI Price. The full weight of the law has reduced and transformed these horrible men into impotent shadows. Frankie glowers at me, his jaw clenched. I raise my chin and confidently hold his gaze.

As the van drives away, I pull out my watch and ensure that he can see it. His eyes widen in disbelief. To my surprise, he actually looks scared.

I check the jump dials again.

14 Minutes

I turn to PC Green. "How did you know to come out here?"

The young policeman's face lights up. "Mr. Brown arrived at the station, told us DI Price was in cahoots with Frankie Shaw and that they were robbing a bank. As you can imagine, we couldn't believe it, but Brown was so insistent, so persuasive, that we rallied the troops and headed out." He frowns, blinking. "And then . . . Well, you saw what he did. He's a hero."

"Yes, he is."

"They're saying it's the biggest robbery in British history. Sarge even handed out pistols." Green bites his lip. "I was too scared to take one."

Police without weapons, the good old days.

"I need you both to come down to the station," he says. "We need to take a statement."

"What's your first name?" I ask him.

"Er, Robert," he says, taken aback.

"You did well tonight, Robert," I tell him. "But listen, I need a minute with Lucy before we go anywhere, OK?"

He rubs the back of his neck and thinks it over. "Sarge won't be happy."

"I know, but it won't take long."

He might be young, but he's smart. "Something odd happened here, didn't it?" He frowns. "Mr. Brown turning up like that, us catching Frankie Shaw."

"Just enjoy it," I tell him. "You caught the bad guys. That's what matters."

I can tell from his expression that he doesn't really believe me, his pale-gray eyes wise beyond his years.

Then it clicks. Those eyes.

This is the man who brought the police box key into Bridgeman Antiques. He was elderly, probably in his eighties, and it's hard to believe he was the same person as this fresh-faced young man in front it me, but I know it was him. It was PC Green. When he came into the shop, I felt as though he recognized me. What must it have been like for him to see me, looking just as I do now, almost sixty years later? What made him bring that key to me, and why then? What did Bill call it? *Subtle serendipity.*

I want to thank him for bringing me the key but I know I can't. Instead, I just say, "Thank you for being here tonight. You're a damn fine policeman."

He shrugs. "All in a day's work. I'll leave you two alone. I'll be back in a couple of minutes." He heads inside the church.

"So what happens now?" Lucy asks me.

"I'm going soon, Lucy. We need to talk. Let's find somewhere away from everyone else. Come with me."

Her confusion is obvious, but she doesn't argue. She follows me around the side of the church to the statue of the broken angel.

"Tommy and Frankie can't hurt you now," I assure her. "It's over."

Her gaze meets mine, and I see raw pain in her expression, but I also feel something deeper. "I put Tommy in that coma," she says, her eyes filling with tears.

"And that is the *last time* you say that." I place my hand on her shoulder. "You were protecting yourself. You had no choice. No matter what they ask, you deny any involvement."

"Frankie will tell them," she says, her voice heavy.

"I'm sure he will, but the police have *nothing* on you, Lucy. Do you understand?"

"I need to atone for what happened," she snaps back. "Now that Frankie is out of the picture, I can tell the police it was an accident . . . they will understand. And anyway, Tommy will tell them when he wakes up. It is the only way."

Time is counting down, and according to my watch, the mission remains incomplete. *Loose ends*, Bill called them.

"Lucy, Tommy Shaw isn't going to wake up," I say, as gently as I can. "He is going to die next year."

Her mouth hangs open. She covers it with both hands, her eyes shimmering. "Who are you?" she asks. "How do you know so much about me? How could you possibly know what's going to happen?"

I have to tell her something she will understand and accept, something that won't freak her out and change her destiny. I try to appear calm. "What I told Frankie is true, in a way."

She swallows, and when she speaks, it's only just loud enough to hear. "You are my guardian angel." I can't tell if it's a question or a statement. Perhaps it's both.

"In a way, I suppose, but I wasn't sent by God. My name is Joseph Bridgeman. I came here to save you because your life is important in ways that I don't fully understand. Frankie and Tommy Shaw were bad news,

Lucy. You got caught up in that, but it wasn't your fault. The Shaws don't matter now, but you do; and Gus needs you. He is very smart. I believe he will go on to do incredible things."

She blinks, her fascination dawning. "But how do you know what's going to happen?"

With an awkward, embarrassed shrug, I say, "I'm from the future. I'm going back soon, but I can't go until you tell me you *understand* what I've said. You won't tell anyone about Tommy."

She considers this, close but not yet sold. "But what will I tell them about why I'm here tonight?"

"You will say Frankie was in love with you, but the feeling was not reciprocated. You tell them that when you snubbed him, he became aggressive and obsessed with you. That's why he kidnapped you tonight."

She shakes her head. "I don't know if I can do that."

"What happened with Tommy can't be changed," I insist, "but it wasn't your fault. You have your own life to live. I know you want to be a doctor." I lean down, ensuring that she fully connects with what I'm saying. "You can do that. You can heal people and achieve whatever you set your mind to, but you also need to be there for Gus. You can only do these things as a free woman."

She wipes away her tears. "Gus has been spending time with the wrong people. I've been so worried he was going down the wrong path."

"I know, but you can change that now."

"How can you be so sure?"

I think back over my old life, the aching loneliness of an absent family. Lucy has fear in her eyes, an unknown future ahead of her. "You just need to be present," I tell her. "You won't always get it right, but all you have to do is be there for Gus. For someone like you, someone with a good heart, that will be easy."

Lucy's shoulders drop a little. She tilts her head to the side and studies me. "You're a good man, Joseph. I wasn't sure there were any of you left."

"So you'll do it?" I ask her gently. "Put what happened to Tommy behind you and stick to the story about Frankie?"

A warm breeze travels over me, totally at odds with the dank chill of the graveyard. Ions crackle in the air, and a bloom of blue spreads over all I see, framing Lucy in a beautiful aura. She regards me, her eyes swimming, and then, with a single nod, changes the course of her entire life.

My watch beeps.

Mission Complete

33

I arrive in exactly the same spot I departed from, the decked terrace of Casa Bridgeman. "Lucy in the Sky with Diamonds" feels like a lifetime ago. The sudden daylight makes me wince.

I need to know whether Amy is safe.

Early indications are good. Casa Bridgeman wouldn't exist if my timeline had been reset, right? I get a brain clench and decide not to think about it too hard.

I slide open the glass door and gaze around the loft—exactly as I left it, down to the half-empty bottle of Bollinger. So far, so familiar. I check the clock. It's Sunday morning, 10:30 a.m.

I make my way downstairs and into Bridgeman Antiques. In the shop all is quiet, deserted. Relief surges through me. Surely, it's confirmed. The present is the same, which must mean my family is still alive and well. *It must.*

My smile becomes a giggle, which in turn becomes a manic laugh.

"I totally did it!" I shout.

A woman screams.

I spin on my heels and almost scream back. It's Molly; she looks terrified. "If your goal was to nearly give me a heart attack, you did it all right!" she scolds me.

"Molly! Gosh . . . sorry, I didn't know you were here."

She takes a step toward me, all focused suspicion. "And *I* didn't hear *you* come in."

"I just got back," I say, almost grinning because it's fun saying cryptic *time-travel* things.

Molly doesn't think I'm clever. "Come over here."

I do as I'm told.

"Goodness!" Her mouth drops open. "What happened to your ear?"

"It's nothing," I assure her. "Molly, is Amy all right?"

"Amy?" She appears confused. "Why wouldn't she be? Have you two fallen out again?"

"Fallen out . . ." Tingles of adrenaline bursting over my shoulders. To fall out with someone, they need to exist. "She's OK!" I cry out.

"As far as I know," Molly replies, "but are you?"

"I'm bloody fantastic!" I grin so wide it hurts. "It's good to see you, Molly!" I feel like Scrooge on Christmas morning: reset, refreshed, appreciative of the small things. "It's good to be alive."

Molly stares at me, deep concern etched on her face. My head pounds as the room takes me for a brief spin. I swallow, try to apologize, and stagger. My mouth is dry. Pulsing red dots prick my vision.

"Are you all right, Mr. Bridgeman?" Molly's voice is sludgy, far away.

I'm clearly not. Zero sleep, borrowed adrenaline, and the constant threat of death are catching up with me. I feel Molly's arm around me. She's stronger than she looks.

"Right," she announces, "we need to clean you up, and then you need to rest."

"I need to see Vinny."

"Absolutely not!" she cries. "Sleep is what you need."

"But it's the morning."

"No more arguments, Mr. Bridgeman." She draws in a breath. "Do as you're told."

Resistance is futile. Molly helps me upstairs to my flat and ushers me into the kitchen. She washes my face and hands and dresses the wound on my ear. She admits she's no nurse but thinks I might get away without stitches. She doesn't ask any questions.

"Right," she says as she finishes. "Get some rest. I'll check on you tomorrow."

"Thank you, Molly. I really appreciate it."

She closes the door, and I'm alone again. I text Amy and let her know that I'm back, that it's all over. I leave a trail of clothes on my way to the shower, where jets of hot water hit me from all directions. I nearly cry, it feels so good.

My thoughts turn to Bill.

My final mission . . . I'm glad it was you, Joseph.

I don't know where he ended up, but I hope, wherever it is, there's someone there who cares, someone to give him a proper burial, worthy of what he's done. I wonder how Iris, the woman I saw at the loch, feels now. Does she know he's gone? And what about Scarlett, the girl with the star-shaped birthmark? He said she had been his student. I wonder what went wrong there. Was he trying to make amends for something when he saved me?

It's going to take years to figure this all out and my poor addled brain can't sort through anything else.

Fatigue consumes me.

Pajamas on, I fall into bed.

It's midday, but Molly is right. I need rest.

I stare at the ceiling, convinced I won't sleep, and immediately pass out.

I wake, still thinking about Bill, to the sound of distant traffic and birdsong. It's 8 a.m., Monday morning, which means I slept for eighteen hours. It's proof that sleep debt is real, and might be a record for me. My ear throbs, but it isn't too bad.

I shower again and get dressed in some of Other Joe's expensive designer gear: shirt, black sweater, jeans made of a clever stretchy material that accommodates my slightly larger frame, and brown desert boots. I stand in front of a tall mirror and assess my outfit. I have no idea if this combination *works*, because I wouldn't know fashion if it slapped me in the face, but I think I look tidy. I shrug and head down to the shop.

Molly is opening up. "Good morning," she says. "How are you feeling?"

"Much better," I tell her. "Thanks for your help yesterday."

"You're welcome." Her tone is amiable but also slightly guarded. If anything like this happens again, Molly will demand an explanation.

"I need to go and see Vinny," I say. "Do you mind looking after the shop?"

She frowns.

"Oh, yeah. I don't ask you, do I?"

"You never *used* to," she says with a quizzical expression, "but something's changed."

"Yes, it has," I reply, cheerfully. "For the better."

Vinny's Vinyl is exactly the same as I remember from my old life. I step inside and soak in the wonderful familiarity of the classic, old-school vibe. Thousands of records are stacked neatly in wooden racks. Handwritten signs denote eras: '60s, '70s, '80s. Posters and classic album covers plaster the walls. Vinny doesn't just stock old vinyl though. "*New stuff brings the kids in,*" he told me once. In the center of the shop, a disco ball hangs over a table covered with thick velvet blankets displaying new CDs and vinyl. The place smells of new plastic and damp, vinegary newspapers.

Some grungy American-sounding garage band that I don't recognize blasts through the speakers. The female singer howls about the importance of understanding how she feels. She sounds angry. I like it.

Nine times out of ten, when I visit the shop, it's empty, and today is no exception. Even though I can't think of a single reason why my actions in the sixties would mess up my friendship with Vinny in the present, I'm still nervous. I don't want to keep starting over with people who matter.

Vinny sits at the back of the shop, reading a music magazine. He's wearing a Guns N' Roses *Appetite for Destruction* T-shirt—an original, frayed at the edges. His knee is bandaged with an ice pack. When he sees me, his entire face breaks into a beaming smile. "Cash!" he says. "Thank the stars. How did it go?"

"You honestly haven't looked it up?"

"I've been waiting for you." He stands up. "And how's Amy? She's all right too?"

"Yes, she's fine."

"Right, into the office with you," he says. "I'm closing the shop. I want to hear everything." He peers at me. "What are you hiding?"

"Hmmm?"

"Behind your back?"

"Oh, I took a detour on the way here." I reveal two humongous breakfast baguettes.

His jaw drops. "Cash, you're an angel."

"Yeah, I've been hearing that a lot lately."

We devour our calorie bombs. When we finish, Vinny wipes his mouth. "Lovely jubbly. Right, come on then," he mumbles, "before we hit the Interweb, I want to hear it from you. Fill me in."

I start at the beginning and tell him everything that led to my arrival at the church. Finally, I pause, trying to decide how best to explain what happened next.

"Come on, Cash, don't keep me in suspenders!"

"The police arrived," I say, "and then . . ." I stare at my hands, replaying the incident for the hundredth time. I look up at Vinny, his pained expression a mirror of my own. "Bill took a bullet for me. He died saving me."

"Who's Bill?"

"Sorry, I mean W. P. Brown." I lean back in my chair. "Vinny, I had him all wrong. He *was* blackmailing me, but it's clear now that he had total conviction, and he was willing to die for it."

"That's a shocker, Cash," Vinny says. After a few seconds of respectful silence, he says, "Listen, Cash, the main thing is that Lucy and Amy are safe, and the bad guys got caught."

"True."

He grabs his laptop. "Right then, shall we catch up on a shedload of history?" We scan the headlines.

Knightsbridge Bank Robbery Foiled!

Mystery Man Shot at Scene.

Vinny gazes at me. "Bill."

"PC Green called him a hero," I reply, "and he was right."

Vinny smiles. "Yeah, he was."

A small boxed article catches my attention.

NEW CRAZE TAKES DANCE HALLS BY STORM!

There's a small grainy photograph of my best friend, doing what the article describes as *The Funky Vincent.*

Vinny chuckles. "Finally, I'm famous."

We continue browsing. Frankie accused Lucy of his brother's attack, but there was insufficient evidence to bring it to trial. Lucy denied everything.

"Mad Harry Hurst got life," Vinny says, tapping the screen. "Says here that he wrote loads of books about his experiences in London's gangland. Great! That's my reading list sorted."

Turns out DI Price bleated like a lamb and cut deals at any and every opportunity. *At least he didn't die this time around.*

Vinny taps at the keyboard. "Interesting . . . During the initial interviews, Frankie claims he was visited by an angel on the night of the robbery." He looks up at me. "Anything to do with you?"

"He was pointing a gun at me. I had to tell him something."

Vinny chuckles. "Nice. Well, it seemed to work. Frankie gave a full confession of all his crimes, including a couple of unsolved murders. He reckoned he was a changed man."

I don't think so. I think he was a scared man, scared of where his soul might end up. "What happened to him?"

Vinny curls his lip. "It appears his religious epiphany didn't last. He changed his story a few times, then hanged himself in prison."

"Same date as last time?"

"No, actually," Vinny says, peering at the screen. "Well, same *day*, April first, but a year earlier."

"April first." Time has a dark sense of humor. "Good riddance to bad rubbish."

Vinny points at a photograph of Lucy leaving the police station, attempting to cover her face. I'm pleased to see a defiant confidence in her expression.

"She looks like a tough lady," Vinny says.

"She was," I agree. "Tough and fiercely independent. What happened to her?"

Vinny searches. "Lucy Romano went on to become a doctor, and then a forensic physician." He turns to me. "Like on *CSI*!"

In one photo Lucy is surrounded by a team of young doctors. It's obvious they revere her. She radiates confidence.

Vinny brings up another article. "She used to give talks to students, and one of them described her as a 'guiding light for women in medicine, and an inspiration to us all.' She got married, apparently, and she said she couldn't have achieved what she did without her husband. She described him as a miracle, one of the good ones." He purses his lips and then respectfully informs me that Lucy died in 2002.

I nod, remembering her. She didn't allow setbacks to define her or to pollute how she viewed other people, men in particular. She balanced hope and determination, and found purpose and inner peace.

Vinny clicks on another article, a retrospective on the robbery written many years after the event. It mentions Lucy Romano and describes her as the mother of the famous physicist Gus Romano.

"Interesting." Vinny opens a few more tabs. "Gus Romano has his own Wikipedia entry." He taps the screen and brings up another article. "Sheesh madeesh!"

I scan through the page. Sheesh madeesh, indeed.

Professor Gus Romano stares out from Vinny's laptop. He is seventy-three years of age and looks colossally intelligent with his salt-and-pepper beard and thick black glasses.

Vinny scans the article, reading parts aloud, his speech faster and higher as he goes. "Gus received the Nobel Prize in Physics in 2010 for his theory on time-translation symmetry." He glances up at me, shrugs, and then continues. "It says here that Romano's Law fundamentally changed the way we think about time. That's so cool. He's properly famous!"

The article focuses on Gus's formative years, working against the odds and the establishment, fighting for recognition. I guess he has his mother's spirit. Most of the science stuff goes over our poor average heads: quantum mechanics, underlying invariances, degeneracies, the second law of thermodynamics.

I rub my face. "I didn't even know there was a *first* law."

Vinny laughs. "Nor me!" He scrolls to a picture of a younger Gus in a lab coat, Lucy at his side. Her hair is gray. She looks proud and beautiful.

I read the caption aloud. "I dedicate this award to my mother, Lucy Romano, who was always there for me and taught me through her own example that I should use my gift to help others."

We are quiet for a few seconds.

"Look at what you made possible," Vinny says, his voice quiet and gentle.

"It's going to take me while to process it all. It's just so much to take in, Vinny, and I have so many questions."

Vinny places a hand on my shoulder. "You might never fully understand what happened, or even why, but you have to let go of it now. You did a good job. You're done."

"I hope so, Vin. I've had enough of time traveling."

EPILOGUE

When I get back from Vinny's, I show my face in the shop, but Molly sends me straight upstairs with strict instructions to relax for the rest of the day. To be honest, it's a relief. There's a kind of decompression that occurs after time travel. It's a bit like a hangover; you know it's coming, it's just part of the deal. The adjustment hurts at first, but then you get that floaty feeling, and a sense of weary calm descends.

I call Amy and tell her everything. She's hugely relieved when I reassure her that the mission is complete, and our family is safe. She explains that, for now at least, her visions have stopped. As our conversation goes on, I become painfully aware of the emotional space that has opened between us. I broke her trust, and all I can do now is hope that she will eventually come around and understand that I had no choice.

I get up early on Tuesday, and I'm in the shop by 8:15 a.m. Molly's due in at 11. Until then, I'm on my own.

I look around Bridgeman Antiques. The clocks tick, and specks of dust float lazily through the morning shafts of sunlight. I stand still for a moment and appreciate the peace of normality. Quiet and mundane will be just fine for a while.

I pull the silver hunter out of my pocket. Although it's felt like a lead weight around my neck since Bill gave it to me, I'm not quite ready to let it go. Apart from the jump dials, which are mercifully blank, it looks and feels to all the world like an unremarkable nineteenth-century pocket watch. I open the back cover and admire the skeleton mechanism within. Cogs whir efficiently, pushing the hands around the face with absolute precision. I wonder: Is there some mysterious universal mechanism manipulating time on a macro scale too?

Maybe Lucy's story, Amy's, mine—maybe they all needed adjusting, like a watch that's running slow. Perhaps Bill's "subtle serendipity" draws each of us into the right place at the right time, like a kind of magnetism. Are Alexia and I like that? I hope so. I want her back in my life. I've been good. I haven't hassled her, haven't texted or called. Loving someone who doesn't love you back is a fool's game, but unfortunately, I'm all in. I pull out my phone, open Facebook, and before I realize what my fingers are doing, I cave and write her a message.

> Dear Alexia,
> You probably think by now that I'm a head case, but I wanted to apologize again about what happened the other day in my shop. I feel terrible. Apparently, what that guy accused me of is true. But it wasn't me who did it—at least, I don't remember it. For what it's worth, I would never knowingly cheat on anyone.

I read the message back and almost delete the whole thing. But this is my truth, unfiltered. I continue to type.

> I also wanted to tell you that I've started to remember some things about our time together, a wedding we went to. You and I had a conversation out on the balcony, remember? You were honest about your feelings, but the old me said some stupid things. I'm sorry.

> If you're still reading, I wanted you to know that I've learned something recently. Sometimes

THE SHADOWS OF LONDON

> mistakes can be put right. Sometimes all it takes
> is honesty and humility. But there are also times
> when mistakes can't be taken back. Life moves
> on, and suddenly it's too late.

> I don't want that to be us. I believe we still have a
> chance. If you can find a way to forgive me, at least
> enough to talk about this, I would appreciate it.
> Joe

My finger hovers over the send button. I change my mind, but my finger disobeys, and I hear the optimistic zinging tone of a sent message.

It's done now. Let's see what happens.

I go into the storeroom to see if Molly's taken in any new items, and I find the boxes from Police Constable Robert Green. Inside are various items of police-related memorabilia: clothing, badges, a notebook, and a rather excellent collection of police manuals. I carry them through the shop, clear a space in one of the cabinets, and arrange the items neatly. They will make someone very happy.

All that's missing is a key to a 1960s police box. The key is lost in time now, but without it, I would never have saved Lucy. It's that simple. Green said he'd had that box in his spare room for months. What drew him here with such perfect timing? It reminds me of when I drove on autopilot to Ludlow and found the camera that helped me get to Amy. How does all of this work?

I dump the empty box back in the storeroom and sit at my desk to go through the pile of mail that Molly's left for me. Among the dull brown envelopes and community leaflets, I spot a white envelope addressed to me. I recognize the handwriting, but I can't quite place it. I open it and begin to read.

Dear Joe,

I've waited a long time to write this letter.

Before I go on, I need to explain that I'm writing to you from the future. Everything I'm telling you comes with the benefit of many years of hindsight. I need you to trust me, Joe. If you listen to me, everything will unfold just as it should.

Who is this *from*? Flipping the paper, I scan to the bottom of the page and see . . . Amy's signature! Is this genuine? The paper and the envelope look ordinary, and try as I might to tune in, they don't give anything away. How on earth could my sister be writing to me from the future? I thought that by completing the Romano mission, I'd put a stop to all of this. I continue to read.

I'm trying to remember how you're feeling just now. Like you're done with time travel, I think? But you probably still have a lot of questions. I want to try to answer them for you.

I know Bill told you he worked with an organized group of time travelers. We call ourselves the Continuum. The work we do is a kind of healing process. Each mission is a part of the healing. Yours, the Romano mission, was an especially important one, which was why we did everything we could to help you succeed. Even though it wasn't supposed to be yours, and you were operating under duress, you stepped up and made the best of a difficult situation. We've now had the benefit of Gus Romano's work—and the brilliant technology it made possible—for many years. Thank you, Joe.

I know you were angry with Bill when he blackmailed you. He didn't want to do it, but once Scarlett bonded you to the mission, we realized it was the only way to get you fully on board and safely out the other side. And things turned full circle in the end. He knew the risk he was taking in going back to save you. He and I talked about it for hours, but he insisted the mission must be his. I feel some guilt for letting him go, but I'll be forever grateful to him for saving your life. Bill told me once that he believed our lives are measured in connections, by our ability to impact others. If that's true, he died a rich man, and he wouldn't want any of us to mourn his passing.

Joe, I need you to do something for me. The younger me, the one that's living in your time, is entering a difficult period in her life. She's going to need your help, although she's not always very good at asking for it. All you need to do is be there for her, for me, like you always have been. But please, don't mention this letter to her. Not yet. She isn't ready, and the effect on the future could be catastrophic. Be patient and try not to worry. She will eventually catch up with her destiny and find light in the darkness.

I also need to ask you to go a step further. I know you've had enough of time travel for now, but there's more you need to understand. You'll be contacted soon by a woman called Iris Mendell. Please, listen to her. You can trust her. She's on our side.

With love, always,
Amy

I stare at the letter, unable to process it all. It sounds like Amy, and it looks like her handwriting, but why is Amy writing from the future? What's she doing there? And what did Gus Romano do that made my mission so critical?

I presume that Iris Mendell is the same Iris that Bill was talking to at the loch, but who is she? And how am I going to keep all of this to myself and pretend that everything's normal?

I read the letter again, slowly piecing together the details, then store it away inside a notebook and lock it in my desk drawer. I look out the window at the pale morning sky. The quality of the light today reminds me of the day Bill arrived. That feels like a long time ago.

You and I are going to have such adventures together. Remember them for me.

Bill told me that he was glad I was his final mission. He sacrificed himself to save me. But why?

I look over at the cabinet containing the Roberts radio. Molly decided to ignore me and hang on to it, apparently. It's old and battered and no longer holds any of the power or darkness that it once did. This particular link to the past is now totally benign. *Its job is done.*

What about me though? When is my job done?

I sip my coffee, watching the world go by on the street outside. Cheltenham. Home.

I breathe, slow and steady. All I can do is take one day at a time. Preferably, in the present. And ideally, in chronological order.

ACKNOWLEDGMENTS

Someone wise told me once that if you aren't growing, you're dying. I think about that all the time. So whenever opportunities arise, before asking the obvious things like effort required or financial gain, I ask myself, Will this help me grow? Well, the process of being published and working with a team of thoroughly excellent people means I've grown a lot in the last couple of years. Mainly because this novel has been through many minds before landing in your hands. There are lots of people for whom I am thankful. Here are just a few who helped me along this time. (If I've forgotten anyone, I'm truly sorry. Just email me, and I'll put you in the next book.)

Thanks, as always, to my brilliant agent, David Fugate. Your sage wisdom is always delivered with positivity and optimism. What more could I ask for? (Apart from a movie or TV deal ASAP.)

Jason Kirk. Your response to the first draft of this novel will forever have a place in my gallery of happy memories. Thank you, as always, for helping shape my vision.

Kathryn Zentgraf. Your attention to detail is the "secret sauce" on the final draft. Thanks!

Everyone at Blackstone Publishing for believing in me and investing in the series. I'm enjoying working with you all.

My beta readers: Some stories arrive almost fully formed. Others need to be revealed, like a sculptor discovering a statue within a piece of stone.

You really helped me find and shape this story, to focus in on what mattered. You're all awesome, particularly my Ninjas (you know who you are).

And finally, Kay. My best friend, my partner in life, and my collaborator on this series. Where and what *Other Nick* would be without you doesn't bear thinking about.

AUTHOR'S NOTE

Thank you for continuing Joe's journey with me. Although I always planned for his story to be a series, writing a follow-up to *And Then She Vanished* presented an interesting challenge. How do I raise the stakes and expand the world, without losing what I felt made the first book special?

It began with something that's been scratching at my subconscious ever since I first watched *Back to the Future*. I saw it three times at the cinema and always loved the ending, when Marty arrives home to a very different version of his family. But it isn't really expanded upon in the films, and I wanted to explore that idea fully, to unpack what it would be like to land right in the middle of a life you don't know.

And what of his mentor, W. P. Brown? Well, things rarely go according to plan, do they? I decided to throw a metaphorical grenade into Joe's orientation, to force him to grow and discover things about himself and his new abilities. It was fun to send him back to the sixties without any backup and watch him panic.

In the end, as the idea took shape, I returned to my original concept: Shine a light on the small hidden stories that occur every day in this crazy world. Write big ideas, but tell them through the lens of a normal, average guy. Oh, and have some fun. I hope you enjoyed reading it as much as I enjoyed writing it.

I like to keep in touch with my readers, so if you're interested, please sign up for my mailing list at http://NickJonesAuthor.com/Signup. Subscribers receive emails about my writing life and stuff I find inspiring. You can also follow me in the usual places:

Website: http://NickJonesAuthor.com/
Facebook: https://www.Facebook.com/AuthorNickJones/
Twitter: https://Twitter.com/AuthorNickJones
Instagram: https://Instagram.com/AuthorNickJones
Goodreads: https://Goodreads.com/AuthorNickJones
BookBub: https://www.BookBub.com/Authors/Nick-Jones

If you like, you can email me at Nick@NickJonesAuthor.com. I read everything I get.